Daughters of Icarus

Alinda Quinn

ISBN-10: 1983692573
ISBN-13: 978-1983692574

DEDICATION

To Zachary, Harmony, and Keegan. You are my favorite stories.

ACKNOWLEDGMENTS

I was fortunate enough (or cursed enough, depending on what day you ask me) to have been born with words burning inside me. Many influential people have woven their stories into mine and encouraged me to tell my truth. So, if you think you deserve some thanks but don't see your name listed here, forgive me and consider yourself deeply loved and appreciated.

First, last, and always—to my father, Douglas, who taught me that I'm a kick-ass girl who could do anything I wanted. Guess what, Dad? I'm doing it!

To my mother, Eileen, for buying me that really expensive poetry writing guide from the door-to-door salesman in 1976. I know you did without something that month so that I could write poetry. I haven't forgotten.

To my brother and sister, Timothy and Saundra, for providing me with a lifetime of crazy funny stories about arguing, screwing up, covering up, making up, and true love. You were my first best friends.

To my grandmother, Lillian, for seeing my beautiful parts, even when I felt ugly.

To my third-grade teacher, Melinda Usey, for letting me read my stories to the class and telling me I must keep writing. You changed my life.

To *Icarus*'s earliest reader, Dee Mullins. You made it from page 1 to page 300 and gave me the fearlessly honest feedback I needed. THAT is love. Thank you.

To my cherished lifelong best friend, Karen Trietsch. You understand my need to make sense of things with my words more than anyone ever has. Your love has carried me through all the events in life that have been worth writing about.

To the other half of my heart, Nikki Ablon. Thank you for introducing me to daiquiri ice and hiding in the corner of the library with me, a couple of bean bags, and a pile of books.

To Pamela Smith and Betty Nelson. You followed Kate cover to cover, and you encouraged me to share her story.

To my Aunt Deb. You bought me my first journal when I was nine years old, and you never stopped pushing me to publish this little book of mine. I love you and Uncle Raymond with all my heart.

To Tracey Bush, my person. The one in charge of my cell phone when I die. God knew I needed you in my life. From 2:00 AM crying sessions to painful belly laughs over a bottle of wine, you give me the best unconditional love a girl could ever want.

To Tim Baker. Thank you for loving Kate and Simon as much as I do. Your friendship has taught me that redemption isn't just for storybooks.

To my soulmate, Leigh. I miss you. I'll always love you.

And to every woman out there who is trying to live her truth. It's worth it. I promise.

I am fire and flesh,

Yearning to taste *the sun*.

PART ONE

EARTH

CHAPTER ONE

October 2049

It was October in Galveston, and Kate wore pink. The previous evening, she had requested her favorite cotton nightgown, the one with small hearts embroidered around the neckline and the thin ribbons down the front. Her tiny hands were folded at her chest. When Simon gently lifted them, he remembered lifting their newborn babies three decades earlier. Her hands were still as warm as they had been the first time he had ever held them, forty years ago, on the porch just one hundred feet away from where she now lay. His huge hands were trembling just about as much as they had then, too.

Before he let his fingers slide away from hers, he leaned in and kissed her wedding band, now a size too large. Aging would have been harsh without Kate by his side. To the casual passerby, she would have seemed small and fragile now, but he knew better. It was he who had been afraid of this day. Of her death. They had spent the previous evening preparing the room after she told him it was time. Kate had used her final burst of life to help him get ready for her death.

She was still breathing now, but just barely, and Simon knew he had to find a way to let her go. It's what she wanted from him. No prolonged suffering for her family. She had seen what that could do to people. Simon Gray, who had always expected to feel a storm of panic rip through his chest when this moment arrived, was surprised at what he now felt instead, and perhaps even more unbearably so—a lifetime of love, bulging, pulsing, ripping at the seams of his heart. So, *this* was grief. He had read about it, watched it in movies, on the news, and even listened to Kate describe it many times for hours that drifted into the sleepy blackness of the night. But this was different—this was *his* grief.

He didn't immediately look at the man standing on the other side of the bed. Abe was here only because Kate asked for him right before she fell asleep for the last time. Through his tears, Simon had managed to find Abe's phone number and summon the decorum to call him. Abe probably thought Simon was jealous, but he was wrong. What Simon felt had no name—it was not pure or solid. It was instead an emotion that jealousy had evolved into after years of being dragged around like a ball and chain. Lesser men would have allowed it to build into something huge, too heavy to manage. Simon had, in his trademark way, learned to direct his energy toward loving Kate, and somehow the huge ball of jealousy had become weightless, like a balloon instead of a boulder. It was ever-present, irritating him, tickling his ankles and bumping into his life, but it was no longer weighing him down. She had given him everything he needed, even if he knew he hadn't done the same for her. It was enough—today, it had to be enough.

Abe was Simon's junior by five years, but looked at least thirty years younger. Not that today's young people could discriminate fifty-four from eighty-four. People hardly looked at each other anymore. But Simon looked at Abe—often—and the man appeared so young, so healthy, *and so God-dam alive*. While Simon had played tennis into his seventies and still swam at five o'clock every morning, Abe had slept late, drank six cups of coffee a day, enjoyed an occasional cocktail in the evening, and stayed out until dawn most of the time. He did everything Simon couldn't, it seemed, and still looked good doing it. But here, today, none of that mattered anymore, as they stood—two men of one heart—over her beautiful dying body.

"You love her." It was Simon who finally broke the silence. "You have been in love with my wife—"

"—Longer than you have," Abe said, and then seemed remorseful for the disrespect. He drummed his fingers on the bible lying next to Kate in the bed. "But she never loved me back. Not like that."

"I think maybe she did, for a moment." Simon's words fell from his lips and slid into that envelope of strained conversation, the one he carried when he spoke with Abe. "Just for a moment, in…" He avoided the other man's gaze. It was a long time ago. What was the point?

"2009," Abe said.

His memory's even better than mine. "All right, 2009. I'll take your word for it. We almost didn't marry, you know?" His eyes never lifted from Kate's peaceful face as he spoke.

"Because of me?" Abe asked. "No—never would have happened. I tried to win her, tried harder than you know, but she didn't want me."

"How can you be sure? All the long nights, the traveling together. I hated it, for damn sure, but no one tells Kate Lasca what to do. Not even you, the man of God. Don't get me wrong now—I've always trusted her." He glanced at Abe now, and continued, "She'd never sleep with another man, not after I slid that ring on her finger. Not my Kate. But loving you—well, no one controls who they love, now do they?"

"No, they don't," Abe said, nodding. "And I love her, Simon. I love her enough to want her to stay right with you and right with God. I have loved her more than anything in this world, or any other world, but after she married you, I never tried to persuade her to leave. On my word—"

"As a man of God, right?"

"As a man."

"You never married, though." Simon realized it sounded more like an accusation than a statement of fact. He tried to temper his words. Kate wouldn't want them to fight. "Was it because of your job? Because of this…*thing* you do? Or because of her?" He clenched his jaw to keep from crying.

"Ministers can marry, Simon. You'd know that if you ever came to church."

"I hoped that tired old argument would die with her." They both chuckled, and the tension eased. After so many years, the envelope's flap now began to close. Simon wondered if it might finally seal itself shut after Kate died. At any rate, Simon felt the relief of finally saying these words, awkward and abrupt as they were. It would soon be done. He would then never have to speak to Abe or look into his eyes again.

"I'm married to my work, you're right, but there just never was another Kate for me. She was it," Abe said, reaching for the faded brown leather bag he had carried since Simon had known him. He seemed suddenly nervous, and kept pulling the antique pocket watch out and glancing at it. "I have to go," he said, "but I'll be back later tonight, when it's time. For now, maybe you should look through this. Kate asked me to give it to you." Abe pulled a large wooden box from his bag and passed it over Kate's still body. The weight of it tempted Simon to bend over just a bit, but his pride forced him to stand up straight in front of the sprightly minister.

"I know what you're thinking," Abe said. "It's true; they didn't know her. The public, I mean. She spent years being maligned—"

"Too many God-damned years…"

"That's what Kate wanted, though. She wanted people to talk about it. She wanted them to question if they were doing the right thing, and not just the palatable thing. That's who she was." He paused a moment. "I think this will answer your questions."

So now he's clairvoyant, too, Simon thought. *What the hell does Abe know about my questions?* He resented the intrusion, but that was nothing new.

"Simon, people talked about Kate, that's for sure. But they also began to talk *because of* Kate. It wasn't wasted. Her pain, I mean—it served a purpose. That was her victory, her salvation."

"She didn't need saving, damn you!"

There was silence. Abe reached across the woman they loved and ran his fingers around the beveled edge of the wooden box that now lay on the bed between her and her husband.

"What is it, anyway?" Simon asked, "And while we're on the subject, why do you have it?"

"It's what you've been waiting for," Abe said. "Kate finally got what she wanted. Now she wants you to have what you need. What you lived without so that she could follow her heart. In the end, I think that was her only regret—that you sacrificed so much for her."

Simon's eyes pierced Abe's now. The balloon snapped at his heels. Abe knew too much about his wife. He always had. Simon lifted a thick smudge of gray eyebrow, as he did whenever he dealt with preachers and pushy salespeople, and he held it there, unsure what to say next. He wasn't much for playing games.

Abe exhaled. "It's the truth," he said, slowly. "The whole truth."

CHAPTER TWO

Daddy, how old are you?
Old, Katie, too old.
And how old is the sun, daddy? Tell me please.
The sun? It was just born yesterday,
And it's yours, Katie—only yours.

December 2008—Dallas

From her office at the Jasper Advertising Agency in Dallas, Kate could look out the window and watch the children playing in the park across the street. And this is precisely how she spent most of her lunch breaks. Today she was mesmerized by the tiny gracefulness of two little girls chasing one another around a giant oak tree, their hot breath swirling in halos over their toboggan-clad heads. In her mind, she could hear their tinkling laughter, and she felt a pang of wondering, of *what ifs*. The girls darted around playing chase; their little pink gloves and soft fuzzy coats were streaks of color against bare trees and a gray December sky.

She missed the summer when the park was full of these enchanting creatures. As Christmas approached, the number of children coming to play diminished. She presumed that they were preoccupied with shopping and holiday festivities. It looked today as if it might snow, but she knew how much Mother Nature enjoyed teasing Texans. She looked down at the half-finished report in her lap and sighed.

"Ham and cheese on wheat, easy on the mayo!" a voice called from behind her. She spun her chair around and smiled at the attractive brunette with her arms full of white paper sacks from Leo's Sub Station.

"Thanks, Hannah," she said, lightly. "You know they don't pay you what you're worth, don't you?"

"Honey, they couldn't afford to!" Hannah cooed in her soft, sweet, southern voice that Kate knew could be deceiving. They both laughed. Hannah's animated facial expression concealed the settling lines around her lively blue eyes and full lips. She whispered, "You know, Jasper's bringing in fresh meat today."

"Don't talk like that!"

"Well, pardon me, Miss Polite Pants." Hannah straightened her posture and thrust her ample bosom forward in mock respect. "The new junior executive is coming in this afternoon for introductions and the tour. Is that better?"

Kate, ignoring Hannah's sarcasm, opened a drawer and placed the report inside. She then stood and began to clear some papers from her desk to make room for her ham and cheese.

"She officially starts in the morning," Hannah added. "The guys are dying to see her. Her interviews were so hush-hush, you know. Jack and Andy are thinking she must be something special."

"Well, I'm just glad they chose a woman this time." Kate sat down now. "Aren't you tired of being a minority around here? We need another woman in this agency."

"No, darling, what you need is a man," Hannah offered, in a playful sex-kitten tone that she knew would get under Kate's skin.

"Can you be serious for one minute, please?" Kate blew a wandering hair from her forehead.

"I know, I know. For solidarity and all that other woman's movement crap." Hannah laughed. "And of course to even up the score a little."

"That's right. You know I'm right." Kate unwrapped her sandwich and removed the top piece of bread. "Don't you get tired of being ogled?" Hannah raised an artfully plucked eyebrow, and Kate remembered whom she was talking to. "And besides," Kate continued, "where do you think we'd be today without all that woman's movement crap?" She sprinkled some salt on her sandwich.

"Married, that's where!" Hannah said.

"You are impossible." Kate was half irritated but half amused. "We need another professional woman here to strengthen our voice and be counted in the decision-making process," she contended for the hundredth time.

"Don't tell me they have fooled you into thinking that this is a democracy." Hannah watched Kate wipe mayonnaise from the corners of her mouth. "Looks like they forgot to go easy on the mayo again."

"We're going to have to stop ordering from them if they can't get it right," Kate said, but before she could work herself into a tirade, they heard the *ding* and slow shrug of elevator doors opening at the end of the hall. Kate watched Hannah's jaw drop open and her eyes widen, which made her look more like one of those caricatures from the carnival than a real person. Considering Hannah's flair for melodrama, Kate only half-heartedly asked what was wrong.

"Well, brace yourself, dear. The new female executive is here, and let's just say you were right...and wrong."

"What are you talking about?" Curiosity compelled her to the door for a peek.

"She looks like a professional woman, but maybe not the profession you meant." Kate nudged her friend into the hall and craned her neck to get a better look.

"They're coming this way. I gotta go." Hannah took off toward the front desk. But Jasper didn't let her get very far.

"Hannah, Kate. I'm glad I caught you together. I'd like to introduce you to Margaret Perkins. She is our newest team member here at Jasper Agency."

He stepped aside, and Kate had a full view of her new colleague. She stood a head taller than Kate and was shockingly thin. She wore a black lace scarf wrapped around her head like a turban, allowing wild wisps of dirt brown hair to escape and fall around her bony shoulders. Her dress, also black lace with its skirt falling just below the midpoint of an emaciated thigh, was accentuated with multicolored rhinestones along the neckline and hemline. Huge silver medallions dangled from her ears and reflected tiny bursts of red, green, and yellow from the dress, like a malfunctioning traffic light. Kate shuddered, hoping the woman didn't sense her dismay and think her ill-mannered. The stranger's intimate gaze stabbed at Kate. She wanted to hide under a piece of furniture.

"Pleased to meet you, Margaret." Kate finally found words, and she offered the woman her hand.

"Call me Greta," she responded, firmly grasping Kate's hand. She felt tugged at as much as greeted.

"Well," Jasper bellowed, "I think you two will get along just fine. Greta is quite the artist, you know?" He was practically beaming. "Kate, you should take a look at her portfolio this afternoon."

"This afternoon?" Kate repeated, incredulous. Jasper knew she had her hands full with the Arlow account.

As if reading her mind, he turned to Greta and said, "Kate here has managed to pull in a gentleman we have been wooing for two years now. Yes, we're very proud of her."

"Well," Kate said, "I just convinced them to give us a chance to earn their business. And they have agreed, quite graciously, to give us until after the holidays to come up with something for them."

"But first you should spend some time familiarizing Greta with office procedures and going over our winter schedule," Jasper said. "Take good care of her, Kate."

Kate grimaced, and she glanced at Hannah, who was silently snickering. Hannah looked straight-faced at them, and said, "Let me know if you need anything, Miss Perkins."

"Please, call me Greta," the woman interrupted, undisturbed by having to repeat her request.

"Greta. It's been a pleasure. I know Kate can't wait to work with you. Why, she was just saying that she couldn't wait to meet the new…person." With these words, she let her gaze lower as if thoughtfully preparing some ominous statement. Kate hoped she wouldn't say anything embarrassing. In her most sarcastic tone, she said, "I know you'll have a good afternoon together." She winked at Kate and strode away.

Kate excused herself and ran after her, catching up quickly. "You should be ashamed," she scolded. "I can't believe how rude you are!" Hannah turned and looked at Kate, her brown eyes narrowing.

"Kate, she has no idea that I was making fun of her."

"Of course she did, or, well…I did, at least. You know, you can't just go through life saying what you think all the time, and making scenes."

"Sweetheart, you're the one making a scene. And you also can't go through life never saying what you think, fighting it, holding it in, like some tiny plug in a great big dam. Next thing you know, you're losing your mind over heavy mayo."

"Back off, Hannah." She had heard it all before. Softening, she asked, "By the way, what makes you think I even want to get married?"

Hannah stood quietly for a minute, arms folded in that motherly *I-know-everything-about-you* way. "Kate," she finally said, "what were you doing when I came into your office today? In fact, what are you doing every day at lunchtime?" Kate thought back to the playing children. Her face and neck felt hot. Hannah patted her on the back and said, "I'll see you later, shug."

CHAPTER THREE

October 2049—Galveston

"Kate…" Simon whispered as he sat down next to his wife. "Kate, darling. I called Maggie. She's on her way. Zeke will be here later, too. I talked to him last night." He took a deep breath and tried to steady his voice. "Kate, I promise. It will be like you wanted. I'll be brave. I'll make the kids understand—we'll do it for you."

He opened the lid to the box and inhaled the piney scent. Why had she given these things to Abe? Hadn't she given him enough, and now—he was the one to deliver her deathbed message to him. What was she thinking?

He lifted to top item from the box. It was an old business card from Jasper Agency. *Kate Lasca, Creative Director*, it said, in dark blue, faded lettering. She had them printed five minutes after the promotion had been offered. He had to laugh. He had always been proud of Kate's accomplishments, even when sometimes the rest of the world hadn't been.

"Well, darling," he told her, "things are going to get crazy here, just like you said. I can feel it in these old bones. But soon the kids will be here, and we'll be putting your plan into action." *Thank God you'll be asleep for all this*, he thought.

The ringing phone startled Simon. He made his way to the front room and picked up the receiver.

"Simon, it's Campbell." A gravelly voice greeted him. Simon could practically smell the Marlboros through the phone line. "Is this a bad time? How are you?" Campbell Cross was born and partly raised in Boston. In spite of his thirty-something years in Galveston, he still occasionally removed the "r" in the endings of words such as "where" and relocated them inexplicably to the ends of words such as "tuna." This was especially evident during high stress times, such as today. In happier days, Simon had teased him about it.

"Well…" Simon paused. "I'd have to say that yes, it's a very bad time."

"Jeez, Simon. Why didn't you call me?"

"So you could do what—interrogate my wife—on her deathbed. Like hell—"

"Now wait a minute. Shit, Simon. You know me better than that. Where's your fuckin' brain? No way I'd disrespect you and yours like that. Not after everything you did for me and my Macy."

"And everything *she* did for Macy. Don't forget that, Camp. Don't you dare forget that."

Both were quiet a moment.

Simon asked impatiently, "So, Detective Cross, what the hell do you want? I need to get back to Kate. And Maggie will be here soon. I need to tidy up."

"Maggie? She's coming in today?"

"Yeah, but leave her out of this. Christ, Camp, leave her out of this."

"Of course. Sorry. What can I do for the family, Simon?"

"Don't pretend to be my friend. We're past that," Simon snapped at him.

"Shit—I'm just doing my job. Even Katie knew…I mean…*knows* that."

"Well, Kate trusted everyone. And forgave everyone. Clearly she's always been a better person than I am."

"Christ, Simon. Just tell me what you need."

"Time. That's all. Just time."

There was an uncomfortably long silence now.

Campbell cleared his throat. "Er…How much time?"

"One more day, Camp. That's it."

"Done." Campbell paused. "Jesus, Simon. I'm so fuckin' sorry."

"Actually, I do need one more thing from you," said Simon, sighing, refusing to acknowledge Cross's condolences.

"Anything. Name it, compadre, and it's yours," Cross said.

"You mean that?" Simon asked.

"Hell yea, I mean it," Cross bellowed. "Name it, I said."

"Good," Simon said. "I want you to leave Maggie alone."

Simon hung up the phone without saying goodbye.

CHAPTER FOUR

December 2008—Dallas

Kate fiddled with the keys to her condo and cursed the maintenance man for not repairing the lock yet. She prayed that she wouldn't get her key stuck again. It was nineteen degrees and windy. The last thing she felt like doing was standing in the cold waiting for Harvey to save her again. "If he would just fix the damned thing," she muttered. She heard Fred's sweet, welcoming voice just inside the door, and she knew he was eager to see her. She couldn't wait to curl up against his soft, warm body. The lock made a small pop when she worked the kink out of it. She slowly swung the door open, looking down at Fred. Then she scooped him up and rubbed her face against his.

"How I missed my sweetheart." She massaged his ears and continued to greet him in baby talk. "Mommy's so happy to see her kitty angel. I missed you so much, yes I did!" She gently placed him on the sofa, so she could shed her coat and other winter accoutrements.

It was an unusually cold December for Dallas. She had never quite understood the term *bitter cold* until this winter. For a born and bred Texan, everything about this cold was bitter, from the taste it left in her mouth to the agitated feelings it stirred inside her. The silence of the empty rooms was broken by short, angry bursts of screaming air pounding the windows, begging to come in. On difficult days, like today, she fought the urge to give herself to it. She saw herself crashing through the glass, shouting, "Take me!" She knew the desire to fly away into that cold solitude as well as most people know the need to breathe. She was always on the brink of departure, toe on the line. But she knew that once she took flight, once she opened her wings and caught that frigid, hateful air, that she might not have the strength to fight her way back again. Every counselor she had seen since her dad died had insisted that she was strong enough to take on anything. She doubted the validity of this claim, however, wondering just how much sincerity one hundred and fifty dollars an hour could purchase.

"What a day I had, Fred. I hope yours was better." The overweight Tabby stared at her with large accepting eyes. "Let's go see if you ate everything Ms. Wakefield gave you today." Purring, he jumped over the arm of the sofa and followed her into the kitchen. Kate paid her rich widowed neighbor, Clara Wakefield, twenty dollars a week, which she didn't need, to feed her cat once a day and share his company, which she did need. Kate had seen the desperation in her eyes that day last spring, during one of her weekly visits with her. Clara's husband had suddenly died of a heart attack early in March, leaving Clara completely alone. Kate had never before, or since, seen Clara even stumble. She and Herbert had loved each other beyond worldly constraints, Clara had told Kate at the funeral. Kate felt comfortable with Clara. She believed in things, and Kate liked that.

"What a good boy you are," Kate told Fred, who was weaving through her legs in a figure eight. He knew the routine and was waiting patiently to be picked up. He didn't have to wait long. Kate carried her companion into the bedroom and while she undressed, she gave him a summary of her day.

After donning her pajamas and scooting her feet into her tattered slippers, she put her dinner in the microwave. The savage wind kept trying to thrust its way in, but the windows held strong, with only a few tiny cracks betraying them, letting in whispers of cold. She pulled the curtains tightly together and sighed. "It's going to be a long winter I'm afraid. But maybe a white Christmas," she told Fred. She fingered the plastic branches of the small artificial tree, decorated in clear bulbs and white lights. The lights and ornaments had been a gift from Clara the year Kate had lost her father. The tiny tree was placed precisely in the middle of the end table. Frank Lasca would have loathed this tree. He always brought home a big bear of a pine tree three weeks before Christmas. The tree was the only item he overspent on, ever. He loved them large and prickly with more colors than the six Lasca eyes could behold, a striking disparity to his otherwise humble nature. And they seldom bought ornaments. The necessary frugality of her earliest years had evolved over time into cherished family traditions. She had never in her life purchased a Christmas ornament.

The Lasca family had always spent much of early December making decorations—stringing popcorn, baking gingerbread, and cutting and pasting. The three of them would huddle around the table in the tiny kitchen, listening to songs like Kate's favorite, "Let It Snow." She hadn't even seen snow until she was six, so the song was for her more a prayer than an exultation. No such thing as a white Christmas in Texas—she had learned that early—yet she maintained her innocent hope year after year, even now. Kate exhumed the images: the large orange and yellow flowers on the wallpaper, the aroma of cookies and popcorn, the intimate laughter. It was all real to her, years later, standing in her own tiny kitchen waiting for her Salisbury steak and mashed potatoes to warm.

Her father had always made a point to be home this time of year. As the regional manager of Tucker's Toys, Kate appreciated how difficult that must have been. In her adult life, she had often wondered how he managed to get the time off from traveling. His frequent extended business trips might have instilled doubts in the mind of a less loyal daughter, but her father's work ethic had instead solidified both her faith in her father's devotion and her condemnation of her mother's thanklessness.

Some of her favorite memories were of December, or specifically, the pre-divorce Decembers. Dad would sneak popcorn when Mom wasn't looking, and he'd wink at Kate from behind the thick lenses he had worn for as long as she could remember. Even with his failing eyesight and silvery temples, to Kate he was eternally youthful and fiercely strong. He would fall asleep on the couch and Mom would gently remove those eyeglasses and then kiss him on the forehead. Every time it was the same—first the glasses, and then the kiss. The tenderness that was her childhood.

The beeping microwave shuffled her back into the present. Exhausted, she retrieved her T.V. dinner and her cat. Before settling on the sofa wrapped in an afghan, she grabbed the remote control. She ate and watched a basketball game in a stupor. She went to bed tired and cold. And she lay there a long time, thinking.

Greta had been with the agency exactly one week. Jasper had made her spend the entire afternoon with her on two occasions, including today. She wondered why in the world he would hire such a person. She had developed a vague idea why, a nasty idea that she wouldn't shape into words. He had never said or done anything inappropriate in Kate's presence, and she had a deep respect for him as a businessman. Really, her respect for him ran deeper than business, but it was nothing sexual. He was in his mid-fifties—a tall man, six and a half feet at least, and he was broad and heavy, with glistening white hair all over, like a big polar bear. His grand personality and magnificent voice projected a dominance very different from her father's simple and quiet, but equal, strength.

Jasper was an effective leader, and a powerful man, but he was warm and personal, as well. He was supportive in her ongoing efforts in getting the center off the ground. She never had to ask his help. It was as if he knew what she needed before she asked. She was very careful, however, to keep their transactions as business-like as possible. The only issue she had ever had with him was that he was a bit old-fashioned, especially about women. She couldn't quite figure out what he and Greta might have in common. Greta was so…bizarre.

The more she thought about her, the angrier she became. Having to compete with Jack and Andy for a strong voice in the agency came as no surprise, but competing with a woman? The irony was unsettling. Kate tried to slow her thoughts, suspecting that she might be getting ahead of herself. But then, there Greta had been, only too eager to spread her portfolio over Kate's desk like a dime-store tablecloth. The most infuriating part was that the work was some of the best that she had ever seen. While she had stood there, Greta's imposing form peeking over her shoulder, she tried to convince herself that her nausea was a result of Greta's cheap perfume and not her own violent envy. She knew, deep down, however, that the intensity was in the sketches and not the fragrance. They were powerful. They were certainly not part of the ad game, at least not the one Kate was playing. She pushed her thoughts away and turned her pillow over again.

The clock on her nightstand read 2:08. She smashed her face into the pillow and again tried to quiet her mind. She pulled Fred close and wondered aloud, "Tomorrow has to be better than today, doesn't it?"

****

"Good morning, Shug!" Hannah cheerfully greeted her.

"Are you always happy?" Kate grunted n response. She stopped at Hannah's desk to pick up messages that she must have retrieved from the answering machine at dawn.

"Well, not always." She turned around in her swivel chair. "But you know, it's never too early in the morning to smile."

Kate shot her a look and thought to herself that it was never too early for Hannah to start lecturing her, either. She turned down the corridor and lumbered the next several yards to her office. She hadn't slept in weeks. By the time she had her key in her door, Hannah was snapping her fingers and singing, "Take Me to the River" along with the radio. She chuckled in spite of her foul mood.

Hannah was the closest thing to a friend that Kate had. They got along fine when Hannah wasn't playing mother. One mother was enough, and besides that, she was a grown woman, only a few years younger than Hannah, who had been married and divorced twice and had a teenage son getting to go away to college. Kate enjoyed being around her because of her free spirit, but she also resented her for encouraging the stereotype of the Texan cowgirl, with her southern drawl, denim skirts, and lace-up ropers. Kate was disgusted by the way Hannah flirted, pretending to be less intelligent than she was. She often reminded Hannah that there were in fact some smart, sophisticated people living in the south. Of course, Hannah reminded her that some sexy people did, too.

Hannah's saving grace, in Kate's mind, was her sense of humor. It was dark like Kate's. No one else seemed to know when Kate was joking. Hannah had once laughed at a sharply critical remark Kate made about the company's holiday decorations, and the flattery had chipped away at Kate's typically stone-like exterior. They had formed a curious bond over the years since then—two apparently different personality types—Hannah bubbly and charming, and Kate civil, but icy cold at times. Kate made jokes with Hannah in the ladies' room, over morning coffee, in the hallway, but rarely in front of the others, and usually not at anyone else's expense.

That was the two diverged. While their humor linked them to one another, their beliefs about when and where to reveal it remained a source of disagreement between them. Kate didn't like gossip, and Hannah thrived on it. Still, Kate took comfort that she and Hannah had a certain understanding—one in which they could just look at each other and laugh. God knows Kate needed laughter. She had tried a few times with other colleagues to make such jokes, but they usually looked at her like she had broccoli stuck in her teeth. So for the most part, she had withdrawn into her own world, the world of advertising. Her outlets from work were Hope Springs Hospice, and its fledgling sister organization.

The Frank Lasca Center was an organization Kate had created to help fund support for people cope with the drain of caring for a loved one with AIDS. She was deeply concerned about young children losing parents to the disease, and as a tribute to her father had decided to create a supportive agency to help these families. The Center was in its infancy. She was raising funds for a building lease and hoping to hire a small staff by next spring. She planned to get it off the ground, then pass the baton but remain on the board. It was her atonement.

Jasper Agency and her hospice work didn't mix. Even when she spoke with Jasper about his donation, it was during their lunch hours. She loved the center, but had very clear plans about how to proceed with its development, and in her mind, it could not be linked to her job at Jasper. The center was important, but just a side note, because Kate felt her feet should be firmly planted on the path to excutivedom.

Kate sat at her desk and began reviewing her messages. She normally returned phone calls around 9:30. Most people were settling in to their offices by then. She fingered the little blue and white slips and groaned when she saw the name on one of them, accompanied by some of Hannah's not so subtle comments. She took a deep breath and marched back to the front desk.

At first, she stood quietly, staring at Hannah's back as she faced her computer. She didn't want to have this conversation again. She watched Hannah's quick, but smooth movements. Her ballerina-like figure and graceful actions made even the most menial tasks seem significant.

"Hannah," she spoke solemnly.

"Hmm?"

"Hannah, may I speak to you, please?"

"Yes dear, what is it?" She didn't turn around. Perched atop a raised reception area, there was no question about her status in this company. Kate opened the door to the short wall surrounding her workspace and stepped inside. She stood beside her for a moment, but Hannah didn't look up. Kate reached over and twisted the volume knob on the radio. When the office busybodies craned their necks, all she wanted them to hear were the Righteous Brothers.

"Damn it, Hannah!" she spat and then lowered her voice to a harsh whisper. "What is this?"

Hannah casually glanced at the small, rectangular paper. "Why, I think it's a message, isn't it?" She kept typing. Kate only lingered a few seconds before she turned to leave. Hannah stopped her with her words. "Shug...You can't avoid this forever."

"That's really none of your damn business, is it?" Kate's shoulders tightened. She wanted to scream, but she refrained. "I know you just want to help." Hannah was looking at her now, expressionless. Kate began to pick up steam. "You have no right to try to guilt me with your little notes. God, you're as bad as she is!"

Hannah's expression began to reflect her growing concern for Kate. "Why won't you just call her? You and I both know that you want to. Why are you—"

"—Just stop," she interrupted her. "This is my problem, and I will solve it. Stay out of this." She stomped off toward her office.

By this time, Jack, whose office was adjacent to the foyer, was observing the prickly exchange. When Kate walked by him, she snapped, "And you mind your own business." Trying to make light of a tense situation, Hannah wrapped her arms around herself, shivered, and said, smiling at him, "Is it cold in here or what?"

Jack guffawed.

"I heard that!" Kate yelled back at her. Hannah turned the radio up even higher and began swaying and humming again. Then Kate heard her cry out, remarkably in tune, "You've lost that loving feeling..."

Kate spent the morning working on Arlow. She knew it was her big break, the break she so desperately wanted, so she battled her exhaustion like the trooper that she was.

"Hey, Kate, got a minute?" Kate recognized Andy's voice and looked up.

"Sure." She really didn't. She buttoned the top button on her blouse.

"I had a question about this invoice," he said, standing just an inch from her side. She tried to discreetly push her chair away.

"That's really a question for Hannah. I'm sure she would be happy to assist you," she said, without even glancing at the paperwork in his hands.

He put the invoice on her desk, in front of her, and bent over her, his chest against her shoulder. "Could you just take a quick look. This is the Madison account. You helped me with it, remember?"

"Hanna really is the person you want to see." Her words were courteous, but her tone was now cold.

"Well, sweetheart, she told me to ask you." He smiled like a hyena about to pounce on an antelope carcass.

She stood up as a polite invitation for him to leave. He didn't understand subtlety; he continued to stand there and smile at her. "My name is Kate," she said.

He still didn't take the hint.

"Well, I know you're not Hannah, but I thought—"

"You misunderstand me." She abandoned tactfulness. "True, I am not Hannah, but I am also not your *sweetheart*. Now, Mr. Spidell, I suggest you go speak with the billing manager, and her name is Hannah, or Mrs. Jones, if you like, but again, also not *sweetheart*."

"Give me a break, Kate." He put his hand on her shoulder now. "We're not *all* dogs, you know."

"No, of course not." She shot back. "Dogs can learn new tricks."

He gave her a condescending smile and then turned and left. She thought she heard him say something under his breath—something like "Better a male dog than a female dog." She wasn't sure. Perhaps he thought it stung, but the truth was that this word that men regarded as the ultimate insult scarcely held meaning anymore. They had used it to such a degree that its bite was barely a lick. It produced no spark of indignity in Kate, and perhaps—if anything—it elicited more pride than upset. There was, after all, no other way to survive in a pack of wolves than to become the bitch.

CHAPTER FIVE

Put me on your shoulders, Daddy. Teach me to fly.
Hold out your arms, Katie, and turn your face to the sun;
Let the angels kiss your cheeks.
Run, Daddy, run. Faster! I can do it if you hold me tight.
Fly, Katie, fly! Never look back!

"Hellooooo, Kate!" called a raspy female voice down the hall at Jasper Agency.

She was jolted from her concentration. Growing tired of interruptions, Kate peered over her rimless glasses at the most recent source of her irritation.

"Hello, Greta." She forced a pleasant tone. "How are you this morning?" She tried to look nonchalant as she glanced at the clock and mentally punched Greta in for the day. 10:28.

"I am good, actually." Greta stepped past the threshold into Kate's office.

"Well, you look very happy." She should at least try to be nice.

"I am. I had the most amazing time yesterday." Greta smiled.

"I'm glad you have enjoyed your first week. Everything went well, then?"

Greta looked surprised. "Oh, you thought I meant that I had an amazing time here!" She threw her head back and laughed heartily, unaware that Kate might be insulted by such a vigorous response. "I was talking about after work. I went to this new club on the corner, what's it called?"

You must be kidding, Kate thought. "I really wouldn't know," she said. Kate felt crowded by Greta's tall figure standing in front of her desk, not moving. As Greta dug around in her purse, Kate drummed her fingers on the desk, glancing at the door. Greta was obviously searching for something. She pulled out first a hairbrush with mats of brown hair stuck to the bristles, and she placed it on the edge of Kate's desk. Next, she pulled out some balled up tissue—unused, Kate hoped—and laid it beside the brush.

"Here it is! Excalibur!" she exclaimed tossing a matchbook onto a pile of marketing reports. "Cool place. You should come with me next time."

Kate cringed at the thought. She smiled at her guest and glanced at the door again. Greta flung herself sideways into an overstuffed chair, worn and comfortable, near the door. She hung her spindly legs over one of its arms and propped her head against the other one, her untamed mane sprawled out like a fan around her. Today Greta wore no scarf, so Kate could see that her hair was as gray as it was brown. Her youthful attitude had been deceiving. Her face today revealed a much older woman than Kate had originally thought.

"Ah, really cozy chair. Where did you get it?"

"My father bought it for me."

"Is that him?" Greta asked, pointing to a photograph on a shelf. "Wow! What a hunk."

Kate stiffened.

"Anyway," Greta said, "about this club. It was great. It was packed—wall to wall party animals, totally wild. They had this band, and the drummer, Oh my God, you should have seen him!"

She was definitely too old to still be chasing drummers, Kate thought. She stopped listening and looked beyond Greta, at the clock on the opposite wall. 10:37. She watched the second hands tick slowly by, dozens of them. The little red hand snapped into place hypnotically, second after second after second, a thin layer of rhythmic sound just beneath Greta's droning voice. Snap. Snap. Snap. The dismal concert was disrupted by Jasper's booming voice from the front of the office. As Jasper spread his *good mornings* throughout the office, Kate looked again at her uninvited guest, assuming she would jump up out of the chair, or at the very least, sit up. But she didn't budge. Kate felt sick as the echoing voice drew nearer. Jasper would come in and find her entertaining this reclining visitor instead of working. She was mortified.

"Hey, there, Katie Girl!" Kate immediately stood to greet him. She hated this nickname, but not as much as she hated the thought of telling Jasper that. His words stretched out over several seconds. Snap. Snap. She cleared her throat and glanced at Greta. For a moment she was embarrassed for her, just lying there, until she realized that this type of behavior might show Jasper just what kind of fruitcake he had hired. He grinned when he saw Greta, and then he reached down to pat her arm.

"Hey, I didn't see you there. How's my newest charge? Is Kate teaching you everything she knows?"

"Good morning, Mr. Jasper." Greta said sweetly, reaching up and putting her hand on his elbow. "How are you?" Kate gasped at the intimate behavior. Didn't Greta know better? Should she mention something to her about office etiquette?

"Well, I'm pretty good. Can't complain, you know? Say, Greta. Why don't we go to lunch today?" Jasper asked.

"Sure. Sounds wonderful."

Kate was speechless. Not that it mattered, since no one was talking to her anyways.

"See you around noon, then. Bye now." Jasper left.

So, she thought to herself, she works an hour and a half and then goes to lunch with the boss, and probably on his dime. And furthermore, how could she act that way in front of Robert Scott Jasper, CEO, and seventh richest man in Dallas? Everyone else knew how high to jump when he said the word. Kate reminded herself to breathe.

Greta jumped up to leave. As she did so, her flowing polka-dotted skirt swept across a stack of business cards on the edge of Kate's desk. As she bent to pick them up, she spied another photo of Frank on a low shelf.

"What's this?" she asked, and helped herself to the photo.

"Oh, just a picture," Kate said.

"Your dad, right" Greta asked. "Is that you and your mom with him?"

"Uh-huh."

"Beautiful. Happy. It's nice," Greta said.

"Thanks, Greta, for the compliment, I mean." She opened a desk drawer and slid the picture inside.

"Well, okay," Greta said. "I guess I'll see you later." On her way out of Kate's office, she nearly bumped into Hannah, who was approaching with two full coffee cups. Hannah stood unnoticed in Kate's doorway for a minute, just watching her.

"You look awful," Hannah said.

"Gee thanks," Kate said, not looking up.

"What was that all about?"

"They're going to lunch. He needs to share something with her." Kate was looking through a file, eager to get back to work.

"Uh huh." Hannah's sarcastic tone again.

Kate looked up now. "God, you are so nasty, Hannah. Why does everything have to be about sex?"

"What else is there? Work?"

"What do you want, Hannah? And why are you staring at me like that? Did I grow a second head or something?"

"The last thing you need is another head." She laughed like that was the funniest thing she had ever heard. Normally it would be funny to Kate also: two heads...someone who thinks too much.... very funny, actually. When Kate didn't laugh in agreement, though, Hannah asked, "What's wrong, Kate? Don't you like the new girl?"

"Leave me alone. I'm busy." Kate looked up now. Hannah was smiling her larger-than-life smile. "Did you bring me extra cream?" Kate asked.

"Of course. Don't I always take care of you?"

"You do. You definitely do."

Lunchtime arrived, and Kate gathered with the others in the conference room, where everyone but Kate usually ate. Hannah had convinced her to come out of her cave and join them for a while. When Kate entered, Andy and Marissa were talking quietly. Marissa, the part-time office clerk, was in her early twenties, and was working her way through college. Kate respected her for that. She also worried about a young, pretty, naïve girl just getting started in the advertising business. Marissa made photocopies and answered phones when they got backed up.

Judging by their whispering voices, Kate felt she was interrupting. They assuaged her fears by excitedly inviting her over.

"Kate! Just the person we want to see. Come join us." Andy called out.

Jack stood and grabbed her arm at the elbow. Kate glared at him and tried to pull away unnoticed.

"Hi, guys. What's up?" She sat down, and Jack sat next to her.

"We were just discussing the new person, what's her name?"

"Greta. Why?"

"Did you get a load of that outfit?" Andy laughed.

She suddenly remembered why she usually ate alone in her office.

"She's pretty nice, though," Kate said. "We have to give her a chance, don't you think?"

"Yeah, we noticed you socializing with her a lot," Andy said.

"We're not socializing, Andrew, we're working. You probably just didn't recognize it." She was in no mood for their gossip today.

"I think I've been insulted, Marissa," Andy retorted, "What do you think?"

"I would have to agree," Marissa said, clearly not wanting to be part of this argument.

Jack rubbed Kate's leg under the table.

"Stop it," she whispered, and moved her chair over.

Everyone was too busy chattering to notice Jack and Kate. Except Marissa. She was hard to read. Was it pity or envy on her face? "Hey, Kate," she said, "Congratulations on Arlow."

Jack grabbed Kate's hand, also under the table, but she didn't dare move. Everyone was watching her now. The smell of pasta and garlic signaled Hannah's arrival. Marissa jumped up to help her distribute lunch.

"I really could do this for you," she told Hannah. "There's no reason for you to go pick up lunch for us every day. I'm available, and I don't mind."

"Oh, no. You're sweet. But what would I tell Antonio? He expects me at noon every day. And you know how impatient those Italian boys are."

Kate shook her head side to side. It was like working on an animal farm. She wrenched her hand free of Jack's grip. He piped in, "Hey, Hannah. You were only gone twenty minutes. Not much of a stud, is he?"

"Jack. Poor little Jack. Lunch is just an appetizer. I'll serve him the main course tonight. Besides, women need a warm up. A real man would know that."

They all laughed uproariously.

"You win again." Jack said, waving a pretend white flag.

"I know, honey," Hannah said.

Andy changed the subject. "So, Hannah, what do you think of the new girl? You know, Kate's new best friend?" he teased.

"I had the baked ziti, Hannah." Kate squirmed in her chair.

"She's hardly a girl," Jack corrected him. He touched Kate's leg again, and she kicked him, harder than she intended, but without remorse.

"Oh, my," Hannah giggled as she handed Kate her lunch and dug for a fork, all the while prattling on, "Can you believe it? I thought yesterday's behavior was odd, but she outdid herself today."

"Where's the salt?" Kate interrupted. Greta wasn't her favorite person, either, but she refused to get sucked into the office gossip, no matter how much she disapproved of Greta.

"Right here, shug." Hannah tossed her a packet and continued, fanning the flames. Kate wanted to leave before they engulfed her. "You know that she and Jasper are having lunch right now," Hannah said, with one eyebrow raised. There was a low murmur, and little titters from the boys.

"Marissa, tell them what you told us this morning," Jack urged her.

"Maybe I shouldn't." Marissa looked nervously at Kate.

"Oh, come on," Andy begged. "It's too good. Tell them."

"Well," Marissa began, "I was at Excalibur last night, you know the new place, and she was there."

Jack and Andy were practically salivating. Jack stood and reached across Kate for a napkin, deliberately brushing his thigh against her arm. By this time, she was having trouble breathing.

"She was a wild woman. I mean, how old is she anyway, forty?" Marissa said.

"Honey, she's fifty, at least," Hannah said. They chuckled at Marissa's innocence. Anyone over twenty-five seemed old to her.

Marissa blushed, but continued. "She danced with every guy in the room. And I don't mean the waltz. It was embarrassing. She hung on them and ran her fingers through their hair, and well, you know, rubbed up against them."

"How drunk was she?" Hannah asked.

"That's the thing," Marissa said. "I never saw her take a drink. And she walked out and drove home. She doesn't seem hung over this morning. I don't think she was drunk."

"No, just horny," Andy said. He thought he was funny. Apparently, the others agreed. Andy leaned back in his chair, proudly stretching his arms and then placing his hands behind his head. Kate resisted the urge to push him and send him sprawling.

"Well," Hannah said, "I wonder what Jasper would think. They seem awfully tight, you know?"

Kate jumped up. "There's nothing going on between Jasper and Greta!" She screamed, unsure why she was angry. There was utter silence as they all stared at her, amazed.

Her appetite was gone. She made a clumsy exit, tripping over the legs of her chair, and ran straight to the ladies' room. She was fuming. Did it occur to anyone that maybe Mr. Jasper just liked Greta's work? Maybe it wasn't about sex at all. It didn't always have to be. For several minutes she tried to catch her breath as she stared into the mirror. She could swear she was looking into her mother's green eyes, flashing with anger as she had seen them only on rare, but memorable, occasions. Kate's dark auburn hair was beginning to turn on her, with thin strings of gray that only she could see, and only in a certain light. She tucked her hair behind her ears and combed it in the back with small, shaking fingers, colorless now except for the rosy pink polish. She leaned over the sink, rubbing her temples, refusing to let her anger become tears.

As she splashed cool water on her face, she felt hot hands on the back of her neck and around the front of her waist, pulling her backward. She jerked her head upright and locked gazes with Jack in the mirror. He tugged the back of her starched white collar down and smashed his warm mouth against the nape of her neck. She lunged forward, her groin shoved hard against the cold sink. She searched her revving mind for a method of escape. Her hands and face were wet, and she was trapped. She thought of screaming, but she and Jack both knew that would be a stupid move.

"What the hell are you doing?" she hissed. He slid a massive hand into the front of her blouse. She tried to kick him, but she couldn't get her balance.

"You didn't finish your lunch."

"Get off me, you lunatic! I'll scream!"

He just smiled.

"Someone is going to walk in," she continued.

"You're so beautiful, Kate." He kissed the top of her head as he spoke, his hands seemingly assaulting her entire body at once. She reached around behind her back and between his legs with cold, wet hands, intending to grab and twist with all her might. This aggressive move served only as an accelerant, though, and he pushed harder against her, forcing her hand crudely into his crotch. She felt her knees begin to weaken.

"Does that excite you?"

"No," she lied. "I told you. It's over. No more."

"Come on, Kate. It's been a month."

"I can't." It had actually been thirty-eight days.

She watched their encounter in the mirror. The scene was disturbingly erotic, like some bizarre carnival sex show. He pressed his face into her hair and inhaled, closing his eyes, still holding her tight. As they moved against one another, his coarse, dark threads of hair weaved themselves in and out of her warmer, cherry-chocolate tresses. The dark strands almost matched at a glance, and in the heat of the moment.

He tried to slow the pace, softly sliding his other hand into her blouse and under her bra with practiced proficiency.

"You and I, Kate. We're the same. We want the same things. Money. Power. Sweaty sex in one of these stalls." His determined hands still grasped her breasts, but she no longer wanted them to stop. His kisses were clever and calculated, and that knowledge broke her heart, but she couldn't pull herself free of them.

Her shame clung to her like the late summer dew, lukewarm and sticky. She wouldn't let him know how much she missed him. No, not him. *It.* The feelings he elicited. The passion at 2:00 AM, that time of day when she ordinarily became acutely aware of her desperate loneliness. That's what she missed—the random and temporary relief of that otherwise ceaseless, gnawing sadness. The recognition of this truth made her sure she would vomit. He kissed her neck again, this time gentler than before, but still unrelenting, never doubting that he was slowly defeating her will. She twisted herself slightly and relaxed against him, grateful now for the sink's support against her buckling knees. His hasty grasp now melted into firm caresses of her breasts. She felt betrayed by their quick response to his groping hands. She returned his kisses, slowly and bashfully at first, sweeping her lips across his eyelids. She was careful to keep her desire at a steady glow, never allowing it to fully blaze. She knew she was about to cry, and she hated herself for it.

"Not now," she whispered. "Not here. 8:00."

She wrenched herself free and ran from the bathroom, suppressing tears all the way back to her office.

Kate kidded herself into thinking she could work all afternoon, her eyes glued to the clock. Her thoughts drifted between the Arlow account and Jack's eager hands all over her. She heard Greta and Jasper step off the elevator a little after two o'clock. A half-hour later, when Greta burst into Kate's office, Kate was on the telephone. But instead of excusing herself, Greta sat down on the edge of the chair and waited. When Kate hung up, Greta greeted her pleasantly.

"Hi, Kate. How is your afternoon going?"

"It's been interesting. How was your lunch?" Kate felt embarrassed, as if Greta had been watching her erotic encounter with Jack.

"Great!" Greta said.

"Mr. Jasper is a good guy, isn't he?" Kate said.

Greta nodded affirmatively.

"Well, Greta, did you need something?" Kate asked.

"Mr. Jasper suggested you might spend the afternoon with me again, you know, showing me the ropes."

"Actually, I am up to my elbows in this Arlow account. As a matter of fact, I was just speaking to Mr. Brody from Arlow when you walked in."

"Marshall Brody. Oh, yeah. Jasper told me about him. He's concerned that Brody will be the toughest sell on this thing," Greta told her.

Surely Greta was confused. "You mean Mr. Jasper spoke with you about the Arlow account?" Kate said. She felt her eyebrows crinkling up in that way they did when she was taken off-guard, which she was careful to not let happen very often.

"Well, yes," Greta said. "Why?"

Kate took a deep breath. "I just wondered. I thought he might wait before filling you in on such a big project. We don't want to overwhelm you, do we?" She wondered if she looked and sounded as plastic as she felt.

"That's so sweet, Kate. I knew I would like you. Listen, you get back to what you were doing. I'll go ask Marissa to show me how to use the phones and copier. I'll get with you tomorrow."

She was gone. Like some horrid West Texas tornado, she blew in unexpectedly, spread her devastation, and abruptly left without apology. Kate sat alone in her office and ruminated on the events of the past months. She had fought hard to get the Arlow account. It was the first major account that Jasper let her head up. Everyone knew it was a test of her competence, both creative and professional. Everyone knew she was first in line for the Creative Director job, and they knew this account would make or break her. She had pushed herself to her limits for months, and she was going to Houston in six weeks to make her mark.

"I thought you'd be thrilled, doing business in your hometown," Jasper had said when he broke the news to her just a few days before Greta's arrival. In her blind race to the top, she hadn't thought about having to go to Houston…and what that would mean. Jasper must have seen terror in her eyes.

"Oh, yes sir, I *am* thrilled. What a great chance for me! I'm feeling a little tired today, that's all."

"Well, you'd better get used to being tired, Katie Girl, because you will get no rest for the next few months. Welcome to the world of advertising."

His remark had made her feel small. She had been with the company for nearly five years, and she knew he would never say something like that to the men. Maybe he wasn't sure of her ability, or worse, maybe he knew about Jack. Or was she getting too old already? She tried not to let her sagging confidence overshadow the excitement of the opportunity. They had been trying to lure Arlow Foods, the largest producer and distributor of pre-packaged foods in the Southwest Region, for two and a half years. She made it happen. Kate was very proud of her effort and she had earned Jasper's respect and trust. Yet, here she was, doubting herself again, and counting the hours until 8:00, like a love-struck adolescent unable to focus on her homework. Jasper certainly hadn't nurtured her confidence by throwing this middle-aged monkey wrench into the mix.

Maybe he's just being friendly and trying to make her feel welcome, she told herself. She knew if she let her mind go to certain places right now that she would destroy her chances for success. They couldn't be doing it, she thought, repulsed by the image. Not Mr. Jasper. The divorce was barely final, though, and he was lonely, she could tell, but still…Greta? She shuddered. Thinking leads to obsession. And that would hurt her work. She absolutely would not risk it. Not for Greta. Not for Jack. Not for anyone.

The doorbell in Kate's condo rang at 8:07. Trembling fingers smoothed the front and sides of the red rayon dress whose scooped neckline merely hinted at her cleavage. On her way to the door, she stopped in front of the gold-framed oval mirror that had been a wedding present to Frank and Emily Lasca forty-seven years ago. Frank's shadow always seemed to linger in its reflection. Kate knew he would never have approved of Jack. *You deserve better, Katie,* he would have said. *Why do you always sell yourself short?*

She studied her likeness in the glass. She hated the freckles across her chest. As was her habit, she patted the caramel-colored dots with perfume, vaguely mindful of a lifelong desire to wipe them away. For some reason, the freckles drove Jack wild. Not that that was difficult. He was on full alert most of the time. Hannah was right, though. She did look tired. Even Kate could see that the usual clarity of her large, sea-green eyes was obscured by the puffy lids beneath them and the suggestion of resignation within them. Thirty-five years old. How much longer would she be doing this kind of thing?

CHAPTER SIX

October 2049—Galveston

"Dad!" Simon heard Maggie's voice call out, excited, but worried. "Dad—oh my God, Dad, where are you?"

"I'm right here, honey," Simon answered. "I'm here. What's wrong?" He shuffled into the living area, gently closing the bedroom door behind him, as if Maggie's screams could wake Kate from her gentle sleep.

"How long have they been here? Better yet, why didn't you tell me they were here? I would have caught an earlier flight or something."

"Who, Maggie? The reporters? Hell, who even cares?" he waved a hand at her, unconcerned. "I'm too old to mess with that crap."

"That's exactly my point. Did you call Campbell? He could come over and—"

"Why the hell would I do that, Maggie?"

"Because, he's your friend, Dad. That's what friends do."

"Oh, is that so? Listen, Maggie...he paused, and decided to let it go. "Not today, okay."

She smiled and hugged Simon tightly. "I just hate that you were alone, and with all these carnivores outside. It's not just press, Dad. It's the zealots and who knows who else. Let me call him. Or someone else on the force. Anyone. You need protection."

"From some newspaper wimps and bible-thumping pansies? I don't think so. Now sit down and let's talk about something else."

They sat on the sofa and Maggie leaned against her father's shoulder.

"Is it really time?" she asked. "Somehow, I'm not ready. We've known for months, waited and watched, and I'm still not ready to let her go. It's like I'm a little girl on the first day of kindergarten. I just need one more day with her, you know?"

"Would you be ready later?" Simon smiled.

"No. But don't try logic with me. You're not good at it. That's mom's department, remember?" She started to cry a little and laugh a little too.

Simon grabbed a tissue from the box on the end table and gently wiped beneath his daughter's eyes. "Don't cry, darling," he whispered, and he kissed her cheek. "She's ready, even if we're not."

"I know, Dad. I know you're right. She's at peace with this."

"Look at this, Maggie," Simon said as he handed his daughter an old photograph from the pine box.

"It's Nurse J and Kevin from Hope Springs. I haven't thought about them in years. Where did you get this?"

The pause said it all.

"Don't tell me Abe was here," Maggie said.

"Now, Maggie, your mother wanted—"

"I don't care. She was never level-headed when it came to Abe Archer."

"You just said she was always logical."

Maggie glared at him. "Not about Abe. I can't believe he would show his face here. He's the reason for these reporters, for the investigation, for everything. I don't want him anywhere near Mom. Dad, you have to promise me."

"I'm afraid I can't honor your request, Maggie. Your mother's over-rides it. Like it or not, and God knows I don't like it, either."

Maggie burrowed herself into Simon's shoulders. "What's he doing with this anyways?"

"Your mom—she gave him a box of—mementos I guess you'd say. He delivered them this morning."

Maggie was quiet. Simon knew what she was thinking. She was just like her mother, which naturally meant she adamantly disagreed with everything Kate did.

"Hey, want some lemonade?" Simon said, trying to change the subject.

"That actually sounds really good," Maggie said, not entirely willing to give up on this fight. She got up and walked toward the kitchen. To do so, she had to pass through her mom's office. Within seconds, she was calling out to Simon, "Dad, have you been watching this?" He entered Kate's office, sheepishly. The small television in the corner had caught Maggie's attention. He knew he was busted.

"Daddy," she scolded gently, "You don't need this right now." She walked over and stood in front of the set. "Oh, my God. Those bottom-feeding…that's our cabin. They've multiplied ten-fold in fifteen minutes." She leaned over to turn the set off, and stopped short. On the screen, a middle-aged man in a gray suit got out of a familiar maroon sedan about forty yards from the cabin and positioned himself quietly at the back of the crowd. She and Simon watched the scene in their front yard unfold on the old TV set.

A scuffle began in front of the man in the suit. "All right, people. Enough is enough," he shouted in a thick Boston accent. "Let these people say goodbye, for Christ's sake. Get out of here now." A few people wandered off, but over half the crowd would not be swayed.

"She's a murderer!" someone yelled.

"Hide your sick loved ones!" another angry voice called out.

The man in the suit had broad shoulders, a tan face, and charcoal eyes. Simon studied Maggie's reaction, and he was sure he saw her eyes soften and her shoulders drop just a little. He imagined that her heart beat a little faster, as well.

"How about that lemonade?" Simon asked.

Maggie sat on the floor, and Simon sat on the couch, with the coffee table between them. The large pine box lay open on the table. Maggie reached inside and retrieved some more photographs, timidly, as if she were disassembling a bomb. There was a series of photos of a young Katherine Lasca and several friends at a black-tie Christmas affair. The most interesting photo was one of her mother and some man Maggie had never seen before, looking quite cozy under the mistletoe. She turned it over and read the words, "Me and Jack, 2008."

"Wow, Dad. Who is this?" Maggie was clearly impressed with the man's good looks. "Jack Finnegan."

"Okay....and?"

"And what, Maggie? His name is Jack Finnegan. Christ, I'm beginning to think Abe gave me this God-damn box just to torment me."

"Dad, come on. Who is Jack Finnegan? Fine looking specimen that he is."

"Your mom and he were...an item," Simon grunted.

"Really?" Maggie asked, incredulous. "Mom was with this guy before you, I mean..."

"I know what you mean." Simon was nearly growling now, and a little surprised by his resentment of her interest. He hadn't thought about Jack in a long time.

"What I was *going* to say was I can't imagine Mom ever being in love with anyone but you. You were born to be together."

"Maggie, let's get this straight right now. Your mother was never in love with Jack Finnegan. *Never.*

CHAPTER SEVEN

Daddy, how long will you live?
A hundred years plus one, Katie.
How long will I live, Daddy?
Forever—in my heart.

December 2008

The nightmares were back. Almost every night. They had been gone for a few months, but as the Houston trip neared, they reappeared. They were variations on a theme. Kate running through a field of high grass, falling and picking herself up again and again, reaching for her father as he blindly ran into the raging wildfire in the distance. Kate rowing a boat as fast as she could, dropping the oars into the water, diving in and swimming her very hardest to catch her drowning father. And the worst one of all, Kate and her father falling at bullet speed from the sky and smacking violently into the ground, with Kate surviving and her father lying next to her in bloody pieces. And in the backdrop of them all, snippets of long-ago, innocent conversations between a little girl and the father she adored.

Kate woke up sweaty and breathless, worn down by the familiarity of the visions. Her chest hurt from the impact of the fall and the breath that was sucked from her lungs during the plummet to earth. She rolled over and reached for Jack, stroking his shoulder. She leaned in and kissed the back of his head, enthralled with the simple feeling of his hair tickling her lips, and loving how his embrace pushed the nightmares into the back of her mind. This was so much better than waking up alone. He began to stir. She kissed him again, wrapping her arms around him from behind, pulling him toward her. He turned and easily found her mouth. His kisses evoked euphoria within her—evidence, she feared, of a great deal of practice on his part. She wished she didn't want him and wondered if he, too, felt any trepidation, but she doubted he did. He turned further and wrapped his legs around hers. Neither of them spoke. He moved in and out of her with a rhythmic splendor she had grown to anticipate. They were two strong individuals struggling to bond and yet remain autonomous, never quite achieving either goal. Her movements against him became more desperate and hurried than usual, but he resisted her frenzy, insisting on a perfectly controlled but powerful union.

Afterward, she lay on the damp sheets listening to Jack's off-key singing muffled by the shower's pounding water. They had spent every night together since their ladies' room encounter. In her heart, she wanted to feel safe and loved when she was with him, but she was not delusional. He was a distraction. A terribly exciting one, but still—a distraction and nothing more. She questioned the wisdom of their relationship, which promised self-destruction, but most of the time she accepted that their lovemaking was the only reason she hadn't gone mad in the past year while she was earning a name at Jasper and raising funds for the center. She could talk to him about work. He was right—they were alike. They craved power, and were willing to sacrifice to achieve it. While he saw this desire to take charge as the basis for their attraction, she saw it as their inevitable point of departure. But for now, she needed him.

He sat beside her on the bed, his hair wet and sticking to him all over.

"Kate." He rested his hand on her hip. "What are you thinking about?"

She drew a feathery circle on his thigh with her index finger, wondering if she should slide her hand into his robe. "I thought the woman was supposed to ask that question."

"And I thought you were a feminist!" His voice was deep and commanding, in contrast to his playful smile.

"I'm thinking about Greta. And Jasper. And your backside."

"In that order?" He smiled again, displaying straight, white, perfect teeth.

"Stop worrying," he continued. "Just let Jasper provide the rope, and she'll hang herself soon enough. She's not like us, Kate. He'll figure that out."

"Jack…what if I don't want to be 'like us' anymore?"

"What do you mean? Of course, you do. You can't just give up." He massaged a towel into his dripping locks.

The work had once been its own reward. Her previous passion for the Arlow account had become a passion to prove herself, but she couldn't say that to Jack.

"Who's giving up?" she said, "It just doesn't feel the same anymore—all the pushing and fighting. I don't know if it's right for me. Maybe I just need a break."

"Well, take a break after the promotion. But not too long, you know?" Jack warned her.

"It's just that, well, isn't there more to life than selling pickles and athletic shoes? Don't you ever wonder if it's worth it?"

"Hell, no. And neither should you. You know that Creative Director position is all but yours. You're too close to the top to start going all girly on me. What's wrong with you? PMS?"

She removed his hand from her side and sat up, gathering the sheets protectively around her bare torso. "God, Jack. Can't you be more imaginative than that?" Her organs twisted themselves into a pretzel, one moment unable to resist, the next moment repulsed.

She encouraged Jack's early departure. Her neighbors all awoke early, and they would love to gobble up another morsel of Kate's love life. Jack was one of her tastier morsels, she had been assured.

Except for having to endure the old ladies' constant chitchat about everyone's personal business, she loved her condominium. It was secluded from the booming intensity of the singles' communities scattered throughout the city. It was quiet, non-threatening. But the gossip amongst her seniors spread faster than the common cold at a nursery school. She didn't want to become fodder for this week's stories, so she convinced Jack to leave discreetly after he extorted a promise that she'd see him before she left for Houston. They played the when-will-I-see-you-again game skillfully, both knowing that they needed these nights together more than they needed food and water. In fact, she was sure she could live off their lovemaking alone for days at a time.

****

Kate showered and dressed, trying to numb herself by chugging hot coffee and watching unspeakable tragedies unfold on the morning news. She pulled up in front of the old empty warehouse at 8:47. The gray metal siding was spotted with round, quarter-sized rust spots here and there, except for one side of the building that she had gotten permission, after much begging, to paint blue last year to cover the words "Fuck You, Gino" sprawled across its surface. Luckily, she had never met Gino or his pen pal, but she feared running into one of them when she occasionally sat out front late at night contemplating her fate and staring at the stars.

From the outside, it didn't appear particularly hospitable, in spite of the colorful mat in front of the door that stated otherwise, each letter comprised of tiny red flowers, arched and angled into the word *Welcome*. Kate had lovingly placed it in front of the shabby building a week earlier, hoping to someday entice the needy and suffering into its doors. She fantasized about getting the place fixed up nice for the families who needed it. Right now, she didn't even have the down payment, but she was dangerously close. This building would become a headquarters for information and intake once she raised the rest of the funds. The real action for now took place at the hospice, a mile and a half down the road, and at the church a few miles from her office. If she had her way, someday it would look like a haven for families and not a drug dealers' hideout.

She approached the building with a familiar ache in the pit of her stomach. She reached into her bag and pulled out a gold rectangular plaque. She held it up to eye level against the splintered wood of the door; in it was the blurry reflection of her face and in the backdrop the words—*The Frank Lasca Center,* and in smaller lettering beneath, *for families living with HIV and AIDS.* She couldn't wait to hang that plaque.

The building had been abandoned for three years, and according to everyone she knew, no one in her right mind would touch it. Thank God, she thought. That bought her some time to pull together funding to open its doors without worrying about someone else snatching it up. She lowered the plaque and took a deep breath. *Someday, Dad,* she silently promised, running her fingers over the engraved words before putting the plaque back into her bag.

Kate usually worked at the church Saturday mornings and spent two nights a week and Sunday afternoon at hospice. She occasionally participated in other functions—too often funerals—during the weekdays as her schedule permitted. Mr. Jasper never questioned her devotion to her hospice work, and she never let it interfere with her commitment to the Arlow account. Robert Jasper's small but consistent donations that year had helped her come one step closer to opening the center, and in fact, he also gave her names and phone numbers of potential contributors, and made several phone calls himself. But most generously, he had agreed to serve on the board of directors alongside her.

A blue Volvo lurched into the driveway. Her 9:00 appointment was ten minutes early. They were usually ten minutes late. It wasn't easy asking for help. Most people, like herself, hesitated before doing so, if they ever did at all. This woman had requested a meeting away from the hospice and had refused to enter the church. Kate suggested they meet here, where the little girl could play on the adjacent playground while they talked. It was cold, but it was emotionally neutral territory. After the car door swung open, Kate saw a woman about her own age step out and smooth her peach silk skirt with her pale hands. She was taller than Kate, but her sadness made her seem smaller. Her thick, almost midnight-purple hair was pulled into a severe bun with a wooden spike forced through it at the back. A well-worn sand-colored wool sweater hung lifelessly across her shoulders, and open at the front, revealing a stark white simple tee shirt beneath. The sweater's ties, hanging in even lengths on each side, dangled loosely at her thighs. Behind her was a little girl, about six years old, clinging to her mother's sweater; the ties swayed with the little girl's slight movements, and allowed Kate random glances at her curly blond hair and intelligent, but also sad, brown eyes. Missy Stone looked just like her father, Kate noted. He had moved into hospice last week, and this was the first time Kate met his wife and daughter. Christopher Stone was a delightful man who had probably been easy to fall in love with.

"Mrs. Stone, I'm so glad you came." Kate spoke cordially and extended a hand. With the daughter's anchoring weight, the woman had to tug a bit to move them both across the gravel drive.

"Now, Missy, stop it," the mother said. She scolded the girl in a weary tone. She turned to meet Kate's gaze. Her eyes were the palest blue, and her skin a soft ivory.

Her modest lips and small teeth gave the impression that they had once been accustomed to smiling. Kate would only ever see that smile in the wedding photo beside Christopher's bed. "I'm sorry, the woman said. She's struggling, you know."

"Of course, Mrs. Stone—"

"Theresa" she said.

Kate nodded. She pulled the folding chairs from the trunk of her Toyota Forerunner and arranged them close to one another. As she did so, she couldn't help thinking about the once ratty office chairs sitting in her apartment, waiting to be moved into this building. The chairs had been re-covered in a silky polyester cloth of vibrant gold and blue. One of her contributors had done the work for free. Kate wished she could offer Theresa and Missy a pretty place to sit. She squatted down and looked closely at the little girl for a moment.

"Hi," she said. "I'm Kate. What's your name?"

The little girl wrapped her arms around the mother's leg. "Is your name Missy?" Kate prodded gently.

"No!" The little girl cried out. She narrowed her eyes into little slits and crossed her arms in response to Kate's question.

"Missy, be nice," the mother said.

"It's okay, really." Kate slid into the chair opposite Mrs. Stone and crossed her legs. She reached into her bag for a clipboard and pen.

"Melissa…" the small voice said.

Kate smiled at her warmly. "Ah, Melissa. Very pretty. Would you like to sit down with us, Melissa? Or maybe go play on the playground?"

"It's Melissa Harmony Stone," she said, louder and with pride. "But everyone calls me Missy."

Kate stayed in her chair, but leaned toward the little girl. "Missy. My name is Anna Katherine, but everyone calls me Kate. My dad called me Katie."

"And your dad died."

"He did."

"So, we're kind of the same," the little girl said.

Kate nodded. "Yes, we are. How about that?"

Melissa's face became serious. "Kate?" said.

"Yes?"

"Were you sad when your daddy died? Mommy told me you took good care of him when he was sick, and it was a long time ago, and you were a big girl when it happened, but I think you were still sad. Even big girls need their daddies, I think."

Kate fought the tears.

"Missy! That's not an appropriate question."

"Sure it is." Kate tried to sound reassuring. "That's why I do this. To help other girls who are hurting when their mommies and daddies are sick."

"So…were you sad?" Missy asked again.

Kate looked at Theresa. Theresa nodded.

"Well, Melissa. Yes. I was very sad. I cried so much that I thought I was drowning in tears sometimes. And you will cry too, I'm sure. And it will be pretty awful at first."

"I cry sometimes now. I wish he wasn't sick."

"I know you do, but I promise that something else will happen. After a few weeks, you notice that you are crying a little less, but just a little. And then a few weeks later, you're crying a little less and maybe even having fun sometimes. And then by the time a year goes by, there are days where you forget to cry, but you never forget your father. How does that sound, Melissa?"

"I like the way you said 'Melissa.' Can she call me that, mom? Is that okay?"

Mrs. Stone looked slightly exasperated, but a little relieved too.

"Well, Mom, what do you think?" Kate asked, smiling. The women's eyes met again. Mrs. Stone's were warmer now, but still as blue, and in them Kate saw something painfully familiar. Frantic hope mingled with angry denial. In those eyes, she saw Mrs. Stone bathing her husband, cleaning up his vomit, carrying him from bath to bed, day after day until he never left his bed again. She also saw herself five years ago—reading to her father late into the night, arranging his pillows, falling asleep in the chair next to his bed, only to be awakened by violent coughing that escalated into hysterical fear for them both. Theresa pulled Melissa into her lap. Missy quietly refused to go to the playground. "I want to listen to the big people talk," she insisted. "I want to help you take care of Daddy, like Kate did. Okay, Mommy?"

Theresa kissed Missy's forehead and pulled her close.

"Kate," the woman began, "Thank you for agreeing to meet with us today. Like I told you on the phone, I have tried and tried, but I'm only one person. Please help us."

They talked for over a half-hour about the services Kate knew of and Kate gave her a folder of resources and they went through it together. Kate felt Theresa Stone's fear begin to ebb just a bit, and that knowledge brightened her own dull spirit a little bit, too.

When it was time to leave, Kate's spirit lifted even more when Melissa wrapped her arms around her.

"When will I see you again Kate?" Melissa asked.

"Probably this week. At Hope Springs Hospice. I look forward to it." Kate said.

"Me too," said Melissa.

"And Melissa, you know what?" Kate bent down and took both the little girl's hands in her own. "I'm glad we are friends. Thank you for talking with me."

"You are welcome," Melissa said, with a huge grin.

"Thank you, Kate." Theresa extended a hand. "We'll see you soon."

CHAPTER EIGHT

Daddy, what's dying?
It's just like going away, somewhere else, somewhere better.
But, are you afraid to die, Daddy?
No Katie. Death isn't an ending. It's just time masquerading,
*   trying to scare us, outlast us. But don't worry, it never will.*

"I thought I'd find you here," Hannah said. She sat down on the park bench next to Kate. "Decide to get a close-up look today? Venture into the lion's cage?"

"Aren't they marvelous little things?" Kate said, pointing to a group of three little girls gathered around a doll carriage near the swing-set, taking turns rocking and singing to a baby doll.

"If you like germ-infested, back talking little creatures," Hannah said.

"You are so full of crap," Kate said. "You love them as much as I do. Look at them...so precious."

"I did the motherhood thing already, shug. I'm over it."

"It's not just a 'thing' and you know it."

"Kate, it's cold out here. Let's go have our lunch inside. We can talk if you want."

"I don't want to talk," Kate said.

So, they sat in silence for a while, watching as the little girls' friendly play heightened into an argument over "who gets to be mommy next." A real mom stepped in and lovingly advised the girls about taking turns. Kate felt Hannah's eyes on her.

"Kate, why are you doing this to yourself?" Hannah asked.

"I don't know what you mean," Kate responded.

"It's okay to have questions about your career. About whether or not you'll ever get married."

"Easy coming from you. You're a pro at marriage."

"A failed pro, need I remind you?"

"The clock is ticking, Hannah. You know, I had a chance to marry an amazing man after college, but no, I was so driven to start my career and determined to let him start his life first. I guess I just thought—"

"There would always be time," Hannah said.

Kate nodded.

"You are about the get that promotion. I just know it. As soon as you guys wrap up Arlow, it's all yours, sweetheart."

"Yeah—I hope you're right. But it could go to Andy."

"Andy? The hard-on with ears? I don't think so."

Kate had to laugh. "You are nuts. I don't know what I'd do without you." She wrapped her arm around Hannah's shoulder.

"Honey, I love being here for you. But I'm no substitute for—"

Kate groaned.

"Call your mother," Hannah said. "It's Christmas. Just call her."

"No."

"Kate, she didn't kill your father, and neither did you. Now just call her, please," Hannah begged. "She is, after all, the only piece of your father you have left."

"Ouch. Nice, Hannah."

Hannah gave her an apologetic, but pleading look.

"On one condition," Kate said.

"Oh, boy," Hannah said.

"Go to hospice with me tomorrow."

"You mean the place with the dying people?" Hannah grimaced, as if someone had shoved rancid cheese under her nose. "No thanks."

Kate had an idea. "How about this, then, Hannah. I will call my mom if you promise to go one week without talking about sex."

"I think I'll just hang out with the dying people instead."

They laughed.

"Fine, whatever it takes, Kate." Hannah gave in. "No sex talk...you are impossible, you know that?"

"That's what my Mom always told me." Kate smiled, rose to her feet, and tugged at the corner of Hannah's pink suede jacket. "Come on, girl. It's cold. Let's go inside and have some lunch."

****

Kate cherished the peaceful, empty chapel that was attached to Hope Springs Hospice, and she always felt tranquil in its haven. There was no sign of Jacob, the rabbi who usually volunteered his time on Tuesday night. He was one of several volunteer clergies at Hope Springs. It was quiet now; the descending sun heralded the end of another day. There was one small stained-glass window north of the makeshift pulpit, the only such window they could afford. It was otherwise a rather non-descript place, but holy, nonetheless. Kate felt a greater communion with God here than she did at her own slightly larger Methodist church on Sunday mornings, but she loved both. One of her church's associate ministers worked here Thursday evenings, and he had told her about the place shortly after she moved to Dallas and begin attending Grace United Methodist Church.

She heard the phone ring in the little room inside the chapel that was reserved for the clergy. Since Jacob was at home sick, she thought she should answer in case someone was in crisis. Just as she entered the office's doorway, the ringing stopped and a young, smooth voice, said, "Hello...Hope Springs Chapel." He had just a suggestion of an accent—British, maybe? She was less sure as she continued to listen.

She watched the somewhat diminutive man from behind. His sweet voice and his generous thatch of honey blonde hair led her to believe he was in his late twenties or early thirties. He spoke gently to whomever was on the other end, and she knew she should back away. Clearly it was a private moment for the caller. But she couldn't pull herself free of the scene unfolding here. The man's narrow but roundish shoulders moved up and down as he spoke, gesturing with one hand as if someone were in the room to read his body language. He was dramatic yet steady in his demeanor, his voice a pitch above the average male perhaps, but solid and convincing.

In the corner stood an easel. It hadn't been there Sunday, she was sure. On it was a nearly completed sketch of children on a carousel. They were laughing and waving, clearly having fun. It was impressive—colorfully exuding joy. It wasn't greeting card colorful, but realistically so, with every detail painstakingly created. As the man turned slightly, she could see that he had smudges of color on his small hands. His skin tone was darker than she had expected, giving him a sort of unusual exotic appeal. She felt like she had been here before, heard his voice, seen this painting She suddenly felt overwhelmed by the sense of it—this moment—this person, like she had been led here. It was crazy, and she knew it. She turned to leave, but didn't get far. He finished his call and turned around.

"Hello, Miss..." The familiar confidence of his voice made Kate hesitate in her response.

"Lasca," she said, turning around. "Kate Lasca." His skin was smooth and tight, but his eyes seemed older—large and knowing. His age was hard to calculate.

"Hi, Kate. I'm Abraham. Did you need something?"

"Have...we...met?" she asked.

"Um, I don't think so," he said.

She was embarrassed that he caught her eavesdropping. "No, I don't need anything. I was just going to answer the phone. I didn't know anyone was here." She smiled nervously.

"Well, thank you for offering to help. Everyone here seems really on top of things—and friendly."

"Thanks...Abraham, you said?"

"Yes—or Abe, whichever you prefer."

"Abraham," she said. "Like Father Abraham. That's nice. And appropriate, I guess. Maybe your mother knew you belonged in ministry."

He laughed. "I doubt that, but it is a fitting name, I suppose. And I guess I was a holy terror as a child." He laughed, in a childish chuckle, at his own pun.

Kate laughed, too. She tried to imagine his transgressions. He had an innocent and reassuring way about him, but a streak of fire flashed in his eyes as well.

"I was just admiring your painting there. It's wonderful. The kids must love it, too," she said, awkwardly.

"Do you paint?" he asked.

"No. I seem to be surrounded by people who do, but me…. no. I'm in advertising."

"So, you're creative, too," he said. "An old friend taught me, actually, to paint, I mean. She was an amazing artist. Well, still is I suppose…"

She shrugged. There was an uneasy silence.

"Forgive me," he said, offering a hand. "Kate, it's nice to meet you. I don't know where my manners are tonight."

The flame in him was a warm glow by the time it reached his extremities. He shook with his left and then generously wound his right hand around her left, delicately, as if holding an injured baby bird within. His touch was safe and reassuring, like her father's. She didn't believe in faith healing, but found herself wishing this man could have touched her father like this. His secure grip was imbued with a peaceful energy that tempered her very breath. She was instantly drawn to him, but as a sister to a brother, and not as a woman to a man.

"I'm sorry I disturbed you, Father, or Reverend—Abe—"

"Just Abe, or Mr. Abe for the kiddos. They like that, you know?"

"So, you're—Baptist?" She ventured a guess.

"Methodist," he said.

"Not that it matters," she said awkwardly. "Methodist, huh? Me, too."

"Yeah? Good. I'm filling in for Jacob tonight, but I think I'll be back. I just interviewed at Grace Methodist on Sexton Street. Do you know it?

"Sort of," she said, with a goofy grin. "That's my church."

"Well, isn't that a wonderful coincidence? Maybe we'll see each other a lot. I'm feeling good about it."

She paused and then said, "Well, again, sorry to interrupt, Reverend. I'll get back to the kids. Nice to meet you."

"Yes, of course. Me too. I hope I see you again."

CHAPTER NINE

October 2049—Galveston

Simon couldn't take his eyes off Maggie. His sweet Maggie. She was so much like her Mother. She looked nothing like either parent, but inside, she was all Kate's. Her brown hair held no traces of the red that were evident in varying shades in Kate, Simon's, and Zeke's. Her eyes were small brown discs that seemed never to blink. Those eyes had a way of getting what she wanted from everyone, most of all Simon. Her milky skin had no freckles and had never been prone to blemishes of any kind.

It was funny, looking through the box, to realize which moments had juxtaposed themselves into Kate's grand picture of their lives. Simon's were so different. They did share a few proud moments, however. He pulled out a newspaper clipping, the one announcing Maggie's large research grant from two years ago:

> *Margaret Frances Gray, Ph.D., professor of Biochemistry and Epidemiology at Tulane University, received news today that her team of researchers has been awarded a $17.6 million grant to further their studies of HIV and its effects on the nervous system. The study has been hailed as the most promising of its kind, and Dr. Gray believes that her team is less than five years away from finding treatments that may spare the brain and spine. Ms. Gray is the youngest female epidemiologist to ever receive a grant of this size, and she has become a household name in the AIDS community.*
>
> *"People all over the world are holding their breath anticipating the progression of my daughter's work to its inevitable conclusion," said Kate Lasca-Gray. Lasca-Gray is also a household name, but for a very different reason....*

"We're on the verge, you know?" Maggie said softly.

"I know, honey. Your mom is so proud. It breaks her heart that they are letting her work tarnish your reputation," Simon said.

"Stop—we've been down that road. You know I don't care what anyone else thinks. I just want a cure. Besides, the hype means more publicity, and more research funds."

"You'll get there. What a gift you are to the world. But I knew that the minute I laid eyes on you. They brought you to me wrapped in that pink frilly blanket. You didn't stop crying for hours. And I figured out.... well....you've heard the story."

"But I still love it," she told him.

"Damn nurses, thought they knew everything. You were my girl, and I knew you didn't like that blanket. So, I slipped in the one I brought from home, the one that was mine."

"The yellow one with small red polka dots." She smiled broadly and tried not to cry.

"Yeah, that's the one. The only one you liked, too." Simon started to shake, and Maggie knew she should leave the room. His pride would be wounded to cry in front of her.

She scurried through the house and made her way to the front room. She stood by the window for several minutes before she was brave enough to push the drapes aside a sliver and look outside. She moved her body without moving the drapes, careful not to draw attention from the hounds outside, until she found him. The feeling started in her face and moved down into her neck and extended through her limbs until she felt like her love for him was pushing its way out of her. She had never known anything but holding it in. She had never expressed it in front of another soul. His face, his eyes, his strong build—they were much like the man in the photo, Jack Finnegan. What an odd surprise. She wondered if Simon saw the resemblance. How much did he know? Like everything else, he probably knew more than she realized, but far less than he thought he did. He wouldn't have stood for it. He would have said she deserved more. But what could be more than complete rapture, total abandonment of logic, and love that pierced into her very being?

She heard Simon's steps approach and she closed the curtain. She dabbed at her flushed face with her blouse, hoping to conceal herself from him. It was going to be a very long day.

CHAPTER TEN

Am I going to die, Daddy?
No, sweetheart, not for a very long time.
        Why do you say such things?
Reverend Tom says everyone dies.
        I don't want to die… I'm afraid.
Never be afraid, Katie. Daddy will be by your side always.
Even when I die?
Especially when you die.

December in Dallas is a happy, hectic time. Kate had one more gift to buy, and she dreaded it. She picked up the small paper from her desk and stared at it. It had been a year since they had spoken, and each silent day seemed to widen the gap between them a little more.

Kate had grown up in Houston and had visited Dallas often as a child. She had been born nearly eleven years after JFK's demise and six years after the murder of Martin Luther King, Jr. During her youth, these two powerful men had been the heroes of her peers. After Kennedy's death, her father told her, people came in droves for several months to see the town that killed the president. Over the years, the fascination had tapered off, with surges of interest recurring in November of every five-year anniversary of his death. She had been visited the Sixth Floor Museum countless times with her parents, who had been devastated by Kennedy's murder.

Kate had always felt that she should have been born thirty years earlier. The events of 1960's America intrigued her. Frank's stories of those times had stirred her interest and elicited tremendous emotion, both positive and negative. Although her respect for JFK, Dr. King, Bobby Kennedy, and others ran deep, and she recognized their roles in improved race relations in her lifetime, her heroes had always been female pilots, and especially Amelia Earhart. Brave, adventurous, willing to risk it all, she was everything Kate wished she could be. She had barely missed Neil Armstrong's moonwalk. His small step for man left the nation in awe. Kate had wished all her life that someone could take a giant leap for womankind. She searched endlessly for details about the life of Valentina Tereshkova, the first female astronaut to go into space, but written information was scarce, until the Internet opened up new avenues for information. She was the only girl she knew who wanted to be an astronaut. While her friends were playing dolls and pretending to prepare dinner for their husbands, Kate was wearing the spacesuit her father got for her at a discounted rate from Tucker's Toys and digging around in the backyard for moon rocks. Later, when the Lascas began visiting the ocean every summer, she fell in love with the water. Torn between worlds. Her father would tell her that she was made of water and of sky, and was not of the earth. She knew it in her heart to be true. She had never felt the normal kinship that most people feel toward others of this planet.

The only typical female activity she could remember engaging in was one that she had held secret for many years. She would go into her bathroom, pull a white towel out of the cabinet, and carefully shape it into a veil, fastening it in the back with a large copper colored diaper pin her mother had held onto for some reason. She would stand in front of the mirror and stare at herself, swaying back and forth as she hummed the wedding song. She had bought a large sparkling silver plastic ring from a machine at the grocery store. Pretending to be disappointed when she put in her dime, turned the latch, and watched the ring pop out, a sparkly strand of excitement had raced through her that day. Although she told her parents she gave the ring to a neighbor, she had kept her treasure in a drawer in her bathroom, careful to never wear it in front of others. She would, during these secluded occasions, slip it onto her finger and hold it up next to her face as she continued to sway and hum. She would smile and nod to her pretend wedding party, and watch herself wink and blow kisses. It felt good, but wrong somehow. Even though her friends were openly playing husband and wife, she was embarrassed by her private sessions, similar to her later feelings of shame during her adolescent self-exploration of her newly acquired body parts. It was private. It was Kate's first secret.

She dialed the phone hesitantly, turning the message slip over and over in her hand. The line picked up after just one ring. This was a mistake, she thought, then hung up. Why didn't she just say, *Hi, mom. Happy Holidays. By the way, what would you like for Christmas?*

Because she already knew her mother's response. *Gosh, I don't know. I'm sure whatever you choose will be lovely.*

Lovely, Kate thought. The catch-all word. There was nothing wrong with the word, technically. When one broke it down: love—ly. Two solid, perfectly normal-sounding syllables. Her mother used it to describe everything from mind-blowing sex to a pair of comfy socks. All of their words to one another were flat, meaningless. Real words, the ones you had to puff life into to speak them, no longer passed between them. Those deflated words were a symbol for everything their relationship had become.

Kate couldn't quite remember when she started detaching from her mother. She had never felt accepted by her, really. Her mother had mourned Kate's disinterest in flowery dresses and shaving her legs. No, Emily had never said a word about it, but the ugly silence, stretched out over the decades, had spoken clearly enough.

Frank, on the other hand, was Kate's biggest fan. He appreciated her interest in the world around her. He took her to the Kennedy Space center dozens of times. He had delighted in her amazement as they read the plaques and examined the displays together.

Frank Lasca had loved his daughter unconditionally. He supported every decision she made, every action she took, every thought she ever had. To be loved like that— Kate knew she would never find it again. And when the time came for her to tell him thank you, the moment where it really mattered, she had failed him. The hole inside her grew larger with each passing year. Now, this December, her fifth Christmas without him, it felt to her as if the winter winds blew right through that hole, reminding her that love was increasingly out of her grasp, that she was detaching from everyone, not just her mother. His death had erased her.

Kate was preparing a marketing report for Arlow when she felt Hannah's presence in her office.

"You did it, didn't you? I can tell by the look on your face."

"What?"

"You either called her or you had great sex last night. Either way, I'm proud of you." Hannah walked in and sat down.

"I called her, but leave me alone about it."

"Come on Kate, this is a good thing. You need to work this out with her."

"I hung up."

"What? This relationship with your mother, you know it's the most important one you'll ever have?" Hannah leaned in toward Kate as she spoke.

"Thank you, Mrs. Freud. Are you finished?"

"Besides reminding you that we had a deal, yeah, I'm finished. Here are your copies for next week. See you tomorrow."

"It's only two o'clock. Don't tell me Antonio is waiting." She winked at Hannah.

"Not unless the dentist changed his name to Antonio, and you said no sex talk." She smiled and stood to leave.

"Hannah, don't go yet."

"Okay, what's up?" Hannah sat on the edge of the armchair.

"Where's Greta? I haven't heard her voice all day."

"Do you miss her?" Hannah asked, tongue in cheek.

"Go to hell, okay? Now, where is she? Is she sick?"

"No." Kate saw in Hannah's face a frantic search for words. "Kate, she's with Mr. Jasper. We didn't want to tell you."

"Who is *we*? And why not?"

"Well, she's in a meeting with Jasper and Mr. Douglas."

"The mattress guy?" Kate was baffled.

"Yes. Apparently, she had this connection. It's a small account, but rumor has it that Jasper wants her to head it up, to get her feet wet." Hannah was clearly uncomfortable having to tell Kate the truth.

"What the hell are you saying?" Kate raised her voice. "Get her feet wet? You mean get them up in the air, don't you?"

Hannah flinched as if she thought Kate might throw something at her.

Kate continued, louder. "She has been here two weeks and he is giving her an account? How did she pull this off? Unbelievable! I guess the question 'Who do I have to screw around here to get ahead?' has now been answered!"

"Kate, I think he gave it to her because she pulled in the business and he felt he had to. Believe me, I am the last person to defend either one of them, and I love your theory that he's porking her. But—don't let this hurt you." Her words trailed off. "I didn't want to tell you."

"Don't let it hurt me, huh? Who, me—the Ice Queen—get hurt? You think I don't know what everyone thinks of me? I have worked my ass off to be a respectable businesswoman. At the cost of..." Kate stopped herself and plopped back down into her chair, defeated. "She's not worth it, is she?"

"Probably not, honey. And everyone here admires you. We all know you're going to be great in Houston."

Kate cocked an eyebrow. "Admire? I think that may be a strong word. As far as Arlow, I hope you're right. I just don't know." She put her head on her desk for a few seconds. "You know, I can't help but wonder if I hurt my career by taking off two years to take care of my dad. It haunts me, you know, some of my decisions. I feel like I have to work harder to catch up, work harder because I'm a woman, work harder—"

"Because working hard means you don't have to feel anything?"

Kate sat quietly.

Hannah continued: "Kate, honey. You wouldn't be the Kate we love if you hadn't done what you did. You devoted yourself to your father. And you did the right thing. Stop torturing yourself. Your dad would be proud, and you were there for him when it mattered most."

Kate knew she really hadn't been. She had let him down at the worst possible moment, and she burned to tell someone about it, to purge her guilt. Also, she felt every minute of those lost two years in advertising. She sat up and faced Hannah and said, "I know you're in a hurry to get going, but can you wait about two minutes?"

"Sure. What do you need?"

"Time to pack my briefcase. I'm going home," Kate said. Hannah didn't believe her at first.

"You're going home? Before 7:00? Do you know the phone number to Hell? I need to call and check the weather down there."

"Very funny," Kate snarled. "Now go get your coat. I need to pack up."

"Let me get this straight, sweetheart. You're going home early to prove a point, but you're taking a load of work home with you?"

"Is that weird?"

"Uh," Hannah paused. "Not in Katie-Land, but here on earth with us normal people, it's pretty weird. Just leave the work here. Go take a walk or go to a movie. Or   even   better—"

"No sex talk, remember? Besides, I can't." Kate's words were softer now.

"Can't or won't?" Hannah asked. Kate didn't answer. "One step at a time, I guess," Hannah added. She circled the desk and put her arms around Kate's shoulders. "Promise me you won't go home and sulk, all right? This Greta thing has nothing to do with you."

"It has everything to do with me," Kate snapped. "We should be working together, not competing."

"Who's competing, you or her?

"Okay, that was kind of mean."

"No. Just honest. Now, get your stuff and let's go."

Kate paced the floor of her apartment. She considered going to visit Jack, but decided against it. Besides, she was too wound up inside to talk right now. She probably wouldn't be coherent. She walked into her bedroom and threw herself across the double bed. The room was filled with images of the sea—on the comforter, the curtains, in the wallpaper. There were waves, lighthouses, sea gulls. But they didn't cheer her up today. She scooted her body back until her head was hanging off the side of the bed. The rush of blood felt invigorating. She remembered lying this way in her parents' room waiting for her mom to get out of the shower and make her breakfast on Saturday morning.

She sat up and opened her portfolio, spreading its contents across her comforter. She had so much work left to do. Her creative energy faded and reappeared inside her, like summer rain in Texas, flooding one day and drying up the next. The contradictory emotions were wearing her down. She liked her job, but here she was on the verge of getting a long sought-after promotion, and she was getting scared, "going girly," as Jack said. Her heart was at hospice, and she passionately longed to open the center office and start generating funds soon. She was being pulled in all these directions, and she had no idea which way to turn.

She drew some sketches unrelated to anything really, hoping to stir some ideas. Nothing came.

She opted to go to bed early. She made herself a large mug of hot chocolate and snuggled into her fluffy comforter, bunching the navy dotted fabric into her chest and shoving her back into overstuffed pillows covered in cases of the palest yellow. She reached into the nightstand, searching for something to read. She always had two or three books going at one time, further evidence of her inability to commit, her mother always told her. Her hand fell upon an old journal, one she had kept by hand at the Galveston cabin. An occasional return to its pages elicited unpredictable responses: sometimes great comfort, and sometimes searing grief. Fear of the emotions kept her at bay for months at a time, but the greater fear of forgetting always urged her back for more. She opened to a random page in the middle.

October 17, 2003

Dad and I are almost finished with our stone path. It has kept us busy, and I've lost four pounds, most assuredly a result of pushing his chair up and down that hill and digging into the dirt and sand on my hands and knees. Unfortunately, Dad has lost ten more pounds—he's down to 165. Thank goodness he was well enough to help me clear the limbs and other items to make a walkway. Ironic word to use: walkway. He was in the chair shortly after we got the path cleared. He holds the rocks in his lap now while we descend, a little further each day, making our little road to the beach. Without its completion to live for, I'm afraid he would have left me already. I'm desperate to find a new project soon. I can stall building our road, but I can't stop the cruel ticking of the clock.

CHAPTER ELEVEN

Daddy, do you believe in God?
Of course, baby. And I know God loves me.
But how do you know?
Because, Katie, He gave you to me.

"Kate, there's someone to see you. Says his name is Abe. Can you see him?" Hannah asked.

"Really? Abe is here?" She paused. "Well, yeah, okay. Let him in."

Hannah usually just pointed and directed visitors, but young handsome ones were personally escorted.

"Here you go, Kate. Mr. Archer, enjoy your visit." Hannah shook her hair a little as she talked. Kate rolled her eyes.

"Abe, I didn't expect to see you again so soon."

"I'm sorry to interrupt—"

"No, no, I didn't mean it that way. It's great to see you. What can I do for you?" she asked.

"You left your watch in the chapel the other night. I thought you might be missing it."

"Oh, my gosh. Yes, I was. So, that's where it was? I feel a little silly. Thank you." She took the watch from his outstretched hand.

"That's odd," Kate continued. "It says 9:33. It's almost 10:00." She held it up to her ear and listened. "It's stopped. I guess the battery is dead. I just replaced it too. Darn it—"

"Let me see," Abe said, taking the watch gently from her. He turned so that his back was to her and held it up to his ear a minute and then shook it slightly. The room was strangely silent.

"Here you go," he said. He turned and faced her. "Good as new. May I?" He reached for her hand, pulled it up close to his chest, and carefully clasped the watch back onto her wrist." The touch felt odd, not quite creepy, but definitely odd.

"Thank you, Abe," she said, wondering if he felt her anxiety.

"It's sort of a hobby I guess…watches I mean. Nothing magical or anything." He waved his hands in the air when he said the word "magical." Then he continued, "You have a nice one, by the way."

"What?" Kate asked.

"Oh, no. Nice watch I mean."

"It was a gift. From my father. He had it custom made."

"Hey, guys. Thought I'd come and see Mr. Archer out for you, Kate. I know you're swamped with work, and it would give me a chance to get to know Mr—"

"It's Abe, ma'am, and I really can see myself out. Pleasure to meet you though." And he was gone.

Kate looked at Hannah. She knew what was coming.

"Meee—ow," Hannah said. "That is some yummy kibble."

"Shush, he can probably hear you," Kate said, a finger at her lips.

"Well, he has a right to know how delicious he is."

"Stop, Hannah."

"I think I may be in heat. Find me a scratching post. Oh, Lord."

"'Oh Lord' is right; he is a minister."

"Tell me he's not. Oh, God—that is *so* hot." Hannah said.

"Besides," Kate said, truthfully, "I don't get that vibe at all. He's just a very nice man. A very gentle, and a very nice man. He feels like a long-lost brother or something. That sounds weird, I know. And besides…"

"Oh, dear, here comes the lecture," Hannah said.

"No lecture. Just news. I'm seeing someone," Kate said. "And I'm not going to tell you who."

"Come on, Kate. That's not fair."

"And you broke your end of our deal—no talking about sex, remember?"

"Was I talking about sex?"

"Purring like a kitten counts."

"Crap—you didn't tell me that. Did you hold up *your* end? Did you call your mom?" Hannah asked.

"Yes, I did. And we talked for twenty minutes. And I sent her a Christmas gift yesterday."

"A sweater?" Hannah asked.

"How did you know?"

"God, you are so boring. Let me check your pulse." She grabbed Kate's hand. "The reason I talk about sex is because you send sweaters."

"That doesn't make any sense. She loves sweaters." Kate said.

"Nobody loves sweaters. Trust me," Hannah argued.

"I do."

Hannah held Kate's hand up, still pretending to take her pulse. "B-O-R-I-N-G— what did I tell you?"

"What would you have me send, a dildo?" Kate asked, much louder than she realized.

"Um, Kate?" It was Abe. He was standing in the doorway.

Both women's eyes widened.

"Yes?" Kate croaked.

"I almost forgot to give this to you. It's a picture that Melissa drew for you and asked me to pass along." He handed her a drawing of two girls standing in the sunlight, hand in hand, and smiling.

"Thanks," she said.

"Well, bye now." He waved and left.

Hannah waited to hear the elevator open and close, and the she howled with laughter.

****

"You're jumping me again? That's four turns in a row!" Kate said.

"Well, I'm just good at this game," Melissa said, giggling.

"Too good, I'm afraid." Kate laughed with her.

"Well, Kate, it looks like you're having a blast. Who's the checker champion these days?" Kate wished she could disappear when she heard that voice.

"Hi, Abe," she said and looked up at him. He had a beautiful little girl holding his hand.

"I'm the champ!" squealed Melissa!

Kate looked at the little girl with round, ruddy cheeks and dark hair. Seven-year-old Lauren Zigler had stolen Kate's heart over the past months. She insisted on playing checkers every time she and Kate were there together, and today she looked a little worried that Melissa was taking her place. During her evening visits, Kate's focus was to keep the children at the hospice occupied while the adults took care of business and had their rare and cherished private visits. Couples with young children like Lauren had little alone time after the illness struck, and by the time they reached hospice, funds for babysitters and sadly, sometimes the generosity of friends and family, began to dry up.

Kate convinced the girls that playing checkers *together* without her was the best idea ever, and then she and Abe sneaked away to chat.

'First of all," she said, unable to look him in the eye, "I am so sorry and so embarrassed about earlier today. I really usually don't talk about such things, and…I am so very sorry."

He took her hand and leaned in, forcing her to face him. "Kate, it's okay. I know what a dildo is."

"Of course you do, I mean, oh God."

"It's really okay," he said, "and actually kind of funny."

"I wish I could agree. I just don't want you to think—"

"What? That you're human…that you're a woman?"

She had no idea what to say. His hand tightened around hers. Her discomfort was melting and she made herself keep steady eye contact.

"Do I know you?" she asked him.

"Well…yes…" He looked confused.

"It's just that, each time I see you there's something—different about you. Not different, actually more familiar I'd say. Did we know each other a long time ago? Where are you from?"

He laughed. "No. You saw me for the first time here in this room a couple of nights ago. I assure you."

"It sounds goofy, but I swear, I know you. When I first heard your voice on the phone, it was like I knew it, but there was an accent or something. And just this weird feeling that I know you."

"I'm glad you feel a connection."

"Okay, don't laugh, but I do. I feel connected to you. And you're virtually a stranger. You don't know this about me, but I don't warm up quickly. And it takes eons for me to connect to someone. So don't take offense, but I'm weirded out that I feel close to you."

"I'm not offended. I'm flattered. It's my job to make people feel safe and comfortable."

"Well, yeah, that makes sense. You're pretty great at it."

"Thanks, Kate. I think you're pretty great, too."

CHAPTER TWELVE

October 2049—Galveston

Maggie turned away from the window and faced Simon.

"Dad, how did you know mom was the one?" she asked.

Simon smiled. "Honey, that's like asking me how I know to breathe every morning. You just know. I saw her….and I knew."

"Do you think love has to make sense?" she asked.

"No…I think love makes everything else make sense," he said. "Where is this coming from?"

"I just—well I just wonder, that's all. You and mom—your love seems so natural, so…uncomplicated."

Simon laughed hard. "You're kidding me, right? Look again outside that window."

"I know. But you know what I mean. It's like your love—"

"Makes everything else make sense?" They spoke in unison.

"Yeah," she said. "I just wonder. Is love always like that?" she asked.

Simon drew a deep breath and sat down. "Well, that's hard to say, seeing how I've only been in love the one time. But, yes, I think it is. If you're lucky."

She came and sat next to her father and put her head on his shoulder.

"Maggie, is there something you want to talk about? I mean, today is probably the day to do it. You know I'll listen."

"Yeah, I know. It's just that—well I'm one of the most successful female scientists—"

"In the country—and not just female, but most successful, period." He smiled his biggest smile of the day.

"Okay, dad. I'm successful. But it doesn't—fill me up, you know?" She looked up at him, and she was twelve again in his mind.

Simon saw the years of hurt in her eyes; he saw it more clearly than he ever had. He wanted to kick the shit out of Campbell Cross.

"Maggie, a man who loves you—loves you completely. Not just when it's convenient, or when it's good for him. Not when it feels ethical or when he just can't be without you for that moment. When he loves you, nothing, and I mean *nothing* will stop him from being with you. Please don't settle for less than that."

"Somehow I knew you'd say that. Maybe we're not all that lucky."

"You don't want to know my opinion on that," he said.

"Yeah, actually I do."

"It will sound harsh."

"I can take it."

"Well," he said. "I think it's better to be alone than to settle. So, if you think you don't have that kind of love, then you clear the decks and wait and see. And in the meantime, you go on living."

"I know—I know in my head, but my heart—"

"Different story, right? Oh, sweetheart. If I could just hold you like when you were a little girl and make it all okay…."

"You could try, couldn't you?"

Simon squeezed his daughter as hard as he could. It's all he could do for her, and they both knew it. She went limp and let him hold her, rocking her gently, as they waited for Zeke to arrive and complete their circle. They didn't dare think beyond that. They sat as quiet as they could, Simon loving his daughter, and Maggie soaking it in like a child running through a lawn sprinkler on an August day.

"I love you, Daddy," she whispered. "I really do.

CHAPTER THIRTEEN

Daddy, is there really a Santa?
Of course, Katie. And he brings you whatever you wish for.
Really? Will he bring me a husband some day?
A man just like you, Daddy?
Yes, just close your eyes and wish for it, and he will bring him.

The Jasper Agency Christmas party took place on December 23rd, as was its custom. Jack spent the entire evening flirting with Marissa and talking football with Andrew. He was a man's man, Kate thought, as she watched him mingle.

"Tie a bow around that and leave it under my tree," she heard Hannah say. She was also watching Jack.

"I don't know," Kate said. "I think he might be too expensive for me."

"Oh, but worth every penny." Hannah then began to claw and scratch the air, growling like a tiger. Kate was too tired to be embarrassed by her antics.

"You know what I think?" Kate asked.

"Hmm?" Hannah murmured, her lips pressed to the rim of her champagne glass. She was getting tipsy.

"I think you're all talk and no action."

"Oh, really?" Hannah said. "Well, Miss Lasca, what exactly would *you* do if left in a room alone with Jack Finnegan? Make pie charts?"

They both stared at the men, who were patting each other on the back and grinning their boys' club smiles. He did look good in his charcoal gray tuxedo, which was just a shade darker than his eyes. Kate watched the laugh lines around his mouth broaden as he spoke, and she thought about how that mouth felt on her skin. His hands—she couldn't stop watching them rise and fall, moving in a circle and cradling his drink, and she shuddered at the thought of them groping her in the middle of the night. He occasionally looked over at her and winked. Hannah must have thought Kate was completely dead from the waist down.

"Now, she has got his number, Katie." Her words were slurred now, and she never called her Katie.

"Who, Marissa?"

"Yeah, look at her. Like a puppy seeking its new owner, eager for the love, honey. You watch out."

Kate stared at Marissa. She was in a tiny swatch of black fabric. Her blonde hair kissed her shoulders like gold silk, and her lips pouted in harlot red. She wasn't exactly "sweet little Marissa" tonight.

"Your boobs are way bigger, though," Hannah stammered.

"Okay—number one, I don't care. And number two, I would never compete with a twenty-year old."

Hannah looked at her and groaned.

"What?" Kate said, defensively.

Hannah kept looking at her, quietly. Her head bobbed a little in response to her fourth glass of champagne, but her eyes were sober.

"What?" Kate said again. "I could compete with her. I just don't choose to. Besides, I don't want him."

"He is mad about you, you know." Hannah giggled and put her arm around Kate.

"You're crazy," Kate said, fidgeting with her drink, feeling no desire to talk about this with Hannah. She knew she was just this year's model anyway; no one loved anyone in this company.

"Please...it is so obvious. Don't pretend you don't know."

"I don't know anything anymore, except that I need more champagne."

****

Kate awoke the next morning with a shrieking headache and her tongue stuck to her teeth. It took a moment for her to remember where she was. Her strapless green dress was crumpled in the floor by the bathroom and her underwear was, well, that was a fine question.

Jack entered looking toothpaste commercial fresh in his fluffy white robe, offering coffee and a bagel. It wasn't like him to be this attentive.

"Just take a bite or two. You'll feel better."

She sipped coffee, nibbled on the bagel, and asked him what had happened the previous night.

"Well, what do you think happened?" He looked down at her naked breasts and back up to her face.

"Besides that, you jerk. How did I get here?"

"You were drunk, Kate. I drove you here."

"Dear Lord, did Jasper see me like this?"

"Yeah, he was here too. We took turns."

"That's just not even funny. Look, Jack, you have to tell me. Did I make a fool of myself?"

She could tell he was considering this once in a lifetime opportunity to one-up her. But he did the right thing and told the truth.

"No. I didn't let you. I pulled up on my white horse and whisked you away to my humble castle to save you the embarrassment of puking in front of your boss."

"Oh…thank God."

"Thank God? What about me? How do you plan to thank me?"

"Jack, I have dried vomit on my face and in my hair, and I'm sure my make-up is smeared everywhere, and…. well, the rest of me smells like a wino."

"Winos don't drink champagne."

She laughed. Her face felt oily, as if she had been eating fried chicken with no hands. She was scared to think how she might look. He kissed her nose, and she put her arms around him.

"Let me shower, and then I'll get out of your way," she said.

She stepped out of the bathroom thirty minutes later, cleaner and slightly less nauseated. Jack's bed had been made. The room smelled like lilies. Her clothes from the previous night were in a little pink tote bag on the bed, and beside them was a fresh change of clothes—shoes, undergarments, and all. Theories flew around in her head while she dressed and dried her hair with the blow-dryer she had found on his dresser, next to her makeup bag and other toiletries. When did he go get these things? Why did he go get them?

She joined him at the table in his breakfast nook. When he noticed that she was squinting, he closed the blinds and took her arm. As he led her to her chair, her curiosity hit the roof. She saw a hug vase of white lilies on the breakfast table.

"The flowers are beautiful," she said. "They brighten the room and smell wonderful."

She was talking, not to communicate, but to prove to her brain that she wasn't dreaming.

"Well, I know they're your favorite, honey. Now sit down. Relax."

Honey? And gladiolas were her favorite.

His effort to be romantic suited him, she was surprised to admit. She sat on the edge of her chair and looked into his eyes, waiting.

"Merry Christmas," he said, as he pulled the napkin off the placemat in front of her to reveal a small, gray box. "I was going to wait until tomorrow, but, well, I just couldn't. And it's Christmas Eve—that's the same thing as Christmas, right?" For the first time in their relationship, Jack seemed nervous. Nervous was pretty cute on him, too.

"Are you going to open it or what?"

"Okay," she whispered, and gently removed the tiny red bow. The box creaked when she gently pried it open, and when she saw its contents, she looked wide-eyed at Jack and back down at the box. Then she ran to the bathroom to lose her bagel.

"Okay, so that was a slightly less romantic scene than I envisioned," Jack told her when she exited his bathroom for the second time in fifteen minutes.

"I'm so sorry," she said. "I just…I don't know what to say, Jack. I'm…overwhelmed."

"Is that *good* overwhelmed or *bad* overwhelmed, because, frankly, accompanied by the vomit, it's a close call."

"Oh, Jack." She kissed him on the cheek. "Thank you, Jack."

His face was serious. They were quiet a moment.

"Thank you, Jack? I give you an engagement ring, and you say, 'Thank you'? A more pleasing response would be, 'Yes, Jack, I'll marry you and have your babies, who would be incredibly good-looking by the way, and then we can grow old watching the sun rise together in my cabin by the ocean.' Try it—it just rolls right off the tongue, I promise."

He took the ring out of the box and slid it onto her finger.

"I love you, Kate."

She couldn't stop herself from laughing.

"Wow! You are a ball-breaker, aren't you?" He stood up and turned his back toward her so that he was facing the mirror.

"Oh, no. Jack. I'm sorry. I didn't mean to upset you." She approached him, lifted his arm, and snuggled herself into his side.

"Thank you. I'm sorry." He jerked away, more hurt than angry. "Who are you? Emily Fucking Post? You are lousy at this, you know?"

"You're right. I am. But it's my first proposal. Forgive me. You have never, in all these months, even hinted that you love me, and now, out of the blue, Christmas Eve, a month before the Houston trip, which you know is stressing me out, you pop the question! Pardon me, Mr. Finnegan, but why the hell are you asking me this now?"

"Why are you angry, Kate?"

"Why are you angry, Jack?"

"Because I love you. And you make me so God-damn mad!"

She couldn't stop looking at the ring. What was he thinking? He didn't love her. He couldn't love her. This was it—this was *the* question, the one whose answer she had rehearsed a million times as a little girl. The moments in the bathroom wearing the white towel had been so different. The clunky plastic ring from the bubble gum machine had felt…well…*perfect*. It had even sparkled more, somehow, than this one. And she had felt so sure. Yeah, she thought, sure of a make believe future husband who worshipped her and gave her everything she ever wanted. Maybe it was time to grow up. Time was marching on, and it would soon be marching across her face, her hips, her ass.…

"Yes, Jack, I'll marry you. But only under one condition."

"Already you have conditions?"

"I'm a good businesswoman. Now do you want to hear this or not?"

He nodded. "Yes, ma'am."

"No one can know about us. Especially no one at Jasper. Not until after Arlow. Maybe longer."

"Counter offer? You have to stay here with me every weekend from now until we tell them."

"Every other weekend?" She paused. "And you can tell your mother." She winked at him and extended a hand.

"You stay here Christmas and New Year's, too?" He winked back.

"My place for Christmas, and you have a deal, Mr. Finnegan." They shook hands.

He pulled her close. She rubbed her hands up and down his robe and stared at the huge gem on her left hand.

"I sure do love doing business with you, Mrs. Finnegan," he said, kissing her softly.

"That's Ms. Lasca-Finnegan." She untied his robe and watched it fall open. "Now, let's get down to some of that business."

CHAPTER FOURTEEN

October 2049—Galveston

Maggie returned to the box and pulled out the Christmas photo of Kate and Jack. She traced with her finger the figure of the lovers in the old picture. Her mother always did look gorgeous in green. She was enchanted by Jack's handsome face and solid build. Simon knew she was imagining his walk, his talk, and his touch. He wasn't stupid—he knew who she was thinking about. Simon had seen the startling resemblance between the two men years ago.

"So, Dad, why didn't mom ever tell us about this Jack person? They look awfully chummy."

"Oh, I don't know," Simon offered playfully, "I guess folks sometimes don't want to share every aspect of their past love life, or even their present entanglements, I suppose. Don't you agree?"

The door burst open and a youthful, angular man tripped through the threshold. The man, wearing a gray sweatshirt with *U of H* printed across the front and a pair of baggy, wrinkled camouflage shorts, was like Simon in his length and strength, and also in his tendency toward clumsiness. Only in the water had Simon ever felt in control of his movements. It was part of his early connection to Kate, and a thread that ran through most of his close relationships, including that which he shared with his son.

Maggie jumped up to greet him.

"Zeke! Oh, God, look at you. I'm so glad you're here." She gave him a huge hug and scolded him for wearing shorts in the cool weather. She also tugged disapprovingly at his pumpkin-orange hair, which had grown past the collar of his sweatshirt.

Simon loved having his children together, and he suddenly felt a jolt of aching awareness that Kate was missing it all, and would continue to miss it. She and Simon had both been only children, and had always loved watching their babies play together. No brother and sister loved each other more, or were more diametrically created, than Maggie and Zeke. They were twins, and Kate had been exhausted during her pregnancy with them. They assumed it was because she was almost forty-five when they were born, but soon after she gave birth, they figured out that it must have been the constant bickering they did in the womb. As infants, they would cry to be together in the playpen and then slap at one another and scream to be separated after just a few minutes of cohabitation. They both said their first words at ten months, an impressive feat until Kate figured out they just couldn't wait to insult each other verbally. The battles grew louder and more complicated over the years, and so did their love and loyalty. *Sweet and sticky*, Kate called it. They would fight each other until the end, but kill anyone who wronged the other in any way. Simon had seen this first-hand many times. He feared a reprise, with all the insanity that today promised.

"Dude, what is up with that crowd?" Zeke said as he plopped down on the sofa next to Simon.

"Did you just say *Dude*? That's new," Maggie said, turning her nose up.

"Yeah, you like it?" Zeke said, laughing. "I'm auditioning new lingo."

Maggie ignored his attempt to antagonize her. It was his second favorite form of affection, right after grabbing her and giving her a good noogie.

"Hey, Zeke. You hungry?" she asked.

Before he could answer, a sphere of flames the size of a soccer ball shattered the glass in the front window and whizzed past Zeke and Maggie, touching Simon's sleeve and crashing against the wall.

"Oh, my God!" Maggie screamed, and Zeke rushed to stomp out the blazing carpet. Maggie realized that her dad's shirt had caught fire, so she grabbed a blanket draping the back of the sofa and tried to extinguish the flames. She and Zeke were astonished by the violent attack. Zeke flew to the window and stuck his head out through the hole in the middle, scraping the glass and cutting his shoulders, as he raged against the crowd outside.

"Bastards!" He exploded with fury. "My mother is dying. Let her die with dignity. And leave my family alone!"

A very young man, short but broad, ran through the crowd. He was wearing a blue tee shirt with "Though shall not kill" printed across the front. He raced straight up toward Zeke, whose long, muscular body was half inside the house and half outside and beginning to bleed more profusely now. Once the young man reached the wrap-around porch, he slowed his stride, met Zeke face-to-face and exclaimed, "Your mother's a murdering bitch. She deserves no peace."

The crowd exploded into cacophony of cheers and boos. Several men and one woman in the front of the crowd lunged, some grabbing the man in the blue tee shirt, and others grabbing and pulling at Zeke. Simon tried to reach the door to save his son, but Maggie pushed him back and threw the door open. Simon stood next to her, and witnessed his worst nightmare coming true.

"Step aside," a commanding and gruff voice rose in the air. "Police…. I said step aside."

CHAPTER FIFTEEN

It's beautiful, Daddy. I love it.
Open it, Katie. Look inside.
It's us, Daddy. It's a picture of us!
Wear it today for Christmas, darling.
I will, Daddy. I'll wear it every Christmas,
                    Right here next to my heart.

The angel sang "O Holy Night" as the congregation gathered in the sanctuary of Grace Methodist Church. Kate and Jack had a child at each elbow, escorting them in for the family Christmas Eve service. It was a yearly celebration of songs, hot chocolate, and the telling of the Christmas story. The Christmas Eve offering went to a different charity each year, and this year's charity was The Frank Lasca Center. With over six hundred in attendance tonight, Kate was hoping that they would raise enough to take a few more baby steps, at least. She worked in close coordination with Hospice and was happy to do so, but she also knew people needed help coping with great loss, and that's what the center could provide.

Jack smiled at her during the telling of the story, and he put his arm around Melissa, who wore a simple ivory A-line dress and sat between him and Kate. Lauren sat on the other side of Kate, wearing an emerald green velvet dress with a big red sash around the waist. The lights were twinkling on the trees, and the sanctuary was full of hope for the coming year. Jack looked surprisingly at ease surrounded by the children and the holiday sparkle. Kate absently toyed with the locket at her breast.

Abraham Archer opened and closed the service, and Kate wasn't surprised to see that he was a dynamic speaker. He gave the center a shining stamp of approval and encouraged everyone to dig deep into those pockets, but in a manner that felt comfortable, not pushy. He talked about the clients she wanted to help, and shared some of Kate's goals with the people of Grace Methodist.

"Kate Lasca and her devoted handful of volunteers want to give the children a voice. They work tirelessly now in outreach at Hope Springs Hospice, where I was fortunate enough to meet her a couple of weeks ago. She has a passion for helping a very special and needy population: families, and especially children, affected by HIV and AIDS. Her hope is to give them expression in the form of art, music, dance, theatre, writing, and any other form that the clients find helpful. To do this, she will need supplies, and she needs to hire a counselor. So, look into your hearts tonight, and if you agree with me and with Kate that there is a need for these families, give what you can."

Jack didn't smile as Abe spoke. He squirmed a little and cleared his throat at one point, but was otherwise silent and still. Kate shrugged it off. While they were waiting in line to get their hot chocolate after the service, Abe approached them.

"Abraham," Kate said, "thank you so much for your kind words. I am speechless!"

Jack extended a hand. "I'm Jack Finnegan. Kate's fiancée. We're grateful for your help."

"Glad to do it," Abe said, a broad, happy grin on his face. He seemed to symbolize pure goodness tonight, with his white robe, in this place, surrounded by tinkling bells and children's laughter, the soft light shining in his yellow hair. "Anyway, I just wanted to come over and wish you a Merry Christmas. It's a special time, isn't it?"

"Yes, it is. And Santa comes tonight!" Melissa piped in. Kate's heart expanded with a tumble of emotions. She became aware that her eyes were watering and that Abe and Jack were staring at her.

"Merry Christmas, Mister Abe," Melissa said, and threw her arms around his legs. Lauren tugged at his robe, wanting a chance to hug him, too. It was a beautiful Christmas moment and Kate allowed herself to feel a little hopeful.

"Group hug!" Melissa screamed, and shoved Abe into Kate and Jack. Abe wrapped an arm around each of them and gave Kate a quick peck on the cheek. Jack stood awkwardly in the minister's embrace, and Kate felt a little sorry for him. She pulled herself free and grabbed Jack's hand to gently pry him loose as well. After a short goodbye, she insisted that they had an early morning and tried to get Jack out of the church quickly and quietly.

Jack tapped his long, thick fingers on the leather-covered steering wheel of his red Saab convertible as he drove Kate back to her condo.

"The kids had a great time, Jack. Thank you for coming with us."

"He likes you," Jack said. His mood had shifted.

"Who?"

"Abraham. The way he looks at you. And what was the kiss about?"

"It's Christmas?"

"Well, yeah, it's Christmas, but you don't see me kissing random women."

"I'm not 'random' and excuse me...you were getting pretty comfy with Marissa last night at the party."

"Hell, Kate, she's just a girl."

Both were quiet a moment.

"Jack, he's a minister. And I hardly know him. Are you jealous of Abe?"

"So, it's Abe now?"

"You are crazy, you know? We have been engaged less than twelve hours and you're already jealous? Of a minister at my church?"

"He sure knows a lot about you. More than I do," Jack said, a hint of pouting in his voice.

Kate exhaled sharply. "Is that what this is about? Do you want to hear about the center? I'd be happy to tell you."

"I'm not jealous, not exactly," he said, calming down a little. "It's just—I guess I don't know you—and I want to," he said.

"Okay," Kate said. "That's easy enough. I'll tell you anything you want to know."

"Really?" His eyes were nearly pleading. She was surprised by his words and actions.

"Really," she said. "What do you want to know?"

"Tell me about your father," he said softly. "His life and his death."

She was silent.

"Kate?" he said. "Kate, tell me about him. What was he like?"

"No. He's off limits."

He wrapped his hand around hers. Her fingers were cold against his as she intertwined them. "I can't talk about him tonight," she said. "It's Christmas. I'll tell you about him soon. I promise."

"Okay," he said. She knew he was hurt.

"I need you to understand," she begged.

"I do. I get it, Kate."

He pulled into the visitors' lot but couldn't find an empty space.

"Go around back," she said. "There's usually room there. Remember our deal? You stay here tonight?"

He didn't say anything at first.

"Did you hear me, Jack? Go around back."

"I better get going," he finally said.

"Okay," she said, almost as a question.

"Merry Christmas, Kate," he said, and he kissed her gently on the lips. He smelled like cinnamon and chocolate. She really wanted him to stay.

"Merry Christmas, Jack," she said and stepped out of the Saab. A blast of cold air hit her in the face and forced her breath back into her chest as she turned to go up the stairs outside her building.

****

Someone knocked on Kate's door just after 8:30 Christmas morning. Kate was surprised to see Abe's smiling face staring back at her through the peephole.

"Come in," she said. "It's really cold out there, isn't it?"

"Morning, Kate. I won't keep you. Sorry to intrude on your holiday."

She smiled. "Would you stop saying that? It's not an intrusion. It's a Christmas gift. I'm glad to see you again."

"Well, speaking of gifts…that's why I'm here." He handed her an envelope. "Merry Christmas."

She stared at him blankly.

"It's a check," he said.

"A check?"

"For $42,000."

She gasped.

"Yes, you heard me. $42,000," he repeated. "Donations from last night."

"But, people—I mean, we're not a wealthy church—and—how—?"

"Well, it's supposed to be a secret, but I'll tell you this much. The church raised $4200 last night."

"And—"

"A donor, who insists on remaining anonymous, came forward after the service and arranged to add a zero at the end of whatever we raised."

"Oh my God." She screamed and jumped up and down, hugging him. "Merry Christmas, kids!" she yelled, in total abandon, dancing and singing and hugging him again.

"I knew you'd be happy," he said. "That's why I couldn't wait until next week to tell you. I had to come today. I guess it's sort of…my Christmas gift."

She grabbed him one more time and planted a huge, smacking kiss on his cheek. "Thank you, thank you, thank you," she said, tears forming in her eyes.

"I didn't do anything. I wish I could take credit. Just seeing the joy on your face—in your eyes. It's the best thank you in the world."

Only he wasn't look at her face anymore. She realized her robe had fallen open and revealed her rather provocative negligee. She had put it on late last night, hoping Jack would cool off and return. Now Abe was watching her, and she sensed his admiration mingled with a little shame. She quickly closed her robe. He turned away, blushing.

"And that's not all," he said. "Here." He handed her a pale-yellow business card. "It's for a therapist. She also came by last night and offered to volunteer five hours a week until you could get someone hired full time. She said she'd try to recruit a few others. They can at least cover group sessions for a while."

Kate sat in one of the newly covered chairs and started to cry. She was embarrassed, but she couldn't stop herself. The tears just came—tears of joy, sadness, grief, and excitement—all in one good cry. She cried for Frank and Emily, and for the Ziglers and Stones, and she cried for Jack and for herself, in the midst of all the confusion and changes. She cried because she was witnessing a Christmas miracle, delivered to her by this mysterious man whom she barely knew.

He knelt beside her, took her in his arms, and let her cry for a long, long time.

CHAPTER SIXTEEN

Kick your feet, Katie girl.
I am, Daddy, I am.
Kick as hard as you can. That's what moves you forward.
Okay, look, Daddy—I am doing it!!
Go, Katie, go! Never stop kicking!

For most people, the first few weeks of January creep along at a snail's pace, but for Kate, their passage was almost instantaneous. During the first week of the New Year, she worked and drank coffee, and worked some more, finalizing plans for the Arlow presentation. Greta had been in and out of her office a lot. Kate was beginning to accept her presence; however, her insides were in disarray. Each day it seemed that Greta was more involved in her business than the day before. Like an earthworm tunneling a hole, her encroachment was barely perceptible a day at a time, but each week ended with Greta burrowed a few inches further into Kate's life. The Arlow account was her baby, and she resented anyone telling her how to raise it. Especially someone like Greta.

The king of clichés, Jasper had told her to hear Greta's suggestions and take them or leave them. He trusted Kate's judgment, he had said. Two heads are better than one, he also had said. Kate believed that the latter sentiment's truth depended entirely upon the heads in question. She finally had admitted that Greta had good, but risky ideas about the project. She didn't know if her heart was softening or if she was lowering her standards, but she sometimes enjoyed their time together. Her reaction to this peculiar woman was beyond explanation, so she wasn't sure she could blame her colleagues for speculating about her. She despised her one minute, and was intrigued by her the next.

One morning in late January, a week before Kate was scheduled to leave for Houston, Kate heard Greta step off the elevator onto the third floor, arms full of bags and parcels, and turn into the corridor that housed Jasper Advertising Agency. As Greta came into her view, she dropped her keys in front of Hannah's desk, and, bracelets jangling, paper bags crumpling, she stooped down to retrieve them. She bumped into the wall, almost knocking down a portrait of the Ryan Scott Jasper, the agency's founder and Bob Jasper's father. She managed to recover, however ungracefully. She laughed at herself as she straightened her blouse. The elder Jasper, portrayed at roughly the same age that his son now was, looked very little like the Jasper she knew. They did, however, have the same firm, thin lips, and both men gave the impression that every word passing between those lips was distinctly important. She had never met the company's original owner, but he had a reputation for living large.

From her desk, Kate watched Greta approach. She was not pretty, Kate thought. She couldn't even call her attractive although, in truth, she did attract attention. Handsome, that's what she was. But in a rough sort of way. Not rugged rough or athletic rough, but a sort of *I've been to hell and back* rough, the handsome part a result of the *coming back from hell* part. Greta appeared to be a survivor. Her confidence emanated from her like a search light and sliced through Kate's insecurity; this was part of Kate's uneasiness in Greta's presence. Unfortunately, it wasn't Greta's confidence that others focused upon. A voice whispered in Kate's ear that this woman was worthy of admiration, regardless of her disapproval of her behavior.

Kate watched as Greta glanced down the hall, and Kate looked down, pretending to read some files, hoping that Greta wouldn't notice her open door. She often mistook Kate's claustrophobia for friendliness and invited herself in to chat. Once Greta started talking, the afternoon was blown. Kate was relieved when Greta dashed down the hall toward her own office instead. Kate listened as the jangling and crumpling grew softer and eventually stopped. Then the tinkle of metal began again, but this time it wasn't the bracelets. Greta's keys clinked against each other as she unlocked her door. Like a Sahara sandstorm, she burst inside. Kate couldn't see this, but she had seen it many times before and now replayed it in her mind to the rhythm of Greta's noise-music.

Kate immersed herself in her files, but by mid-afternoon she had grown restless. She watched the clock tick 3:15…3:16. Then her mind began to wander. She listened for the faint but familiar clackety-clunk of Greta's keyboard. She could usually just make it out in the slow, still, afternoon hours. *I wonder if she's writing another story,* she asked herself.

Greta had written countless short stories and a couple of plays. One of the plays had even been picked up and performed by a local community theatre last summer. No big deal, she told herself. As if the plays and stories weren't enough though, she could paint, too. She was sick of hearing about it—*the plays, the stories, the boyfriends,* she mumbled through clinched teeth. Frustrated, she tossed the thick Arlow file onto the corner of her desk, and when some of the papers caught the air and flew, Kate frantically began to chase them.

"What boyfriends?"

Kate heard her voice and, while on her knees between a file cabinet and a wall, stretching for the last unruly page, she twisted her neck around and came eye level with Greta's crossed legs. Her colleague was comfortably seated in her now-favorite chair opposite Kate's desk, swinging her leg casually up and down, revealing with each upward motion the early stages of a run in her shimmering black nylons just where they intersected with her black go-go boots.

Weren't those things outlawed in 1978? Kate asked herself, and she struggled to pull herself to standing with as much dignity as possible. Damp stray hairs were pasted to her cheeks, and she tried to rearrange them back into some order. She pretended not to watch her guest pull a package of Juicy Fruit from the pocket of her red, oversized, rather sheer smock, which hung only a half inch higher than her dangerously short black skirt.

"What did you say?" Kate asked, a bit dazed, tugging at her jacket, which, like Greta's skirt, had inched slowly upward.

"What boyfriends?" Greta laughed. "When I came in, you were saying…"

"Oh, that." Kate laughed, but not with the same ease as Greta's laughter. She twisted her ruby earrings, trying to devise some clever remark, but her mind kept repeating, Just how much did I say out loud?

"Good God. Don't' worry." Greta smiled again, this time showing her large, white teeth. "You act as if I asked you to murder my cat or something. If you don't want to talk about it, just say so."

Kate exhaled in relief. "Thank you, Greta. I really don't."

"But while we're on the subject of boyfriends, you know, I heard that Hank in payroll thinks you are hot!"

Kate tried to be delicate. "Look, Greta. I appreciate your coming by, but I really have a lot of work to do, and…Hank thinks I'm hot?" She silently chastised herself for getting distracted. "Greta, I really am trying to work, you know, deadline and everything." She knew her tone was condescending.

"Well, that's exactly why I'm here. Jasper says you're quite busy, you know, with the Arlow thing looming and all."

Silence. Then Kate finally realized that she was being baited. "And?" she asked.

"Well…" Greta wrung her hands and swung her boot anxiously, as if she were about to make a big announcement.

"Well?" Kate asked.

Greta took a deep breath and blurted it all out, like a child announcing to her parents that she had just won the fourth grade spelling bee. "I'm-going-with-you-to-Houston-next-week!" They weren't words. They were one long ugly pronouncement, sharpened to a dagger's point.

Kate's mind swam. She could almost feel her hands tightening around Greta's throat, squeezing the wretched life right out of her. Pure pleasurable release.

"How nice," she said.

"Isn't it? We have so many plans to make. Where to eat, what sights to see. You know, I love basketball like you do—we could go to a Rockets' game. I've never been to Houston, but Jasper told me you grew up there. We'll have a lot of fun, won't we?"

"A lot of fun. Yes." Kate thought about how tough the Houston trip would be anyway without Ms. Go-Go Boots hanging around. She somehow managed to be gentle in her request.

"Greta. It's 3:30, and I'm in the middle of this thing I'm working on and if you don't mind, can we talk tomorrow?"

"Of course. Tomorrow. Sure." She stood up and spat her gum into the wastebasket. "Kate…"

"Hmm?" Kate was looking out the window now, counting to ten under her breath.

"I knew we'd be friends."

Kate nodded and escorted her to the door. She watched the back of Greta's head as she strolled back to her office, and she wondered how in God's name this could have happened. She shut her office door and sat back down at her desk. She started counting again. One…two…the volcanic rage built over the next few minutes, and then spewed.

"The Rockets!" she screamed, and she picked up her files and flung them hard against the wall and once again, papers flew.

I will be calm, I will be calm, she chanted to herself. The anger, however, could not be quelled with a simple mantra. She stalked down the hall to Jasper's office. He was with someone. She paced back and forth outside his office, cracking her knuckles. Fortunately, within three minutes he was finished with his meeting.

"Katie Girl, come in. What can I do for you?"

She stomped into his office. "You can explain something to me," she said between gritted teeth. "Explain to me why the hell Greta has been assigned to the Arlow account."

He tried, unsuccessfully, to interrupt.

"With all due respect, why are you doing this to me?" she asked. The cork had popped, and there was no stuffing it back in. It hit Jasper right between the eyes.

"After months of hard work, how could you do this? I have waited and worked and slaved for five years. I have given my life to this place and you are putting her on this account?"

"I'm not exactly giving her the account, Kate," he managed to squeeze in.

"Then how do you explain this? Huh? Explain!" She couldn't believe she was talking to him like this, but she also couldn't stop herself.

"She's going with you to watch, and to help. She has some good advice to give. I told you before, take it or leave it—her suggestions, I mean. You are a good team. You have the right qualities together to be fantastic. There is more to Greta than you see, Kate, and besides, she is just going to help."

"She is just going to screw up the biggest opportunity in my life. And one of the biggest accounts this agency has right now. I can't work with her. I refuse to work with her. And that's my final word!" In one angry fluid motion, she turned and strode away.

She slammed the door behind her when she entered her office. Out of control, she grabbed a vase of silk sunflowers from the shelf and smashed it against the wall. Then she threw herself onto her father's chair and screamed into a throw pillow until she couldn't breathe. There was a soft tap at the door. It was Jasper.

"Listen, Kate. I should have consulted you. I just assumed…well, I know I shouldn't have. But Greta likes you so much. I assumed you felt the same. I will break the news to her. She will be disappointed, but clearly this means more to you than to her. Now go clean yourself up." He handed her his handkerchief.

More self-loathing. How could she sink low enough to play the father-daughter game with her boss?

"Mr. Jasper," she said softly. She didn't want to say it, but felt she had to. "You're right. She should go. I don't know why I reacted this way."

"Because you care about your work. That's why I gave you this chance. But Katie, you've gotta remember that work is work—it's not life. Whatever you decide will be fine with me. Take a day or two, but no longer." She could see by the look on his face that their conversation was over.

****

Kate twisted her shoulders and neck under the stabbing hot water and hung her head so that a flood ran through her hair, encircling her face, but not touching it. She thought about Jasper. He would expect an answer tomorrow. Should she take Greta to Houston? The question that kept coming to her mind wasn't about her feelings for Greta or how Jasper would view her if she told him no. Instead, she wondered why Greta wanted to be around her at all. Kate had been civil, polite, but rarely friendly or inviting to her. Greta didn't seem to care, and in fact simply enjoyed whatever life was giving her, and according to rumors, it was giving her lots and lots of parties and very young men. Kate wondered why she wasn't enjoying her own life. She had a dream job, she was moving up quickly, and one of the most handsome, successful men she knew had just proposed. What else could a girl want? She could be Mrs. Jack Finnegan and Creative Director in less than six months. What else could a woman ask for?

While Kate was drying off, the doorbell rang.

"You're early." Kate stood in the doorway in a robe and towel.

Jack eyed her seductively. "Apparently I am right on time." He playfully punctuated the last three syllables.

"We have dinner reservations." Kate shut the door behind him.

He was surprisingly agreeable about waiting. She dressed quickly while they chatted about his current projects at work. She promised herself they would have a pleasant dinner with no talk of Greta. After arriving ten minutes late at Frederico's, the restaurant of their first date, they were seated right away and within minutes were working on their first glass of wine.

"Where's the ring?" Jack asked.

"I carry it in my purse," she said.

"Well, can you at least wear it when we're out together?"

His token, she thought to herself, and she quickly pushed the thought away. He was trying so hard. His hand grabbed hers as she reached into her bag, and they came out clutching the box together.

"Let me do this," he said.

"But you already—"

"I know, but it never gets old." He slipped the band onto her finger, and the metal felt cold against her skin.

"It really is beautiful," she said. "You know what I like, don't you?"

"Yeah, I do." He smiled, proud of his efforts.

They finished eating and arrived back at her door before 10:00. While she dug for her keys, he grabbed her and kissed her unexpectedly. All she wanted was for him to warm up every inch of her cold neck and face with his hot breath, but she resisted, forcing her body to go stiff.

"What's wrong, Kate?"

I don't know. I'm just worried about tomorrow, I guess. What am I going to say to Jasper?"

"Let's go inside and talk about it," he whispered in her ear, and then took her gold earring into his mouth and licked her earlobes. He really does know what I like, she thought. Still, she wouldn't yield.

"Do I take Greta to Houston? Is he right about her?"

"Jasper's always right. He signs the paychecks, doesn't he?" He looked into her eyes now.

"Life really is that simple for you, isn't it?" She was surprised by the edginess in her voice.

"Yeah, it is. I work. I play. Then I work and play some more." He kissed her again. "And I always know who is calling the shots. It has paid off so far."

"Don't you care about anything else?"

"Like what? Doing the right thing?"

"For starters."

"Kate, c'mon. Listen to me. Greta is fine. She probably was great at one time. But she's what? Fifty-five or so? She is on her way out. This is a pity job and you know it."

"So that's how you feel about middle-aged women? That they should be pitied?"

"Don't make this about women's rights okay?"

"Okay, Jack, so this isn't about *women*, it's about *me*. How are you going to feel about *me* when I'm fifty-five?"

"Like you are the hottest fifty-five-year-old chick I've ever seen."

"Seriously, Jack? I mean seriously, that's your response?"

"That's your problem, Kate, you take yourself way too seriously. Let her go with you, or cut her loose. Either way, this is your account, not hers. And I do care about something else—you."

"I don't want to hurt her feelings, or look inflexible."

"But you *are* inflexible." He laughed. "Look how hard you're fighting me now, even though you know it's the right thing to do." He gently pushed her against the door and hovered over her, as if he could intimidate his way into her house.

"What if I say no?"

"To me?"

"No! Jack, stop. Are you listening to me?" One of her neighbors' doors was eased open, and a slant of yellow light fell across Jack's dark face.

"Just let her go with you." He lowered his voice to a whisper. "What harm can she do? Who knows? She might be entertaining." He pulled her into his firm chest, and she laid her head against his collarbone.

"I can be entertaining, too, you know," she said, in a small voice, lifting her face. She kissed his chin and neck, waiting for him to reciprocate.

"So I've heard," he said, tilting his face down into hers. "I promise you, Kate, everything will work out." He took the keys from her hand and reached behind her to unlock the door, never letting their bodies separate. He pushed her through the door and immediately onto the sofa.

She used to believe that Jack only cared if things worked out for himself, but he had been different since the proposal, more loving and passionate than ever before. He was considerate, even sensitive on occasion. Although in a lot of ways he was still the same old Jack, at the same time he was full of wonderful surprises. She desperately wanted to make this relationship work. Enraptured by his hard, warm body on hers, she kissed him again and again.

CHAPTER SEVENTEEN

October 2049—Galveston

"What is he doing here?" Zeke grumbled as Maggie and Simon tried to gingerly pull him back inside through the window. The crowd had dwindled slightly and quieted down momentarily. "Maggie, I said what is he doing here? Did you call him?"

"No, Zeke. Don't start," Maggie said.

"No one called me," Campbell said. He was standing in their living room now. "I told your dad earlier I'd keep an eye on the house, from a distance. Give you your space and all." Detective Cross folded his arms across his broad chest and shifted his weight. He was clearly a very fit man, as firm and trim as Zeke, but even more muscular, in spite of their thirteen-year age difference. His dark hair and eyes and his genuine smile made him a favorite among the females on the force. He did look like Jack, but unlike Jack, he seemed unaware of the affect he had on women.

"So, get the hell out of our space," Zeke growled at him. "You're not needed or welcome."

"Zeke—" Maggie began.

"You shut up!" Zeke yelled. "You are part of the problem here."

"That's not fair," Maggie said. "Zeke, you're being a real jerk—"

"God—I can't believe this," Zeke muttered. "I thought that was his car—I thought I saw him skulking around in the yard. I should have punched you in the nose—"

"That's enough!" Simon yelled. Both Maggie and Zeke were stunned into silence. Simon almost never raised his voice. "That's enough," he said again, softer. "If Camp hadn't been here, Zeke, you'd be shredded meat right now."

"I can take care of myself," Zeke said under his breath.

"Yeah, clearly," Maggie taunted.

Oh, grow up!" Zeke shouted.

"I said no more! Get out of here, both of you. Now," Simon urged.

The twins left the room, whispering angry words at one another. Maggie stopped in front of Campbell on her way out and took his hand.

"Detective Cross," she said, cordially, and too obviously, "Thank you for coming."

Zeke jerked her by the arm and pulled her from the room.

Cross chuckled. Simon did not.

"She is still pretending that I don't know about you two," Simon told him.

"Let it go, Simon. It's over," Cross said.

"Not for her, it's not. Do you see the way she looks at you? Damn you, Camp. Do you have any idea what you've done to my baby girl?"

"She's a grown woman—"

"She was eighteen years old!" Simon screamed for the second time today.

"Eleven years ago!" Cross yelled back. Then he drew in a slow breath. "I told you I don't want to disrespect you, Simon. You meant the world to my father, and you were the best damn swim coach University of Houston has ever seen. Three national championships, coach. I'll never forget swimming for you."

"You swam for yourself. Don't fuck with me," Simon said. "And you've got a room full of trophies to prove it. But my daughter wasn't supposed to be one of them. You have ruined her life. She hasn't been on a date in—"

"Holy Christ, Simon, I apologized how many times?"

Simon shook with rage. "Is that what you're here for? Forgiveness? Absolution? Well, Minister Abe will be here later tonight, and you can ask him for help. Leave my wife and children out of this."

"I know I made some bad choices, Simon. But, shit, can't you get it? Macy was dying, on her deathbed, do you have any—" His words stopped short. Simon saw true remorse in Cross's eyes for the first time. And he knew that pain. But he wasn't willing to budge This was Maggie they were talking about.

"I'm sorry, Simon. Jesus...I'll be outside if you need me." Campbell turned to leave. "And I'll call someone to fix that window," he said as he shut the front door quietly behind him.

CHAPTER EIGHTEEN

February 2009—Houston

"Thank God that's over," Greta moaned as she grabbed her suitcase from the baggage claim platform at the airport in Houston. "I detest airplanes."

"I know," Kate said. Greta had mentioned it several times today. "You seemed fine; you did great."

Greta changed the subject. "Let's go get the car," she said.

They walked to the rental counter and took care of some paperwork.

"The hotel is about six miles from here," Kate said as she turned the key in the ignition of the blue Honda Civic. "It's a little bit of a drive in this traffic, but it's a beautiful hotel. I love to stay there. And this is a nice car. I think we'll enjoy the ride."

Greta stared out the window in silence as Kate drove.

"It's a pretty day," Kate said, feeling an odd need to chat.

"Yeah, nice," Greta answered. "I've never been to Houston. Did I already tell you that? It seems really warm for February. Is it always this warm?" She rattled on.

"Oh, my God. I forgot, it's Groundhog Day. Let's find out if it is warming up for good." Greta bombarded Kate with questions about Houston, and Kate reached for the radio dial and started flipping stations looking for news about Punxsutawney Phil and his shadow. She stopped when she heard "Same Old Lang Syne" by Dan Fogelberg. Greta hummed and sang along with the words and music. This song had always been one of Kate's favorites, and it sprinkled the airways this time each year.

Kate wondered if this tune held any significance for Greta. For Kate, it was one of those songs that are so inextricably linked to a piece of herself that she couldn't imagine it being written for anyone else. The first love of Kate's life, Lucas Salazar, had slipped from her grasp during her first year of graduate school. The song captured that moment for her—when he had finally said goodbye, standing at gate 49 of DFW International Airport in the late summer of 1995. For years, she had dreamt of a reunion like the one Fogelberg depicted in the lyrics. But then, slowly, bit by bit, he had floated from her memory until he was just a misty instant from her past, like that few seconds of sprinkling rain before the bottom drops out—the sweet spray of liquid turning to a violent gush, washing it all away. Many of the details of their courtship were hazy, but an overall impression remained—intense, stomach wrenching, hand sweating, passionate love. He had been an athlete, like Kate. She swam; he ran cross-country. When he decided to seriously train for the Olympics, they had parted. He had a dream to follow, and she had a career to create. But his dark eyes were always following her, even now sometimes in her dreams. Their parting was the beginning of a very long stretch of sadness in her young life, and she couldn't help but wonder if she shouldn't have let him go. And since that day, letting go, as a general rule, had become impossible in her life.

"His name was Lucas," she said, shocked at the release of his name into the air, shocked by the vibration of the word on her lips. She wasn't sure she had spoken the name aloud since that day at DFW Airport.

"Lucas?" Greta said. And then, quite naturally, she said to Kate, "Tell me about him."

Kate told her the story. She had met Lucas at freshman orientation at Southern Methodist University in the fall semester of 1991. She was seventeen years old, and Lucas had strolled into the huge auditorium with a humble bravado that reminded her of the heroes in her dad's western movies. There she sat, alone, miles of empty chairs on either side. She knew no one. Some of her friends were scattered all over the country by that time, but most of them were back in Houston, seniors in high school with plans to graduate the same year she should have. They were buying class rings, getting senior photos made, and a few she thought of were probably beginning to fret about a date for Homecoming. Meanwhile, Kate sat here, at the outset of her adult life, scared out of her wits. Always in a hurry, she had finished a year early and had been awarded a scholarship, but she was nonetheless uneasy about fitting in with the upper-middle class students who were there on daddy's dime.

More than a thousand young people gathered in the sweaty auditorium that day, some wandering aimlessly, others trickling in with friends on each arm. Then there was Lucas. Solitary. Purposeful. Dark. She saw him walk through the double doors at the back. Something had made her turn and look just as he entered. At the time, in her teenage heart, she just knew it was fate whispering in her ear, telling her to lighten the path of this beautiful boy with warm caramel skin, distant black eyes, and shaggy brown hair.

He had walked in her direction—intentionally, she believed—and he told her as much on their first date. That he too had felt drawn to her. Looking back, she had realized how goofy she had been to believe that, but every girl needed a fairy tale romance, didn't she? God bless him for giving her one. She fell in love with him in about seven seconds. For four years, the sun didn't rise without his consent. She gave everything to him—her love, her soul, her innocence. And so much more. He handled it all with great care and affection. Her passions in college were Lucas first, and swimming second. Nothing else existed for her.

A private coach, Olen Victor, had watched her swim at a regional meet and asked her to train with him during her sophomore year. Had Kate known then what she would discover over the next two years, she would have done things differently. But the lenses through which she gazed at the world at age nineteen had not yet been darkened by distrust. Olen would take her to the Olympics, he promised. He would make her a champion, he swore. She believed him. After all, he had taken two other young swimmers all the way in 1976. Indeed, he had put her on a pedestal at first. And then, like any good coach, he pushed her harder and harder, and she began to be transformed. While she viewed this change as that of a caterpillar into a butterfly, Lucas saw it as something much less natural. He became suspicious during the spring of their junior year—she had known that. He asked odd questions. He didn't approve of her transformation—she knew that also. Her practice sessions with Olen had stretched into something more demanding, obsessive even, and she was secretive, he accused. Kate was defensive, charging him with jealousy of her athletic opportunities. Later, when Lucas was picked up by the US world team, Kate could no longer ignore the truth. It was Olen whom he didn't trust. He wasn't jealous of her swimming. He was jealous of her relationship with her coach. He thought she encouraged his advances. She wondered how much Lucas knew, how much he understood. It wasn't like him to be insecure. At the deepest level, she had known how Lucas felt, and believed it wise not to tell him everything. She had kept it inside, like any frightened young woman in love might do. And in love with Lucas she was. So, she kept this secret, and many others that followed.

Then, over the long months of their final semester together, they silently and solitarily prepared to part. They made love with less frequency and passion, and she told herself it was just her way of preparing to say goodbye. They both made the expected promises of *We'll visit on holidays*, and *we'll meet in South Padre during spring break*. She held the intent of those promises in her heart the first few weeks after he left. When the fall arrived, he was in Colorado training for the Olympics, and she was in Lubbock, earning an MBA on an academic scholarship. She had dropped Olen and her Olympic dream by the time Lucas was flying over Oklahoma City. Sometimes great courage comes from great loss, her father had often said. He was right in this case—losing Lucas made her rebel against Olen, something she should have done months earlier. Watching Lucas leave had propelled her into action. However, sometimes loss cripples us, not just momentarily, but for a very long time.

Kate had never managed to completely shake her love for him. One day, two years after he left, she had written his name on a tiny piece of paper, folded it carefully into a miniscule square, and stuffed it into the dark recess of consciousness only accessible during times such as this, when "Same Old Lang Syne" played on the radio.

"I love this song," Greta said, as the last few mournful notes of the saxophone wept to a conclusion." She looked at Kate, and for the first time since they met, Kate really looked at Greta. Not the wild hair or the short skirt, but Greta. Few people managed to break through the stone gates Kate had erected, once she had decided not to let them in. At that moment, she thought she heard the hinges creak and the door swing open, but just a tad. There it stood, though, barely ajar, swaying an inch forward and an inch back in the cool breeze of her heart. Greta's reaction to Kate at this vulnerable moment would be critical in pushing Kate to turn a corner and offer her friendship to her.

Kate looked back at the road. "His name was Lucas," she heard herself say again, "And I'll never love anyone the way I loved him."

Greta turned off the radio, and they rode in silence, forgetting about the groundhog. That night, there were no doubts lingering in Kate's mind about her decision to embrace Greta as her partner in the project. As the women parted ways at their rooms and made plans to meet at 6:00 to have dinner and prepare for the next day's presentation, Kate already knew that Arlow was no longer hers. It was theirs, together.

CHAPTER NINETEEN

Kate and Greta were back in Dallas, just miles from Jasper Agency, before noon. Houston had been even more difficult than she had imagined. They had driven past many familiar places and eaten in one of her favorite childhood restaurants the evening before—a celebratory dinner for her and Greta.

Mr. Brody from Arlow had loved them. She was relieved that soon she could move on with her life. Arlow had been sitting on her shoulder for almost three years now. After their meeting, he had asked simply to meet with them at the end of the week to present to Peter Arlow himself. She just wanted it to be over.

When they arrived at Jasper Agency that afternoon, the conference room was decorated, and everyone was standing around drinking punch. Jack was standing in a corner talking with Marissa. Kate watched him lean in and whisper in her ear. His hand was on her waist, and Marissa glanced at the door in anxious anticipation. When she saw Kate, she pulled away from Jack, and he immediately came to Kate, and everyone began cheering. Kate was very touched, and very tired.

"Thank you everyone," she said, holding up a hand in protest. "Thank you for your support, not just today, but over the past months. It really has been a team effort, and I'm grateful to all of you."

Jack shoved a glass of punch into her hand and put his arm around her shoulder. Hannah winked at her and raised a glass. "Congratulations, Kate," she said.

"…And Greta," Kate added, raising her glass to her and smiled broadly. Greta gave Kate a quick peck on the cheek, and Kate wasn't embarrassed by it. She was truly grateful to Greta for her help. It was her charm that had won Arlow, and surprisingly, that was okay with her.

"And congratulations to me…" Jack said, "for landing an even bigger account."

A new account in just a few days? Kate wondered. *Why didn't he mention anything to me?*

"…You are looking at a new and highly lucrative partnership in the making…"

Kate was happy to hear about Jack's success. He had been working hard, too, and it was time for her to support him for a while. So what if he flirted with the office intern while she was away?

"After many months of playing cat and mouse, finally, Kate has agreed to take me on as a client…a permanent client…."

Kate was astonished. He was about to tell them everything. She nudged him, hoping he would stop. But it was too late. She looked around the room, watching as expressions of confusion turned to surprise, and then joy as he spoke. Everyone clapped and sang out their congratulations and best wishes. Andy grabbed Jack's hand and made some stupid macho remark. Marisa stood alone in the corner she and Jack had occupied together, her expression unreadable. Kate felt sad for her, so young and so naïve about men. Greta hugged Kate and kissed her again. Hannah did the same, and whispered in her ear, "I told you he's crazy about you. Have dinner with me tonight." Kate felt like she was in an airless tunnel, and she just wanted to run to the end and breathe.

She was smiling quietly as they cut the cake and passed the pieces around. After a few minutes, Jasper suggested that they leave Jack and Kate alone to celebrate privately. So they all filed out, still hugging and shaking hands with the newly engaged couple as they made their way to the door. Jasper was the last one to leave, and he smiled at her just before he shut the door behind him. There was something in his smile, a hint of pride maybe, that made her feel brave enough to confront Jack. He grabbed her and kissed her after Jasper was gone. "Congratulations, Kate," he said.

She waited a few seconds for Jasper to get out of earshot. Then she slapped Jack in the face as hard as she could.

"What the hell?" He staggered backward a couple of steps. He reached up and rubbed his cheek and stared hard at her.

"How could you do that to me?" She was furious. "You promised…"

"Hey, I promised to wait till after Arlow. Nothing more," he protested. "Damn, Kate, that hurt."

"But the spirit of the promise," she continued, "You broke the spirit of it, Jack."

"What are you talking about?" he said.

"You should have waited. You should have warned me."

"Well…" he began, "I guess I thought you were ready."

"But you still should have warned me," she argued again.

"Warning?" he said, "Isn't that something you do when something bad is going to happen?"

Kate thought about the implications of her word choice. He had a point. He looked betrayed, and she was a little surprised by her reaction. Was she ready? She put her hand on his face. It was still hot from her slap. She stood on tiptoe and kissed the bright red spot.

"You're right, Jack. I'm sorry. I—there's no excuse for my behavior," she said.

"I'm very tired, and I want to go home."

"Okay, I'll meet you at your car. It shouldn't be a problem to knock off early."

"Wait, Jack. I'll call you later, okay? We'll get together tomorrow." she forced a smile for him. He kissed her and told her he understood.

A few hours later, after a nap and hot bath, Kate was sitting at her kitchen table, chatting with Hannah and waiting for pizza to arrive.

"You have been a very naughty girl," Hannah said, "and I love it when Santa rewards naughty little girls at Christmas with diamonds. Jack told us the story after you left today."

Kate's face must have looked panicked. "Wait, honey," Hannah said, "Not the whole story. I was hoping you would fill in the blanks."

"We just didn't want to tell people yet. Not until after Arlow." Kate tried to play it cool.

"You are so sneaky, though. How on earth did you keep such juicy news to yourself?" Hannah sipped her wine.

It didn't seem appropriate to tell her that it had been surprisingly easy.

"But the big question is, well..." Hannah's voice dropped a full octave. "...How is he?" she asked.

Kate took a sip of wine. "He's fine. Just fine." She was sure she was blushing.

The doorbell rang and Kate collected the pizza.

Hannah slumped down in her chair. "C'mon. Don't be a tease. I have been hot and bothered all day since I heard. The one thing I want to know...well you just can't hold out on me, Kate. I must know. I've been imagining—"

"—Stop! That's so gross. You have not!" Kate said.

"Not you, darling—him. Jack Finnegan. The Adonis of Jasper Agency. So tell me, is it, you know?" She held up a breadstick, looked at it, and back at Kate. "Is it...big?" she whispered. Kate looked away, but giggled, the wine beginning to warm her insides.

"So, darling, tell me. Is there a lot of meat on his pizza, or is it just cold cheese and bland sauce with a stale floppy crust?" Hannah said.

Kate opened the pizza box and savored the warm garlicky smell for a moment, trying to devise just the right response. "Hannah Dear, his pizza not only has a very firm crust with loads of meat piled on it, but the sauce...ooh la la." She licked her lips and sighed. In a bad Italian accent, she continued, "The sauce—it is much too spicy for the average consumer. Are you sure your taste buds can ...how do you say...survive the experience?"

"Bring it on, baby," Hannah said, and they both cackled.

In a much more convincing southern drawl, Kate said, her mouth full of sausage and mushrooms, "Then honey-child, let me tell you all about this here pizza..."

****

83

"You know, Mr. Finnegan, I really should get to bed." Kate lay with her head on Jack's chest, drumming her fingers softly on his abdomen. The sheet was twisted around their bottom halves, cool against their warm and damp legs. It had been thirty-two hours since his big announcement at Jasper.

"You are in bed." He chuckled.

She looked at the huge bouquet of lilies he had brought over that evening.

"Tomorrow is a big day," he said. "You and Greta in Houston again. By the way, what's up with you two?"

"Nothing. We just like each other now, I guess. What's wrong with that?" She knew she sounded a little defensive.

"You *like* her? That's rich, Kate, really rich."

She glared at him.

He continued. "You mean you're not pissed off that Brody insisted that she be part of the team? And now she's stealing your thunder."

"It didn't happen that way, Jack. She's sharing the thunder, not sealing it. You're overstating her importance on the account." Kate knew he wasn't. What she didn't know, or couldn't come to terms with, was why she wasn't really bothered by it.

"What's going on, Kate?" He put his arm around her and she pulled away. She wasn't angry. She just wanted to talk as co-workers, or even as friends, but not as lovers.

"Look, Jack. She is a creative person. And Brody wants her. There's nothing I can do."

He laughed. "Since when does that stop you? I can't believe you are taking this lying down."

"Taking what? I'm not taking anything. It's just work, Jack, not life."

"Oh, boy, what are you now—Jasper's mouthpiece?" he said in that tone that rode just above a chuckle and made her want to choke him.

"It doesn't matter," she said curtly, "because tomorrow, it will all be over, and I can move on."

He put his arm around her again, and she leaned into him this time. He kissed her hair, and said, "We can move on, too, or forward actually. Which means you have to decide." The words of an ultimatum, but he said them so softly, so gently, that she didn't recognize him for a moment.

"Decide?" she asked.

"Decide if you want to be engaged or not," he said.

"But you know I do. I said yes."

"Then where's the ring?" he asked.

She pursed her lips and didn't speak.

"Kate," he continued, "no one's twisting your arm, you know. But you have to decide. And soon. I think I deserve that much."

"Of course you do," she said. "It's just that, between the Lasca Center and Hospice and Arlow, and us, I just feel...confused. But I know I want to be with you, right here, and right now."

"What about tomorrow and the day after, Kate?" He reached into the nightstand for her handbag. "Here," he said. "Take it out."

She retrieved the ring and looked at it a moment. He grabbed it from her and held her hand. "Look," he said as he slipped it onto her finger. "This is the last time I will slip a ring on your finger until our wedding day. It's up to you to let it be part of your life now. But I won't ask again."

"Jack, I wish I could make you understand," she said.

"It's all right," he said. "I'll see you in a couple of days, and we'll go from there. For now, I should go and let you rest. Good luck tomorrow."

****

This time, they were in a red Civic, headed for the same Houston hotel at nearly the same time of day. But the comfort level in the car was different. Kate was agitated. Jack had struck a nerve, and he knew it. Was she going soft? Should she be more worried or envious? Greta was flipping through radio stations again, fueling Kate's edgy mood. She wanted to make sure Greta knew her place and didn't blow the promotion for her. Kate cleared her throat and tried to sound professional. "Look, Greta, I think we should lay some ground rules here, about the meeting today, I mean."

Greta glanced at Kate and responded, "Well, that sounds official." She went back to the tuner.

"That's because this is very important business. Will you please stop with the radio? This is my life here, months of it anyways." Kate resisted the impulse to slap Greta's hand.

Greta stared at Kate. "Why do you do that?"

"Do what?"

"Treat me like a child. And not even your child. Like your third cousin's step-child from out of town. I am a grown woman. Just say what you want to say."

Kate was a little offended but not surprised by her frankness. She thought that perhaps their relationship had reached that level where they could say such things to one another. Maybe that was a good thing.

"You don't seem to have any trouble saying it when I'm not around," Greta added.

"Greta, that's not fair!" Where was this coming from? Kate hadn't intended to the let the flames leap this high.

"Do you think I don't know what you and the others say? About my choice of clothing, leisure activities, men? Just because I am easygoing doesn't mean I'm easy, and I'm not blind or deaf. I would tell you or any of them anything you want to know. If anyone had the courtesy to ask." It was a flood of emotion. Greta must have been holding this back for weeks.

Kate tried to be delicate, then realized that that was exactly what Greta didn't want. Might as well plow ahead and get it all out on the table. "Well, then, why don't you try to be more discrete?"

"I don't have anything to hide. Why should I pretend that I do? Because it might hurt me professionally?" She laughed at the idea. "Besides, you guys don't know anything about me. You just think you do."

They traveled in silence for minutes that felt like hours. Kate routed potential words and phrases through her brain, filtering them for flavor and intensity. Finally convinced she had found the perfect punch, she turned to Greta.

"You're right," Kate began, and Greta turned to face her. "I should—"

And that's when everything changed.

Kate witnessed pure horror on Greta's face. Then she heard her scream Kate's name. Or maybe it was tires screeching. She couldn't be sure. There was roaring, screaming, and then eerie silence. But that didn't make sense. Noise, but not noise. All thoughts and sounds had been compressed into a fraction of a second.

One-tenth of second, maybe. That's how long it took for the world to spin around several times and stop. Kate couldn't move, and everything was blurry. She looked to her right, past Greta who seemed to simply be napping, her head propped gently against the airbag, her hair swirled around her head. Why was there a tree in her window? As the fog cleared, she saw that it was a telephone pole, not a tree, that was smashed into Greta's door. As Kate's air bag deflated and her lungs fought through smoke and powder, she saw that a truck was smashed into the front left of the little Honda. Where did it come from? She had seen Greta's face and then heard the most horrible sound imaginable. But those were the only pieces she had.

She managed to pull her hand free from under the dash. There was still no sound, and now everything moved in slow motion. Tiny bits of debris floated in the air around them like dirty snow. Within seconds, dozens of eyes were staring at them through a shattered glass waiting to crumble. It reminded her of the time she broke the glass in the back sliding door with a baseball when she was nine. Jesus, was her life flashing before her eyes? Some awful smell drifted in the air. It was faint, but nauseating. Blood. Did blood have an odor? She looked down and saw no blood on herself. Thank God.

Then she looked at Greta. Her hair was filled with bright red fluid. Without thinking, she grabbed Greta's head and started screaming for her to wake up. But Greta didn't move. Kate watched the blood trickle down her fingers. Overwhelmingly drowsy, she let go of Greta and stared up at the headliner of the car. She tried not to look at Greta again, fearing she would vomit. *Head wounds bleed a lot,* she thought. *It's not as bad as it looks.*

And for the first time in five years, she said a prayer: "God, let her be okay," she whispered into the stillness before she lost consciousness.

PART TWO

SKY

CHAPTER TWENTY

October 2049—Galveston

Mercy killing is still killing—
Thou shall not kill!
Mercy killing is still killing—
Thou shall not kill....

The chanting had been going on for over an hour, with no foreseeable end. Simon hoped that Kate couldn't hear the noise or feel the insanity outside their cabin. He had hoped the crowd would grow tired, but instead they just grew. He sat by Kate's side quietly for a while, and then spoke lovingly to her.

"The kids are here, honey," he said. He touched her arm lightly and then re-tied the pink bow on her nightgown. "They're here and they're…fighting with one another. I guess I can't lie to you, can I?"

He smoothed her long silver hair and ran the back of his hand across her cheek.

"Campbell is here, but I don't want you to worry. Everyone's being nice to him." Okay, so maybe he could lie.

"I don't know why Cross deserves to even be in our home. He has chased for you for so long. How can he not know what kind of person you are?"

He paused.

"Maggie still loves him. I just don't get it. How is she going to survive him if you leave? You're the only one she'll talk to about him. How did this happen to my baby girl? She is so much like you—strong in her professional life, and terrible taste in men." He laughed. He knew she would have laughed too, if she could.

She would also have said, "Love is a good thing. Let her keep loving." Kate was goodness through and through. It was impossible to understand how the predators outside their home believed anything else about his wife. She took care of the terminally ill. People were suspicious; they questioned what she and Abe did inside the homes of the dying. The secret final words and actions. But there had never been a shred of evidence against her or Abe, and not for lack of looking. Campbell Cross had seen to that.

It was human nature, he guessed, to not trust one another, to always see the worst. He certainly had his doubts at times, too, or maybe not doubts as much as questions. But looking at her now, laying here, so prepared for death, he was actually grateful that she has seen so much behind those closed doors. He held his breath every time the investigations started up, but Kate never blinked. "I've done nothing wrong," she told him simply. This secret life of hers should have torn their marriage apart. But he worshipped Kate Gray, from the first seconds to the very last. He had learned, over the years, how to tuck that jealousy away for another time, another life, maybe.

"I've been looking though this box, and honestly, darling, I'm not sure what you're trying to tell me. I am enjoying the memories, though. Maggie found the photo of Jack. Did I ever tell you how much he looks like Campbell? Disturbing, really. What is it with you Lasca girls and tall, dark, and handsome?"

He opened the lid to the box and pulled out a series of newspaper clippings from the past several years. The first one was particularly harsh:

> Yesterday evening renowned pianist Janet Harding was found dead in her home after a four-year battle with cancer. Her children were stunned, saying that they believed she had begun to turn a corner and test results looked promising at her last oncologist visit. When asked to confirm speculations that the deadly duo of Abe Archer and Kate Gray (also known as the macabre minister and his mistress) may have had something to do with it, Harding's children refused to comment.

Simon had been arrested after he beat the holy hell out of the reporter, breaking the guy's nose and dislocating his shoulder.

"Fucking scumbag deserved it," he told Campbell Cross when he arranged for his release after convincing the reporter to drop the charges.

"Damn it, Gray!" Cross had told him. "You can't do this. We're not the bad guys here. If the guy didn't owe me a favor, you'd be doing serious time for assault. Jeez— don't be a fucking idiot. Let me run this investigation."

"Daddy, can I come in?" Maggie's voice was small and sweet, and he wanted to grab her and pull her close like when she was a baby.

"Of course, Maggie. Come sit with us."

Maggie looked at her mother for several minutes before speaking. Simon studied her face and prepared to console her.

"You know what, Dad? I'm okay. She looks…beautiful. Really peaceful and beautiful."

"She loves you Margaret. You, me, Zeke. She loves us more than anything," Simon said.

"I know, Dad. I love us too." She leaned over and kissed Simon. It was he who needed consoling.

"I'll leave you alone," Simon told Maggie. "Just come out when you're ready. I have a feeling that you two have a lot to talk about."

CHAPTER TWENTY-ONE

February 2009—Houston

"Kate, can you hear me? I got here as fast as I could. Everything's going to be fine." She recognized Jasper's voice, and he sounded like he was in father mode more than ever. She slowly opened her eyes and turned her head toward him. A pain shot through her neck, and her eyes stung with tears.

"Hi, Mr. Jasper," she croaked. He gave her a sip of water.

"I'm so glad you're okay. It looks like you will be sore for a few days, and then you'll be fine. You must have had an angel in the car with you."

The images began to return to her in pieces. Warped metal. Smoke. Blood. Lots of blood. She looked down at her hands, and saw traces of Greta's blood around her cuticles and behind her nails. "I don't feel so good," she told Jasper. What time is it?"

"It's 8:30. Actually, visiting hours are ending. Your mom will come soon, I think. Hannah has been trying to reach her all day. Do you know where she is?" If she didn't know better, she'd say he had been crying. That can't be a good sign, she thought.

"No. But I'll be okay. We shouldn't bother her with this. When can I leave?"

"They want you to stay overnight. The x-rays don't show anything broken, but you're pretty shaken up. The crash was, well, it was bad, Kate." She recognized the tone of someone trying to be strong.

She thought of Greta. "Oh, my God!" She tried to sit up, but the pain wouldn't allow it. "Did I kill her?"

"No, no Katie Girl. Do you know any of her relatives? We'd like to try to reach someone."

"I'm sorry," she answered. She began dozing off again.

"Well, we'll talk more tomorrow. Try to rest."

Early the next morning, Emily Lasca was at her daughter's side, holding her hand and stroking her hair.

"Mom?" Kate's voice was a little stronger than the night before.

"I'm here, sweetheart. Right here. You're going to be all right."

Kate chuckled. "Why does everyone keep telling me that? It makes me nervous." She looked into Emily's face, smiling, but with tears streaming down each cheek. "Oh, mom. Don't cry. Please don't cry."

"I'm just so relieved that you're okay. Hannah didn't know any details, really. She tried to reassure me that it wasn't serious…" she paused and then whispered, "for you, that is."

Kate began to shake. "Is Greta okay, Mom? Where is she? What's going on?"

"Kate, honey. She hasn't regained consciousness. She has suffered a head trauma, and she's not doing so well. There's not much we can do but pray, and…"

Kate couldn't believe what she was hearing. "What are you saying, Mom? Is she in a coma? Is she dying?"

"No, she's not dying. They don't really know yet. These first couple of days are critical. They just won't speculate right now." She hesitated before she spoke again. "They do want your help finding her family."

"I—I don't know anything about her family. She mentioned a sister once. I'm not sure where she lives. I don't even know if they have the same last name." She remembered her last conversation with Greta and felt angry with herself.

"Kate, don't worry. We can talk more about that later. You need to get well. You just need a couple of days' rest."

"She's right, you know?" Jasper's voice sang out from behind Emily. He put a vase of flowers on the table beside Kate. It was just like him to be by her side right now. She hoped she never took him for granted.

"Oh," Kate almost cried, "they're so pretty. Thank you, Mr. Jasper."

"Well," he laughed, "they're from everyone, not just me." For a moment no one spoke. Then Jasper began again, "Everyone sends their love."

She wondered if everyone included Jack. Had he called the hospital? Why wasn't he here?

"You know, you'll be going home this afternoon," Jasper said. "I bet you'll be glad to get out of here, won't you?"

"Yes!" Kate said. "And I can still make the Arlow presentation on time."

Jasper and Emily looked at her in surprise, their eyes like colored marbles peeking out from the snow. "Kate, it's Saturday. Your meeting was yesterday, and I rescheduled it."

"Are you crazy?" her mother added. Then she and Jasper lectured her simultaneously.

"Okay, okay. You're giving me a headache. I'll ask for an extension to rest a few days."

"You'll do no such thing," Jasper snapped. "I told them they can wait a couple of weeks."

Kate managed to scoot herself up two inches in bed. "Mr. Jasper, we need this account. I need this account," she said.

"And we need you," he retorted. "How could you be thinking about this right now? They can wait. They understand. I made them understand. I've got to get my two girls healthy again."

She didn't want to think about Greta anymore. The pain was searing through her neck again. She wondered how long recovery would take. When Jasper left, she asked her mother to help her get to the bathroom. Preparing to stand, she pulled back the bed sheets and gasped. Her legs were covered in large, purple bruises. She was sure she would faint. Her mother grabbed her and held her, stroking her hair. "It's okay, Katie. I'm here now."

Kate stayed with Emily that night, in the house where she had grown up, and she was hurting enough to let her eager mother nurse her back to health. She was able to move quite well by the next morning. She was stiff and pretty sore, but she noticed that walking made it easier to cope with. It was only after sitting for long intervals that the aching surged. So she spent the next twelve hours being babied and shoving Greta into the depths of her mind. But guilt wouldn't let her forget for long. And Emily wasn't going to let her forget either.

"Kate, dear. I hate to bring this up today. I just keep thinking of Greta's family, and how I'd want to know if I were in their shoes. It's been almost two days now…" her voice wavered. She bit her lip. "Look. I have to tell you. The hospital called this morning. They really need your help finding Greta's family. She has never filed a living will it seems, and there's just no paperwork on her anywhere."

"A living will? My God, Mom, has it come to that?"

"Not yet. They have been running in circles, and they need you. It seems of all the people she knew in Dallas, you are the one who knew the most about her."

"How is that so?" Kate was flabbergasted by this information. "What about Jasper? He has her personnel files."

"Yes, and he has told them all he knows."

"Well, I'm sure he knows more than I do. We barely spoke. She went out every night. She has boyfriends out the nose—where are her friends?"

Emily was silent.

"Oh." Kate was not proud of herself. She had merely tolerated Greta. In her self-absorption, she had assumed that she was the only one who had trouble liking her. Apparently she was fun to party with, but no one bothered to get to know her. She felt very sad at this realization. "I'll try," she told Emily.

"That's all anyone expects, Katie." Her mother sat close to her and held her hand.

"Thank you, mom. I'm glad I'm here."

"Me, too sweetheart. Me too."

On the second morning, Kate awoke to the smell of bacon frying and coffee brewing. She felt ten years old again, sitting in front of the television watching

Scooby-Doo cartoons. She rolled over and looked at the clock. She hadn't slept late in months. She took a quick shower and dressed. Her mother was setting the table when she walked into the kitchen.

"Hi, Mom. Everything smells great."

"Good morning. I hope you still eat bacon."

"Unfortunately." Kate chuckled. "But I don't expect you to take care of me."

"I know. That's why it's so fun. I miss taking care of you."

Kate watched her mother turn and reach into the cabinet for a cream pitcher. From Kate's vantage point, she hadn't changed at all. For a flash of a moment she believed she actually was a child again. She expected to hear the front door open and her father step in with the morning paper.

"Mom, let me help."

"Nope. I'm just about done. Hope you're hungry."

Kate studied her mother's face while they ate. In a matter of minutes, her mother had morphed into an old woman. How did this happen? She hadn't been away that long. Kate wondered about her mother's happiness. It was sad seeing how old she had become, and a bit disturbing to know that she was looking into the face of her older self.

Emily Lasca had been thirty-eight years old the day she found out she was pregnant with Kate. In 1974, that was unheard of. Her friends had been worried and scolded her for letting it happen. Emily and Frank had been trying for thirteen years to conceive, so they were overjoyed at the news.

Kate thought about what Emily had always said to her when she was a little girl: "My friends and family told me how crazy the whole thing was. How I was too old to be having a baby. It was too dangerous—it could kill me, they kept saying. But they were wrong. Being without a child was what was killing me. Now God had given me this miracle. I knew he wouldn't let me die before I could pay him back."

Kate had wished for a miracle for her father, but none came. She was trying to honor him with the family center. But it certainly couldn't replace touching him, wrapping her arms around him.

"What are you thinking about?" Emily asked.

"Oh, just remembering. I can't believe what you have done with the house. It's beautiful. I hope you didn't push yourself too hard."

"No, no. It was good for me to do it. A little painful, but most important things are."

"How is your knee since the surgery?" Kate asked.

"I don't mean that kind of painful, Kate."

Kate knew what she meant. But she didn't want to take that road. It was full of twists and turns and ugly detours. She wanted to speak only in present tense. Safer that way. They finished breakfast in generic chitchat.

Kate grabbed a magazine and sat down in the living room to read while her mom washed dishes. She had refused her help, and Kate did not have the energy to argue about it. The huge maple tree visible through the front window kept catching the corner of her eye. She couldn't resist the temptation to look. She walked over and stood next to the window, allowing her arm to brush against the cold glass. It was surprising that their tree had grown so large. It didn't seem right, somehow, that the tree got to live. Pieces of anger traveled up into her throat. She swallowed them.

Kate suddenly realized that her mother probably had asked for help with the house. Or that she had people in her life to look after her, maybe even a boyfriend. Astonishingly enough, Kate had never thought of that before. She had believed that she was the only one who could help her. After much argument against it, Emily had accepted a small check from her each month. The check helped Kate more than it did Emily, and perhaps because Emily had been wise enough to know that, she finally gave in to Kate's insistence that she accept the money.

"Mom!" she yelled. "I'm going outside." She grabbed a sweater from the hook near the door and pushed her arms through it in spite of the lingering pain in her stiff muscles. Her home became a time machine. Standing in the small front yard, feet firmly planted in grass that she had tossed about with her father in, she let her hand slide easily over the branches. Flashes of the past blew through her brain like a lightning storm: planting, watering, and eventually learning to climb it—falling again and again. She remembered clearly the first day she made it to the very highest branches. She had sat very still, spread her arms wide, and thrust her face upward into the sun, smiling. Her chest was squeezing her heart inside it in response to the memory.

"What do you think?" Emily asked.

Kate spun around. "It's very pretty," she said.

"I know you miss him," Emily whispered, as if she needed to say the words, but wasn't sure she wanted Kate to hear them.

"Yes." Kate resisted the urge to add, *But you don't, do you?*

"He was a good father to you. And the best husband he knew—"

"Mom, I can't do this. Not today."

"Then when, Kate? When would be a good time? When I see you next? We can't talk at my funeral, you know? I'll be a little out of sorts that day."

"Please!" Kate shook as she spoke.

"All right. All right. Let's not spoil your visit. I am so glad you're here. We don't have to talk about your father today. But only because I don't want you upset. I want you to enjoy being in Houston."

"I do too, Mom. I really do."

They decided to see a play that afternoon. Emily had the connections to get last minute tickets. Apparently Emily served on the Arts Council and had many such connections. Life had gone on for Emily.

They sat through the play in silence. In her heart, Kate was dimly aware that something had to change in her life. She was miserable. She had continued to ignore the signs, not really hoping they would go away, but hoping she could survive until after the Arlow presentation. And then the second Arlow presentation. She had been so terrified of failing with Arlow that she had never considered how it would feel to succeed.

Kate had her mom drop her off at the hospital to meet Jasper and check on Greta. As she entered the ICU area, she was told that Greta could only have one visitor at a time. She was early, so she assumed she had beaten Jasper there. To her surprise, she found him shuffling around in Greta's room. She hung back out of sight and watched, looking for a hint of a relationship she had heard gossip about. He was arranging some flowers in the corner. Then she watched as he ran a cloth under the tap for a minute and then delicately washed her face and hands. Ashamed of her voyeurism, she returned to the waiting room to give them their privacy.

She sat and listened to Katie Couric talk about the most recent events in the Middle East. An American soldier had been captured neared the Pakistan border.

"That stuff'l depress you, you know?"

She was happy to see him smiling.

"How is she?" she asked.

"Hanging on. How are you?" Jasper inquired.

"I'll heal. Can I see her now?"

"I think she'd like that, Kate."

Bleach, she thought, as she reentered the ICU. She remembered bleach. The unit was relatively quiet, except for beeping machines and the sound of air being whooshed through ventilators, into chests, and back into ventilators again. It was life—pulsing veins, beating hearts, expanding lungs—but a distorted version of life. Life that had once been depicted in paintings, stories, and photographs, but it was being recorded instead on tapes and monitors. A sterile measurement. The push/pull of air: in and out, tracking the seconds. How many seconds did Greta have left?

Greta's skin looked pink and healthy. If it weren't for the tubes and wires, one would mistake her for a woman sleeping peacefully. Kate was scared to touch her. She pulled up a chair and sat next to her in silence. *What do you say to someone in a coma? To someone who you have treated like shit for the past two months?*

"She likes when you talk to her," the nurse said. She came in with a pocketful of needles and vials. Kate watched her remove each vial, suck its contents out with a needle, and then inject them into one of Greta's tubes.

"That's the problem," Kate said. "I don't know what to say."

"The other gentleman talked to her about work. Do you work with her too?"

"Yes, I do." Kate waited for the nurse to leave. Then she started talking, quietly, near Greta's face.

"Well, they gave us an extension on Arlow," Kate said. "You gotta get well so we can be ready next week. You know they want you on this account, Greta. I can't do it without you." She felt awkward. She talked about work, about the flowers Jasper brought, about the weather…. she made herself keep talking until her throat hurt. It was all she knew how to do at the moment. And she knew she must do something. Anything.

Later that evening, while Emily was sitting at her vanity rubbing on cold cream, Kate came in and sat down on the bed her parents had shared for thirty-two years.

"Mom, I have to tell you something."

"What is it, sweetheart?" Behind the cold cream, all Kate could see were Emily's eyes, again giving her mother the youthful look she remembered.

"I just got off the phone with the airline. I'm going back to Dallas tomorrow."

"But what about Arlow?"

"I'll be back in a few days."

"Are you sure you're able to travel? Maybe you should wait."

"Mom, I can't wait. It's about Greta. I need to go to her apartment. I need to try to find her sister. I went to the hospital today. It was awful. Oh, God." She started to break down, then pulled it together.

"What's wrong, Katie?"

"I just need to go see what I can find out."

Emily put her hand on Kate's knee. "Honey, I think you're doing the right thing. Just take it easy okay? When will you be back?"

"Tuesday."

"Okay, I'll see you then."

"Um, no you won't."

"Well, what do you mean? Surely you're not getting a hotel or something. Kate, that's ridiculous. Save your money—"

"No. I'm staying at the cabin."

"Oh," Emily said, her face lengthening and eyes widening. Then there was a long silence.

Kate had not expected Emily to take it well. She was scared to death of going back there herself, but she couldn't stand being here either. She wanted to be alone, and thought it was time to face some very old ghosts. She kissed her mother on the cheek and returned to her room to pack her suitcase.

Twelve hours later, Kate was on a plane, ordering a gin and tonic and then pulling down the tray in front of her. In one more hour, she would be back in Dallas. She thought about how tired she was of traveling after only four plane trips. She had yearned to live in the sky when she was a little girl. What had happened to her? She looked at the huge clouds floating around her in soft clumps and wished she could jump on one and disappear forever. When she was a little girl, she and her father would pretend they were cotton candy, and act as if they could bite off sweet mouthfuls together. Her drink arrived, and she washed the cotton candy memory down in one long swig. These days she just wanted her feet firmly planted on the ground.

She had met with Greta's doctor and one of the hospital's attorneys before leaving town, and after making several phone calls had discovered that there truly were no records to be found that would help her locate Greta's family. The next logical step seemed to be going to Greta's apartment. Jasper had asked Hannah to fax some files to him at the hospital, and he shared with the doctors what he knew. She had been in Dallas for the past few years, and prior to that had spent at least twenty years in West Texas. She was sure Greta had mentioned being raised in a neighborhood near Jasper Agency, though.

"So, where's home—Houston or Dallas?" the man in the seat next to her asked.

"Both," she said.

"Well, they're both great towns. Business or pleasure?"

"Neither," she said.

That answer seemed to satisfy him. *Thank God*, she thought, as he put on his headphones and leaned his seat back slightly.

"Have a nice trip," he said.

Kate gave him a quick smile and nod. She closed her eyes and tried to think of something peaceful in between sips of her second gin and tonic. She used to never drink. Lately, though, she had found many excuses to partake, and today she added flying to the list.

The first time she had been on an airplane, she was eight, and her father and mother had taken her to Colorado. They had saved for a couple of years to afford a week-long ski trip. Kate had begged her father to teach her to ski, and she had loved the snow. By the time she was finishing drink number two, she was lost in the memory of her father's warm hands on her waist as he knelt on the ground in front of her, icy flakes crunching under his knees, explaining the basics and reminding her to be careful. She hadn't listened to a word he had said. She hadn't known how to be careful, how to slow down. Where was that little girl?

She remembered the pure ecstasy of the cold air whipping at her face. It was as close to flying as she could imagine. But they couldn't afford to go again. Thank goodness they hadn't had to save money to go to the beach. There was freedom there, and space. She longed to go back to her cabin on the beach, but she feared it, too.

She pulled the diamond ring out of her purse and slipped it on her finger. It was magnificent, even in the shade, but it really came to life when it reflected the light. Unfortunately, her life was much less glorious than the ring suggested. She thought about her current situation: she preferred the term *situation* because to think of this as her *life* would be unbearable. The truth was that Kate was alone.

CHAPTER TWENTY-TWO

February 2009—Dallas

Kate pushed number nine on the elevator control panel and leaned against the wall as she made her slow climb to Jasper Agency. She glanced up at the mirrored ceiling and thought that something seemed different about her appearance. Would others notice? Silly thought. One accident couldn't change anyone that much. She thought about those movies where people were terribly disfigured in accidents and had plastic surgery and went back to wreak havoc on the lives of those who had hurt them.

She got online in her office and within minutes had a list of twelve phone numbers for people with the last name Perkins in Dallas with reasonable birth dates to be a sister to Greta. She dialed number four as she twisted her chair around to face her window. It rang two times, three times…. Dollops of snow shimmered on the ground outside, and children pushed each other on the swings. The snow had begun to fall just as her plane was landing. She felt a firm hand on her shoulder, and she spun around.

"Mr. Jas…. Oh, Jack."

"Nice greeting. Good to see you, too."

The touch of his hand was warm and familiar, but she still jumped a little. He took the receiver from her hand and hung it up.

"What's wrong, Kate? Didn't you miss me?" He leaned in to kiss her.

She rolled her chair back and turned her head away from him. "Not now, okay? I'm not up to it."

He grabbed the arms of the chair and pulled her closer. "My God, Kate. You're covered with bruises. Let me look at you." Jack held one of her arms into the window's light and studied it, while Kate studied his face. Everything in the world felt strange and new, and his touch, while gentle, confused her. Jack got down on his knees and took her face into his large, warm hands. "Do you know how much you scared us?" She wanted to lean in and kiss him, and she also wanted to punch him in the throat.

"Us?" She put her hands on his and raised an eyebrow as she spoke.

"Me. You scared *me*. I thought I'd lost you." He cradled her head and again tried to kiss her. She let him this time, holding her lips firm all the while.

"So why didn't you call?" She started talking before he was finished kissing. "Or my God, why didn't you come? I'm your fiancée, for fuck's sake!" she said, her chest tight.

He didn't respond at first.

"It will sound silly." He paused. "I—in my heart, I wondered if you really would want me there."

Was that the old Jack slithering into the room? She lifted a hand to stop him. "I'm busy, Jack. I'll have to talk with you later."

"Come on, Kate." He sounded a little pathetic, and part of her felt sorry for him, but just for a second. She was the victim here. "Come on, now, give me some credit," he continued. "Jasper was with you, and I knew he would take care of you. I knew you were safe and that he'd call if—"

"I said I'd see you later," she inserted.

"When?"

"Call me. If you remember my number."

"Come on, honey. Don't do this. I need to see you."

"Then meet me at Hope Springs tonight."

"Tonight?" he said. "I mean, isn't it early for you to be hitting it full stride? You should rest." He did sound concerned. One point for Jack.

"You mean, I should be at home in bed with you," she said.

"Well, sure, but I mean that in a good way." He laughed.

"I'll be at Hospice from 7:00 until 10:00. If you need me, you know the address

"It's a date then. I'll bring dinner at 8:00." He touched her hair. "Chinese okay?"

"Sure. I'll see you then."

"Kate—"

"Yes, Jack?"

"Thank you for wearing the ring."

Kate stood in front of Greta's door for several minutes, turning the key over and over in her palm like a magic token. She hadn't asked Jasper why he had a key to begin with. She had rationalized that he must have taken it from her purse at the hospital. When she finally opened the door and stepped inside, she felt like a prowler. Tentatively walking from room to room, she tried to get a feel for the small apartment. There were no immediate surprises. Artwork—probably Greta's—on the walls. Books strewn about. A huge stack of newspapers in one corner, next to an ancient Kimball upright. The apartment even smelled like Greta, an unusual helix of musty old books and fresh tulips.

Kate wasn't quite sure where to begin looking, or what she was looking for. As the hours had lumbered on since the accident, she had felt an increasing sense of responsibility. She had been the one driving. It didn't matter that the police told her it was the other guy's fault. She had seriously injured another person by not paying careful attention behind the wheel. And deep down, she knew she had hurt her, as well, by her actions during the previous months, by not paying careful attention to Greta's feelings. A stone of guilt had wedged itself into her gut, so she found herself here, rifling through Greta's personal items, examining the contents of each nook and cranny, seeking Greta's identity as if it might be hidden in a sock drawer.

She decided to look for an address book or similar item containing phone numbers of family and friends. Then she would move on to legal documents. It wouldn't take more than a few hours. Then she could fly back to Houston, take a day to prepare for Arlow, present, and be back in Dallas in four days, tops. She didn't care what Jasper said—no way was she going to drag this out for two more weeks. As guilty as she felt, she knew she couldn't do this for long: she knew she wasn't strong enough.

She started in the kitchen and intuited that she would work in a circular motion to cover the entire apartment. It was funny to her how a tiny place could become unbearably large under certain circumstances.

She opened a drawer. It creaked, and she felt a little ill at ease. She dug through a variety of gadgets—of course she had started with the junk drawer. How revealing could it be? She pulled out a long white extension cord and then two screwdrivers and some blank index cards, followed by matchbooks from every restaurant and club in the area. When she had emptied the drawer, she reached her hand far into the backside where she couldn't see and found some flat thick pieces of paper. More index cards, no doubt. She yanked them free, dropping them on the floor in the process. They scattered, and among the smooth white cards, a small blue one stood out. She knelt and touched the card, carefully, as if her fingers might erase the contents written upon the ordinary square of paper.

She flipped it over and read:

Isabella Marquez
(602) 62*-*515
#46 Windswept Road
Phoenix, Arizona

The card looked as if it had been dark blue once upon a time, but the years had faded it unevenly, and spills had smudged two of the numbers beyond recognition. Could this be something? Really something? Kate rarely trusted things that came so easily. She toyed with the paper's edges, softened by handling. She ran her fingers over the letters of the name, *Isabella Marquez*. She shuddered. Not one to go with gut instincts, she was surprised to find herself sensing some cosmic connection between these two women—between the three of them, even. It must be the pain meds at work.

As cold fingers toyed with the top buttons on her sweater, she wondered what lay ahead for Greta. She ventured a few steps out of the kitchen, and her eyes scanned the adjacent room for a thermostat. Nearly every inch of wall space was occupied with prints and artifacts whose origins she couldn't place. The walls were painted a garish tangerine and trimmed in turquoise. Eight bookcases, each identical in their sandstone color, but varying in size, took residence in the corners under suspended silver cylindrical lamps. Their shelves burst with books and magazines. The bookcases cramped the already small room but also created a warm and embracing mood.

Once she had spotted the thermostat and turned it up to seventy-six degrees, she ditched her previous plan to search the kitchen. All those books beckoned her. Her excitement rose with the temperature of the room. The abundant possibility in Greta's living room began to melt Kate's discomfort.

She had arranged her literature in categories: novels, magazines, poetry. Kate ran her hands over the volumes of poetry first, starting with the American classics—Walt Whitman, Emily Dickinson, moving forward in time—Langston Hughes, Maya Angelou. Poetry had been Kate's first love in terms of her creative endeavors. The poems she had written in her youth had been of a merely satisfactory quality. Lack of skill, however, had not been the reason she had abandoned her verses. She had lost touch with poetry as she entered high school, too impatient for its careful rhythm and extended foreplay, preferring instead the heady rush of love affairs like Heathcliff and Catherine's, and eventually moving on, much to her later embarrassment, to the full throttle experience of bodice-ripping dime-store romances.

She remembered Dickinson most fondly. She forced readers to wait, with her thoughtfully inserted dashes and layered linguistic meanings. Kate couldn't resist reading her favorite poem any time she stumbled across a Dickinson collection, so she slid the volume out of the shelf and opened to number fifty-two. As she did so, a Polaroid fell from between the pages, twirled to the ground, and slid across the scuffed oak floor before it caught the rug's edge.

Kate quickly retrieved it and eagerly flipped it right side up. Staring back at her was a young Greta standing next to another woman, forty-ish, a beautiful woman with flawless olive skin and soulful eyes. Kate felt another surge of anticipation. She was unable to take her eyes off the two women in the photograph. They wore matching scarves completely covering their hair. In spite of the dulled images, Kate could see that the silk had once been shiny and vibrant with wild patches of color. She thought about the simple black scarf Greta had worn the day they met.

In the white space beneath the photo, in Greta's sprawling script was written *Izzie and Me, 1984.* She slid the picture into her handbag next to the blue card. She held those images in her mind as she turned back to poem number fifty-two and read:

> Whether my bark went down at sea—
> Whether she met with gales—
> Whether to aisles enchanted
> She bent her docile sails—
>
> By what mystic mooring
> She is held today—
> This is the errand of the eye
> Out upon the Bay.

How serendipitous was it that the photo had been placed against this particular poem? Kate was beginning to feel a little creepy—too many coincidences in one evening. She shook it off, imagining that her near death experience had likely upset her senses. She envisioned Greta standing out on the Bay, watching, waiting for her ship's return, and wondering about its location. Kate knew that in her vision of herself, she was waiting for her father. But who or what was Greta's ship?

She pulled the picture out and looked again. Greta must have been in her late twenties. Life's indignities had aged her unfairly. She focused her attention on the wide-open, hazel eyes—somehow gray, green, brown, and orange all at the same time, like cat's eyes. What the photo couldn't capture, Kate filled in with her mind's eye. She had spent many hours trying to avoid those eyes at work. And she felt them penetrate her once again, from a twenty-five-year-old photograph. Was Greta trying to speak to her? Those young eyes were full of hopes and plans—that detail was still visible. Kate tried to extract from them what Greta's future had in fact contained up to this point. She looked so happy, happier than she had ever seen her in person. "Who are you, Margaret Perkins?" she whispered.

Kate pulled a quilt from the back of a leather sofa where it had been carelessly draped. She wrapped the soft, worn fabric around herself and continued searching the bookcases. Two rows along the bottom of the largest cabinet looked promising. It was lined with personal books of some kind, journals maybe. She flipped the switch on a small lamp on a nearby table to aid her vision in the fading evening sun. The lamplight cast a circle of gray mist into the dark room, much like a spotlight in a black theatre. She squinted as her eyes adjusted, and she could see that the spine of each volume was labeled with a number: a year. They had to be journals.

The numbers began with 1963 and progressed to 1969. Some years had as many as four volumes, and some had only one. Where to begin? A teenage girl love to bitch about her mother in her diary, right? So she grabbed a volume from 1968, surmising that it would be a year of mother-daughter drama.

She pulled the blanket tight, held the lamp in one hand, and clutched the journal to her breast with the other. She waddled toward the kitchen to get her purse and her notepad. As the lamp's cord reached its limit, she placed it on another small table with a wooden base. Still hugging the journal, she dug through her purse and retrieved her eyeglasses. Using her free hand, she pushed them absently onto her ears and nose.

As she reached for the lamp, she noticed a framed photograph on the table. She picked it up and examined it. It was Greta, roughly the same age as in the first photo, standing next to a young boy. Thirteen, maybe, or fourteen? Kate knew nothing about children and was dreadful at guessing their ages. He was about six inches shorter than Greta's five-foot-eleven frame, and he had the same cat's eyes. A brother? Kate tingled with anticipation. She carefully removed the frame's back and pulled the photograph free. On the back was Greta's familiar handwriting: Arizona, 1985. That was it—no names. But what a find!

She curled up in the rocker in the living area after gathering pillows of a multitude of colors—lime green, violet, and burgundy—that were strewn about the room. The apartment clearly belonged to someone with plans to return, but she didn't let herself linger on that thought. She arranged the pillows beside and behind her until she was settled and comfortable.

As she opened the journal's front cover, it creaked a peculiar welcome, like every seldom-visited, but never-forgotten book. A wave of uneasiness returned when she reminded herself that she was actually reading someone else's diary. She suspected, however, that she was going to have to move beyond those feelings—and do so quickly—if she ever wanted to get back to Houston, and more importantly, to Arlow. She moved the tiny lamp into place and focused her eyes on page one, and read, in Greta's childish handwriting:

January 5, 1968

I am so happy to be turning thirteen next month! I am hoping for a new guitar and some pretty jewelry that Elise and I saw in the Village Shop at Christmas. I hope they still have it. B. J. came over today. He still doesn't understand why I won't come to his house anymore. Dumb boys, can't figure anything out on their own. I wanted to get out of his life without a fuss, but he keeps pushing me harder and harder. Finally I got mad and yelled that he can come see me anytime he wants, but I'm never coming next door again! He looked like he might cry. I don't want to hurt him. He's my friend. But I'm never going back there.

Kate skimmed through the next dozen pages or so and learned that Greta had in fact received the guitar she so desperately wanted. She had used babysitting money to pay for a few lessons to get her started. Kate's eyes stopped again several pages later.

> February 14, 1968
>
> B. J. gave me a box of candy today and told me he loved me. He said since I'm thirteen now and never been kissed, and since he's already fourteen, that he should be the first. I told him to go away and never come back. But he'll be back. He's my best friend.

And again later.

> March 28, 1968
>
> Elise's birthday was today. She got a pretty new skirt and belt and some perfume. It's her favorite. It smells like flowers. She's sixteen, so Dad said she could wear some lipstick today. Mom had a fit, but Dad wouldn't give in. She looks so beautiful. I want to be just like her when I'm sixteen. B. J. told me I should never want to be someone else, no matter how bad life gets. But what does he know? He's just a stupid boy with a creepy dad.
>
> B. J.'s dad came to the party with him. Everyone was surprised to see him. He smelled like beer. Aunt Josie whispered to Momma that she felt sorry for poor B. J. and wonders why his dad keeps embarrassing him. But I don't think B. J. cares. He never talks about it. Elise says that's just the boy in him, and he cares plenty. She should know. She's smart, and she's sixteen now.
>
> P.S. I am thinking about letting B. J. hold my hand.

Kate woke up freezing to the sound of her cell phone ringing. The clock said 7:39. "Shit!" she yelled into the phone. She had fallen asleep reading the journals.

"Hello…Kate?"

It was Abe.

"Hello, Abe. Sorry…I was asleep."

"Kate, I'm at Hope Springs. I have bad news."

"What's happened?" She was nearly awake now.

"It's Chris Stone. He's…well, it's almost time. Melissa's asking for you."

Kate threw on some clothes and looked at the clock again. She had been napping for nearly two hours and now she was late. She was worried about Melissa. They knew Chris would go soon, but hoped for a few more weeks.

Her forays into Greta's life hadn't been completely fruitless. She had discovered that Greta had an Aunt Josie and a sister Elise and a friend B.J. But that was forty years ago. Where were they now? She also had some birth dates, which would help. And a mystery woman and child in Arizona—were they relevant? She scribbled some notes in her pad before rushing out the door.

She turned her tan Toyota Forerunner onto Rainy Lane and headed south toward Hope Springs Hospice. She picked up her cell and said "Jack" loudly and clearly. It dialed Jack's number. No answer. She tried again. No answer.

"Damn!" She made an unplanned left on Oak Bridge, and then she called Abe to tell him she would be there as soon as she could. She pulled up to the gate at Jack's apartment, quickly entered the security code, and raced toward Jack's building. It was quarter to 8:00. He should be home, or on his way to Hope Springs with Chinese food. She hadn't caught him in time. The sun had gone down, and there were no lights on. She peeked into his window, but saw nothing. She hoped to stop him before he brought dinner. She called his home number. No answer. She called his cell. Jack's voice mail picked up. She hurriedly tried again. About to give up, she turned to walk away, and thought she heard music inside. Then it was gone. She stood in front of his window and tried his cell again. Yes, definitely music. She stuck her ear to the window and recognized the tune from Jack's ring tone. Why was his cell phone in there when he wasn't?

She didn't have time to bother with it. She hopped back into her Toyota and drove as fast as she could to Hospice.

"I'm sorry I'm late," she said, breathlessly. She looked at her watch. Then she compared it to the clock on the wall. Her watch had stopped again.

"How was it?" Kate asked. "I mean, I heard you were the last to see him. Again, I'm sorry I was late. I—"

"It was peaceful. You're here now," Abe said. "Theresa is grateful for that. Now is when she needs you."

"It was just—so quick," Kate said sadly. Of course it wasn't quick. It was months of agony, and she knew that better than anyone.

Abe smiled and put his arm around her. "Melissa doesn't know yet. Theresa asked if you'd help her talk to her. They're in the playroom now."

"Of course," Kate said. "Of course. Thank you, Abe. I'm glad you were here for him."

CHAPTER TWENTY-THREE

October 2049

Simon held another photo in his shaking hands. "Kate," he said, "She was beautiful, wasn't she?" He laid the picture gently across her breast, as one would place a crying newborn. They hadn't spoken of the child in many years. The photo was in the box, so he knew Kate wanted to talk about her today.

"You know it never mattered to me," Simon said, "Your past I mean. I know you loved her. You were so young, Kate. Barely more than a girl. Think about Maggie. You'd forgive her, right?"

He sighed. He wasn't sure what Kate wanted him to say about the child he never knew, the little girl whose memory hadn't left her. He looked again at the picture of the child whose eyes had never opened to look into those of his amazing mother. Kate's heart hadn't ever mended. She had never fully let her go. Simon was sure he had seen the lost child's reflection in Kate's eyes the day Maggie and Zeke were born. Now he had a similar task before him. Letting go of the woman he loved. The woman who was inside him. The woman who willed his heart to beat, who urged his lungs to breathe.

Zeke stepped into the room. He was smiling. Thank God for Zeke and his smile. He approached his parents, bent down, and took Kate's hand.

"Do you think she's happy?" Zeke asked.

"More than you know," Simon said. "Yes, she has had a tremendously happy life, thanks to you and Maggie."

Zeke looked at the photo and commented, "Have I seen this?" He picked it up and examined it. "This is me, isn't it?"

Simon didn't correct him. He had vowed never to tell a soul about the child Kate had lost.

"I was a cute little guy, wasn't I?" Zeke said.

Simon scratched the side of his nose. "You were beautiful," he said.

Zeke looked at Simon and saw grief forming along the naturally easy lines of his son's face. He would give anything to stop it, or to at least slow its course.

"How are you holding up, Dad?" Zeke asked.

"I'm okay," Simon said. "I'm an old man, Zeke, and this is part of the job."

Simon could see that Zeke didn't buy it.

"Dad, she loved you so much. I never told you this, but, well…. never mind."

"Now, don't be that way. What is it, son?"

"I guess it's just that I am envious of what you have. The way Mom looks at you, even now after all these years together. I want that, too, someday."

"I want it for you, too, Zeke. There's nothing like it. And I know you'll find it."

"Mom always told me not to settle for less, but I can't help but wonder. I mean, I'm almost thirty. Maybe I missed it. You think maybe it happened when I wasn't looking?"

Simon laughed, "It always does, Zeke. Trust me on that."

CHAPTER TWENTY-FOUR

Katie? Please help me, Katie.
Daddy, I can't. Not like this.
You're my girl. You're the only one.
I know—and I'll always love you,
                              but I can't.

February 2009—Galveston

Kate drove toward the cabin in Galveston in a rented Chevy Tahoe. She wanted to ensure that she was one of the biggest vehicles on the road, and that she would have room to transport items back and forth for a few days. She had landed in Houston a few hours earlier, all her supplies in tow. She had a stack of Greta's journals and books, and several photo albums and personal papers alongside her own items. It seemed a little nuts to bring everything here instead of just staying in Dallas where she knew Greta had at least some kind of past. But Greta was here now, and she needed someone by her side. It was maybe the craziest thing Kate had ever done, but crazy was becoming the new normal.

   She had no trouble finding the place. It hadn't gone anywhere, after all—she had. After pulling into the small sandy driveway and unloading her bags, she decided to unpack. That way, she couldn't change her mind and go to a hotel without some effort. She hadn't eaten all day and hadn't stopped to get anything. The closest open restaurant was at least a twenty-minute drive, and being more tired than hungry, she decided to go to bed without dinner.

   Kate slipped out of the white tee shirt and stretched her long arms over her head, leaning gently back until silky strands covered her shoulder blades. She savored the feeling of her hair against her skin for a moment. Gathering courage, she opened the closet door and began to hang up her clothes. There were only a few items in the bedroom closet before she started. She pushed those toward the back and added a handful of her own, more recent clothes. That's when she spotted it—from behind a sea of navy and taupe she had just hung in the small space, a tiny orange thread

111

peeked out. The sundress she had worn that summer. She tugged it from the wardrobe and nearly fell backward when it popped off the hanger. The faded orange material grazed the side of her face, and the familiar fragrance, gently mingled traces of sand and Old Spice, overtook her. My God, had it been that long?

She pulled the cotton to her face and inhaled its delicious smell until she felt dizzy with nostalgia. She longed to return to the water, to feel its waves lap at her toes as she inched herself easily along the shore, wandering gradually deeper into the soul of the water. Of all her years of swimming in high school and college, the water here at the Bay still held the most charm for her.

The old feelings burned her chest and face as she scanned the room. Feelings she thought she had outgrown, outdistanced, leapt like flames into her new life. She laid the sundress on the bed and sat down to catch her breath. *This was a mistake,* she told herself. *I'm not ready.* She fought the impulse to run. She had to prove she could do this, to stay here at least one night alone. She was so tired that it couldn't be that difficult to just go to sleep soon, and all the memories could wait until tomorrow.

She pulled her jeans down to her ankles and then kicked them a few inches away. She stepped over her powder blue panties, leaving them lying on the floor behind her as she walked toward the window. She pushed the drapes open, and, gazing into the darkness, she saw only her reflection in the glass. She didn't recognize herself at first, and she jumped as if she had seen an intruder. She watched herself pull one bra strap over her shoulder, then the other. Embarrassed and yet delighted by the sight of her own nudity in the window, she continued the striptease for some pretend lover in the night. She stood tall and sucked in her stomach, even though she knew no one was there to see or judge her slight bulge.

She raised one long leg and gracefully rested it on the bed. It wasn't as muscular as when she was training in college, but it wasn't bad for her age, she thought. Slowly, she rolled down her thigh-high stocking to her ankle, all the while pouting her lips and fluttering her eyelids a la Marilyn Monroe into the reflective darkness, broken only by the outline of a half-moon. As she tugged at the end of her nylons to pull them off her foot, she lost her balance, and came crashing to the floor. As she fell, she grabbed the curtains and pulled them down with her. She laughed out loud and looked again into the blackness, grateful no one was watching. Then she wrapped the coarse, burgundy drapes around herself like a baby in a blanket and fell asleep on the rug.

She awoke early the next morning to sounds of the birds and the faint glare of the sun just peeking into the bare window. She sat up, resting her hand on the table beside her and gathering her thoughts. Then she pulled herself up and sat on the edge of the bed, where she used to sit for hours at a time listening for her father's breathing, contemplating the harshness of their world. She spread her hands across the quilt as if she could reach into that past and grab onto it. She lifted the sundress to her neck, wrapped it around her shoulders like a scarf, and let its worn softness stroke her tired skin. Becoming ill at ease with her naked body, she rose and quickly pulled it over her head, past her shoulders, and finally down past her waist. She slipped into her sandals and took a cursory glance around the room. As she walked past the mirror, out of habit, she stopped to examine her face. She opened the top bureau drawer and pulled out her powder, opened it, and mechanically dabbed three puffs—one for her nose and one for each cheek. Then she stared at herself long and hard, hoping to find some clarity in her image. Even though a few wrinkles had crept across her eyes, it was the same face as five years ago. It was as if she hadn't lived a moment in all that time, but instead had hit the pause button on her life.

She opened the door and walked out onto the deck, which served as a sort of cliff to the rustling water below. The picnic table she had bought was shoved against the house. It had changed—its edges splintered from neglect. She pulled it to the middle of the deck and sat and listened to the water for over an hour; its sweet symphony swept across her and calmed her. She had slept too late to watch the sunrise, but the view was stunning, nonetheless. She gazed across the expanse of water, and into that place where ocean meets sky—that place that only exists conceptually—that place where she used to go looking for herself.

"Hi!" A man jumped out from beside her, and she flinched. "I'm sorry Ma'am," he continued. "I didn't mean to scare you."

She went rigid. Her eyes darted from the intruder to her cell phone. Should she grab it or play it cool? No one ever came this far out from the main road.

A tall, somewhat lanky man made his way up the steps and stopped in front of her. "I'm Simon Gray." He offered his hand. "Forgive me for startling you."

"It's okay," she said, pausing between each syllable. She didn't take his hand.

He stared at her, unblinking, and she kept staring back, until she became self-conscious and looked away. "I'm sorry, Ms. Lasca, is it? Pardon me. I didn't know you were here. No one told me."

She hoped she could keep a steady voice. "Well, sir. I know that you are Mr. Gray, and that you are apparently sorry quite often, but you seem to know a great deal more than that about me."

"Gosh, I'm…oops! Almost said it again." He laughed, but she wasn't amused. He pointed a finger at himself and pretended to shoot. "You got me! Yes, you did."

Great, I'm being accosted by the urban cowboy, she thought.

"Mr. Gray…" It came out in a shout as she attempted to hide her shakiness. She suddenly remembered that she was naked beneath her sundress.

"Oh, call me Simon, please. And can I call you Kate?"

"I don't know you well enough to call you Simon. Now how exactly do you know my name, Mr. Gray?" She looked at her cell phone again.

"Well, I…or, your mom…. you see now…that's a long story."

"Mr. Gray, are you aware that this is private property and you are trespassing?"

"Well, you see, Ms. Lasca…" He seemed lost at what to say next.

"No. I don't see—that apparently is the problem."

"I'm not supposed to tell you. My mom asked me not to. And your mom, too."

"Okay, then. That's settled." She picked up her cell phone and began to dial. "If you can't talk to me, then I'll let you talk to the police. They can be here pretty quickly. You'd be surprised."

"No!" He put a hand on her arm and she jerked away, sending the cell phone tumbling down the steps of the deck. She knew she had to stay calm. He couldn't be that big a threat, she told herself. He knew her mother, and he said "Gosh" and "Pardon me." Still, she hadn't actually dialed 911 yet, and now she had to get past him to get to the phone. Or maybe he didn't know her mother. Murderers have been known to lie, she told herself. She hadn't realized how frightened she was until he grabbed her arm.

"Look, why don't we calm down and talk about this?" he asked.

"Fine," she said. "You have sixty seconds to explain what the hell you are doing on my property or I go into the house and get my gun."

"Okay, okay. Your mom knows my mom, and they know I like to come out this way and swim. Your mom told me about your place here and how much it means to you, so I offered to look in on it once a week."

"Why didn't you just say that?" She suspected she was receiving a heavily abridged version, but it sounded reasonable enough.

"Your mom worries about you. She thought you might get angry if you knew. And clearly, well…"

She thought his last remark was a bit haughty. "I am angry, Mr. Gray, because a stranger is on my porch speaking to me in a rather personal manner, and up until thirty seconds ago, I had no idea why."

"Well, now you do." He winked at her.

Haughty. Yes, definitely. He rocked back and forth on his heels and toes, hands shoved deep into his pockets. She noticed that his boots were rather shabby. Then her eyes traveled upward and examined his long lean legs, and thin but muscular torso and arms. It was then that she looked at his face for the first time. She realized she would have made a terrible witness to a crime. He had reddish-blonde hair and freckles, huge blue eyes, and a Howdy Doody smile. She hadn't noticed anything about him until that moment—about two minutes after his arrival. She could have been in twenty pieces in the freezer by then. Well, maybe not in pieces, but dead and in the freezer, for sure.

"Mr. Gray, how about this? You tell me what my mom is paying you, and I'll double it to get you the hell out of here."

"You must have misunderstood me, ma'am. She doesn't pay me."

Kate just stared at him.

"Mrs. Lasca, or Emily, your mom that is, well she's a nice lady, and she said you were nice, too, and that I'd like you."

"Apparently, she was wrong, wasn't she?"

"No, ma'am. Not at all, she wasn't. I like you just fine, Kate. I figure I can call you Kate now since you've threatened my life and tried to pay me off in the time it normally takes me to brush my teeth. And we've only just met. Imagine how I'll feel about you in a week or two." He winked at her again.

Kate shot up out of the chair and ran past him down the steps. She grabbed her cell phone and shook it at him like a mean old lady with a stick, threatening the bratty neighborhood kids. She knew how ridiculous she probably looked, with her odd behavior and her tattered orange sundress.

"Get out, Mr. Gray. And don't come back!"

He smiled at her as he descended the steps and brushed against her just slightly as he hit the sand. He walked casually down her driveway and headed for the water below. A dozen yards out, he turned back and smiled again.

"Hey, Kate," he said, looking her up and down, "I like your dress."

"Get out!" She screamed again.

He kept walking, never looking back again. He did, however, raise one arm high in the air and wave goodbye to her as he strolled away.

CHAPTER TWENTY-FIVE

Kate survived two nights in the cabin. On the third day, she met with Mr. Brody and dropped off the last of the paperwork necessary to seal the deal. He was very understanding and patient. The work was finished essentially, and she assured him that she would make herself available for further questions. She was eager to get back to Dallas.

"Actually, I understand that a Mr. Finnegan is our new point of contact," Brody said, just as she was seating herself in a black suede armchair opposite his desk.

"What?" she said.

He thumbed through some files on his desk, pulled one out, and opened it. "Oh, yes. He said. Jack Finnegan. I just spoke with Rob this morning. And Jack is meeting with me in the morning."

"You mean, Mr. Jasper told you this?"

"Why yes, Kate. He called this morning, said you would be in before noon, and that after today I should call Jack Finnegan for information. I'm sure I won't need to call for a while anyway, so it hardly matters to me, but Rob implied that you would be taking a few weeks off."

Kate was quiet.

"Kate, are you okay? Are you well?"

She nodded.

"Can I offer you some professional advice?" he asked.

She nodded again.

"Take a break. You and Greta did a damn good job here, but move on. Let Jack finish it out—it's all tedious grunt work from here on out anyway. Don't make an issue of this. We are being flexible because your company has suffered a terrible tragedy. Don't push your luck."

"Are you threatening me, Mr. Brody?"

"Of course not, Kate. In fact, we are launching a new product line in the fall—baby food. We want you on it. That gives you plenty of time to rest and do some other things. We'd like to start talking again in July. Are you up for it?"

Kate stepped from the building that housed Arlow Foods and into the glare of sunlight. She quickly dialed Jasper's number.

"Katie Girl! I'm glad you called in. I'm having trouble getting through on your cell. All that humidity, I guess." He chuckled. "Don't be mad. I put Jack on the case, but it's nothing. You did the work—you get the credit. Besides, did Brody tell you he wants you again in the fall?"

"Yes, he did," she said, careful to not say too much. Her emotions were all riding along the top of her skin, and she was nervous about exposing herself.

"Super! Now, you understand that this was for your own good and it all worked out."

She sighed, resentful of Jasper's treatment.

"So," he continued, "let's get you hooked up with an Internet phone this afternoon so we can reach you more easily. And you might want to reconnect service in the cabin."

"But, Mr. Jasper, I'm coming back tomorrow."

"No, you're not." He was hiding something.

"What is it Mr. Jasper?" she asked.

"Hell, Jack is standing right here. I don't want to blow the surprise. Let him do it. Here he is."

"Jack, is that you?" She knew her voice sounded irritated, but she didn't care.

"Hey, honey? How's Houston?"

"Well, good, I guess."

"I have some good news." He sounded casual but happy.

"Really?" She was deliberately snotty. He deserved it.

"Yeah, babe. I'm coming into town tomorrow. I want to spend Valentine weekend with you. Isn't that fabulous?"

"I'm at the cabin, you know, Jack, and I—"

"That's even better. It's about time I saw the infamous cabin, don't you think? What a great place for a romantic weekend."

She was contemplating telling him how she felt about his recent professional tactics and asking him where the hell he was the last night she was in town, and that's when she saw him. Simon Gray was approaching her cabin, slowly and happily strolling up the path with the sun shining behind his shoulders.

"Jack, honey. I have to go now. But I'll see you tomorrow morning around 11:00. Is that okay?" Her voice was sweet and welcoming now.

"Sure thing. See you tomorrow."

"I, um, I love you, Jack," she said loudly, after Jack hung up. Simon stood at the foot of the cabin steps now.

"Ms. Lasca."

"Mr. Gray?"

Simon smiled sheepishly. "I think I owe you an apology, Ms. Lasca. I didn't mean to tease you the other day. I…it's just that—"

"It's no big deal," she told him. His eyes were amazing. Had they been this amazing before? And had his shoulders been that broad?

"Of course it is," he said. "One should never treat a lady in such a manner. I was hoping maybe I could take you to dinner to apologize."

"I don't know," she said.

"Please ma'am. You'd be doing me a favor."

"How so?" she asked.

"You'd be giving me a chance to redeem myself, and apologize like a gentleman." He smiled. His eyes were definitely not that amazing last week.

"Okay," she agreed. What the hell was she doing?

Twenty minutes later, they were entering Beau's Burgers, and he held the door open for her. Then he pulled out her chair and asked her if she'd like some iced tea from the pitcher sitting on the table, which appeared to be a wheelbarrow with a glass top. Bits of straw and peanut hulls were scattered on the floor, and the smell of smoked brisket and fried chicken wafted through the air.

"Tea would be nice," she said. "Thank you, Mr. Gray."

"Could you call me Simon, please? Would that be okay?"

"As long as you call me Kate," she said, smiling as he poured. He smiled again too, a very genuine smile. His lips were full, and his face was over-run by freckles. His clear blue eyes stared at her between chunks of thick strawberry blonde hair that needed a trim.

"What brought you all the way out here from town?" she asked.

He grinned a little. She felt a little tingle of hope that the answer would be "I came to see you, Kate."

"I thought maybe I would come out tomorrow and clear some brush for you. I usually come on Friday. It's my morning off. I wanted to make sure it would be okay, though, now that you're staying here and all."

"You come every Friday?" she asked. "And my mom doesn't pay you?"

"Not really," he said.

"I wouldn't feel right, Mr. Gray, I mean Simon, letting you come now that I'm here. I can do it, or pay someone—"

He looked a little offended. She realized she must sound like a snob.

"It's no bother," he told her. "I like to do it. It's great exercise, and I love to go for a swim after. I consider that my payment. It beats the pool at U of H."

He did have great shoulders.

"You swim? That's great. I used to swim—"

"I know," he said. "Remember, your mom and my mom…"

"Oh, yeah. Well, why don't you come and swim, anyway?"

They talked for three hours.

He told her he was the assistant swim coach at University of Houston, and that he had lived in the same house all his life. He was left-handed and couldn't snap his fingers or whistle. He was an only child. His mom had met Emily Lasca a few years back and they had become instant friends. That's how he knew about Kate and her cabin. She told him about swimming in high school and college and how she gave it up in grad school and even mentioned her father. It was the first conversation she could remember that wasn't about work or anyone with whom she worked.

"So, you guys spent summers at the cabin when you were little?" he asked.

"Yes. It belonged to my Uncle Pat back then. But he let me buy it from him when dad was diagnosed. HIV."

"I'm so sorry."

"Yes, me too," she said. "Pat let me make a very small down payment and fair payment arrangements because he 'just knew I'd make it big in advertising soon.'"

"Did you?"

"I don't really know, that's a good question. I think maybe I'm about to. Then I can pay the thing off."

"So," he said, "what do you love most about the cabin?"

"Everything! But it's hard too, full of memories. I do love my book collection there though. Lots of my favorites, and a lot of my books from when I was a kid. That's pretty nice."

"What's your favorite book?" he asked her.

"I—I don't know," she replied.

"No fair, you already used that once. Come on, everyone knows. What's the book you've read a hundred times? The one whose lines you can recite?"

She thought about it a minute. Then she replied:

"It is only with the heart that one can see rightly; what is essential is invisible to the eye."

"What do you think?" she asked. Do you recognize it?

"No. Tell me—what is it?" Simon asked, genuinely interested.

"The Little Prince. Have you read it?" she asked

"No, but maybe I should. It sounds beautiful," he said.

"I'd loan it to you, but I can't. I used to have a very old, very tattered copy, but I lost it in the move to Dallas five years ago. I hoped I might come across it in the cabin, but no luck yet. What about you? What's your favorite book?"

"Sneetches, and Other Stories, by Dr. Seuss, of course!" His eyes sparkled as he spoke.

"Oh, yes. A good one," she said, laughing.

"When the star bellied sneetches had frankfurter roasts," he began.

"Or picnics or parties or marshmallow toasts," she continued.

"They never invited the plain bellied sneetches," he chuckled.

"They left them out cold in the dark of the beaches!" She frowned her biggest sad face, and they laughed together.

His red Ford pick-up hit every bump in the road between Beau's Burgers and her cabin, and she was reminded of traveling this road in her dad's truck before Beau had ever flipped his first burger. Simon mentioned needing to wash his truck and said he was a little embarrassed by the soda cans in the floorboard.

When they pulled up in front of the cabin, he ran around to open the door for her again. He walked her up to the porch and waited to make sure she got it unlocked okay.

"I'll be back around 9:00 tomorrow morning, but I'll stay out of your way," he told her.

She would be at the hospital in the morning, but she just couldn't make herself tell him. Instead, she reached up and gently moved the strands of red hair out of his eyes. It was as if someone else were controlling her movements.

"Thanks for dinner, Simon Gray," she said. Then she quickly went inside and shut the door tightly behind her.

****

"How is she today?" Kate stopped at the ICU nurse's station and asked Reagan, her favorite nurse.

"The same, Kate. I wish I could tell you more."

"I know you do." Kate sighed and tried to smile. "When do you expect the neurologist?" she asked.

"Around 10:00, he usually comes through. Will you be here? I think he can answer your questions better than I can," Reagan said.

She thought about it. It was 9:00. She knew Simon would be at the cabin any minute. And she was meeting Jack at 11:00 at the airport. No way she would get to see Simon today.

"Yes, I'll be here a while," she told Reagan.

She entered Greta's room and put her bag of supplies next to the bed. She straightened her sheets and fluffed her pillows, careful not to jiggle her.

"Hi, Greta," she said. "Reagan says you are stable—that's good news, you know?" Kate pulled a chair closer to the bed and sat down. "I thought you might like some company while I wait for Dr. D'Angelo. How does that sound?"

Kate shifted in her chair and started thumbing through her bag.

"I thought I'd read to you for a while. You know I've been reading your journals. I'm so sorry. I feel awful snooping into your life. I've been looking for family information and thought you might enjoy listening as I read. Might as well kill two birds…." She stopped herself. "Well, how about December 1968?"

She leaned the chair back a little and opened the journal to the marked page, and began to read:

> December 31, 1968
> Dad, Elise, and I went to the New Year's Eve block party tonight. There were fireworks and champagne. Mom went to church instead. As the clock struck twelve, I let B.J. kiss me. No tongue, though. Gross! His lips were softer than I thought a boy's lips would be. It was sweet. He smelled like oranges.

The words from Greta's journals had taken hold of her. Childlike, but wise, she kept thinking. Greta was not so different from herself at thirteen.

Jasper needed an update, but she found herself not wanting to tell him anything, which she fully realized ran counter to her goal of getting past this and moving on with her life. It was like she had come across some fantastic secret treasure map that would lead her to Greta's hidden past. Or even more pathetically, like she was in some secret club with this little girl who didn't exist anymore. Getting lost in Greta's life made her believe maybe she could reinvest in her own.

She was vague when she gave Jasper news, telling him only that she had a few names and a possible phone number. There, after all, wasn't much to tell. But she knew that she had to find something soon to help her friend.

She began looking up phone numbers in Arizona, searching for Isabella Marquez from the photograph and the partial phone number on the blue card. Of the two missing numbers, one looked like an eight or maybe a six, so she would start there. The other questionable digit was unrecognizable. She had scribbled out all the possible combinations and called them. She had been hopeful when she found a Marquez attached to one of the numbers, but they claimed to have never heard of an Isabella.

In the meantime, she devoted her mornings to sitting by Greta's side and reading journals to her. Today, they made it to spring 1969.

> April 17, 1969
> I'm actually 14 now—not as exciting as thirteen, becoming a teenager, but one year closer to sixteen!
>
> B.J.'s dad stopped drinking. Momma made us kneel in prayer of gratitude when I told her. Thank God the gratitude prayers are the shortest! I have known for a few weeks, but I've kept it a secret since he's quit so many times before and started again a few days later. He's doing okay this time, I guess. He doesn't stink anymore, and B.J. is happy. He goes to work every day, too. B.J. says his dad may become a partner in his firm, but Pop says that's putting the cart before the horse.

Speaking of B. J., I've kissed him every day after school since January 20. He always says, "thank you for letting me kiss you," but I want it as much as he does. Elise says not to let him know that. She said I should play hard to get, whatever that means. Lately, I've even started kissing first instead of waiting for him. Momma would make me pray for six hours! But she'll never find my diary. It's very well hidden. So she'll never know. I love B. J.'s orangey smell and the salty taste of the skin around his mouth. The first time he used his tongue I almost gagged, but now it's okay. It just tastes like B. J. Maybe I love him?

Kate paused a minute here and thought about her own first kiss, and her first "tongue" experience. She had to laugh. She was in ninth grade and had been in love with Todd Randall for four whole months. She just knew she would throw up when he suggested meeting her behind the football field after school to use their tongues for the first time. How wonderful to be so blindly in love and worried about nothing in the universe except whether you will be a good French-kisser. She continued reading:

June 15, 1969

Pop was mowing the lawn today and he fainted. Momma was afraid he had a heart attack, so she called an ambulance. The ambulance came and took him. He looked white as a ghost. Momma followed them in the car, which is strange because she hates to drive and only drives to church. She said this was almost as important as church and for us to stay by the phone. She hasn't called yet.

B. J. and I had to move our kissing into the shed out behind his house. His dad started to get suspicious. I was getting more comfortable at his house again, but lately he looks at me funny. Elise says be careful, especially since my boobs are growing. Why is it that as soon as a girl puts on a bra, all the men treat her differently? Like she changed species or something. Anyways, they're only kisses, even though B. J. wants to do more. He doesn't force me. He knows I'd punch his lights out. I'm waiting. I want my first time to be special.

"Miss Lasca?" A man's voice said her name. It was 9:40.

"Yes?" She stood and extended her hand to the doctor.

"Rick D'Angelo. I'm the neurologist on Ms. Perkins' case." He took her hand and shook gently.

"She would prefer Greta," she said.

He smiled. "Greta, okay." "Ms. Lasca—"

"And I prefer Kate." She chuckled.

"Kate, how much do you know about head injuries?" he asked.

"Not a lot unfortunately," she said.

"Well, they are tricky. And there's really no such thing as a 'typical head injury.' There are some common scenarios—"

"And hers is common? So, we might know what to expect?" she interrupted.

"Not exactly. We often see this kind of injury, but there's a huge variance in response."

"Are you saying you have no idea how long she'll be in coma, or what life will be like when she wakes up?" Kate asked, trying to take it all in and stay calm.

"Well, yes. That is correct. What we do know…" he pulled films from a huge manila file and slid it into the light frame on the wall. The scene was familiar. She listened intently; she was highly skilled at listening to test results.

"What we know is that there is swelling around her brain stem that suggests damage there." He pointed and talked, and she took mental notes.

"That sounds bad," she said, feeling a little stupid. "So, what does that mean for her prognosis?"

"The brain stem controls heart function and breathing," he said.
She sat back down in her chair, her stomach churning.

"But it's only swelling…what does that imply, as far as treatment I mean?"

"Brain swelling is actually very serious. She's on meds right now for it, but they're only helping slightly. Ideally, they will continue to work so we won't have to open her up to drain the fluid. Then we get into issues with infection, especially since she's sedentary right now."

He gave her a minute to let her process everything he was saying. Then he continued: "I'm sorry. Like I said, we've reduced some of the swelling, but it's wait-and-see for at least a few more days. That's what we know for now. In a couple of days, we'll be able to better gauge where most of the damage is. We'll continue to monitor her and keep you posted." He turned to leave.

"Dr. D'Angelo. Wait. How much are you telling me? I mean, are you holding back for legal reasons?"

"Holding back?" He smiled. "No, quite the opposite. I shouldn't be telling you anything. I think you know that since you met with the hospital legal team."

"I don't want you to get into trouble. I'm looking for her sister. I think that would be best for her."

"Ms. Lasca, I'm a big boy. Let me worry about my legal trouble. You just keep reading to her. And praying for her."

"Okay," she said softly.

"You do pray, Ms. Lasca?"

She was unsettled by the question and his tone. "Yes, I do—um, I will. I promise."

It was an odd thing to promise, but Kate knew she must keep it.

CHAPTER TWENTY-SIX

February 14, 2009—Galveston

"I've missed you, Kate," Jack said as he held her close. The afternoon sun was streaming in the window of her bedroom in the cabin. "It's chilly out there. Why don't we just stay in bed the rest of the day?"

"Don't you want to go celebrate Valentine's Day?" she asked.

"Didn't we just do that? In fact, can we do that again?"

She snuggled into him. It was a little cold outside, but she had grown addicted to being in the sunlight, watching the ocean, tidying the lawn.

"I know a really sweet burger place just on the edge of town. C'mon, it'd be fun!" she said.

"A burger place? Are you serious? I thought you'd make reservations somewhere nice. How about some seafood—I've been looking forward to shrimp and lobster all week."

"I guess I've gotten hooked on burgers and fries," she said.

"I thought you looked a little pudgy." He pinched a tiny fold of fat around her abdomen.

"Don't be a jerk," she said. Perturbed, she threw the sheets off and stood up. She didn't care if he had a full view of her naked pudgy body.

"Hey, I was just kidding. You look gorgeous, as always. I'm sorry. I didn't mean anything."

She began to get dressed and didn't look at him or speak.

"So…let's plan to get a burger after you show me around. Let's go see some of your favorite places when you were growing up. What did you used to do?"

She still didn't speak.

"Or…I could meet your mom."

"Are you crazy?" she snapped.

"Again, a joke. But it's quite revealing how you are flipping out. We are getting married, remember? Maybe she'd like to meet me first."

"Sarcasm doesn't work for you." She began to let her guard down a little. She opened a box on the nightstand and pulled out the red silk blouse he brought her for Valentine's Day. It was beautiful, and expensive. "It's really something," she said, leaning in to kiss him. "I love it. Thank you Jack."

"My pleasure. Leave that top button open, will you?"

"Are you trying to piss me off?" she asked.

"Yeah, cause you are sizzling hot in bed when you're angry."

"Is that so, Mr. Finnegan?"

"Oh, yeah," he said, rubbing his hands together. "Come back to bed...please?"

She walked to the edge of the bed, and stood there in her pink lace bra and panties, hands on her hips. She stared at him a minute.

"Come here," he whispered, and beckoned with his index finger. "I need you for something."

"You don't need me," she said.

"Oh, yes, I do. Very much. Come here, my little Cupid."

She leaned over and kissed him, and then slid back onto the bed. She lay on her back and arched her entire body upward into his. She wished he needed her. She knew she still needed him. Even now, with her world in chaos and taking her on a wild ride, that one thing hadn't changed.

They spent a few hours that afternoon at the Kennedy Space Center, and she was proud of how Jack endured it, even though she knew he was bored out of his mind. They stopped at Beau's Burgers around 7:00. She was famished, but eager to get back to the cabin, so they ordered two burgers to go.

"What is this place?" Jack looked around, incredulous, as they stood in line to pick up their order. He looked out of place in his polo shirt and khakis.

"It's the place that makes the best burger you'll ever eat," she said and wrapped her arms around his neck. As she looked past his shoulder, she saw Simon sitting in a corner, alone. He had his eyes closed and his head laid back, resting on the back of the bench that they had occupied together a few nights earlier. She prayed he wouldn't open his eyes before they could get their food and get out. Her prayer was answered.

As they approached her porch, she saw a package sitting on the picnic table. It was small and wrapped in plain white paper and tied with thin pink ribbon.

"What is it?" Jack asked.

"I can't imagine," she said, gently tearing at the seams of the paper. There was no tag or note. She pulled at the delicate ribbon, which had been woven with a fresh twig of baby's breath. She was quiet when she saw its contents, and then she smiled and looked out at the road leading away from her cabin and into town.

"Okay, so what is it?" Jack asked, a little more impatiently this time.

"A book. *The Little Prince*," she said.

"Uh...I don't get it," he said.

She kept looking at the road and smiling. Then she looked at Jack. "I know you don't, Jack. I know you don't."

Kate stayed up late that night reading from Greta's journal.

June 26, 1969

Dad came home from the hospital a few days ago. I've been too busy to write. I'm so glad he's home. I missed him terribly. He can't do much. He's very weak. I have moved into Elise's room with her, and I sleep on a cot. Dad is in my room. Mom says it's just easier for him to have his own room. She hardly goes in there. Elise and I care for him. Mom's too busy kneeling in the closet, praying and lighting candles. Stupid. God can't heal him if he starves! Elise and I make his favorite, chicken noodle soup and grilled cheese sandwiches. After his nap, he will play cards with us, he promised. I just know in my heart he'll be okay. I pray too, in my way, in my cot at night, and sitting beside dad's bed watching him sleep. And I know that chicken noodle soup, and not candles, will heal him.

I have a secret. I haven't told anyone, because I know they won't believe me. When I was praying beside Dad's bed, really my bed, last night, I saw a shape in the corner. I think it was God watching us. It was a beautiful man who looked like God. I felt warm all over, and my fear went away for a few minutes. As soon as I looked at him, he faded away. I know Elise will laugh at me. She'll say I imagined it, seeing shapes like when I was little and scared of the dark. I don't know what mom would say. But I can't tell a soul. I just know that God came to save Dad.

CHAPTER TWENTY-SEVEN

October 2049—Galveston

"Well, Kate. I guess there are things that need saying." Simon began, with no clear plan for where he would go with his words. "It's strange. You're the only person I've ever known how to talk to, but I don't have a clue how to do this.

"Forty years ago, can you believe it? Forty years. I remember— I just kept hearing about the amazing Kate Lasca. It's funny to think how your mom was so spot-on about you. You think I fell for you in 2009, but I loved you before I met you. I just had to wait for you to show up and love me too. Emily knew you so well, and she filled me up with wonderful stories about you and your life and all your passion. She loved you, Kate. I know it's so complicated, and I know you never fully worked through it all with her. You were just beginning…and I know you wish you could have finished…. shit—I don't know what to say to you.

"I love you. I've always loved you. That first day, at the cabin, on the porch. It sealed the deal. I would go home and just pray, dear God, make her love me, please God, let her love me. Betcha didn't know I secretly believe in God, did you? How could I not? Look at what He has given me. No mere mortal could make such things happen, especially a mortal such as myself. I knew you were out of my league…. hell, the world knew it. Me a swim coach, you an ad exec? Brilliant as fuck, and legs that…well, you know. And you were drop-dead gorgeous. Still are…." He stroked her cheek and tried not to cry.

"How could it happen, *us* I mean, without a God? I know it couldn't have. So, I am counting on Him to get me through, to show me the way. You asked me to do three things. It's in the note." He took the paper from the box and unfolded it slowly, and then read it aloud as if it might be unfamiliar to her.

Dear Simon,

In the past year since my diagnosis, we have talked a lot and I have told you everything I could. If you're reading this, then today is my last day in this life. Don't ask how I know—I just do, and so does Abe. The world has a lot of questions about me and Abe—and so do you. You will know your answers by day's end. It is my one regret that I couldn't tell you sooner. Please believe that it was only to protect you and the children. Many times, I have almost told you, but ultimately knew I couldn't, or shouldn't. I asked you to trust me and to trust Abe, and you did, even though I know it almost broke you as a man to do so. You have to believe that your trust only proves that you are a man, and a good man. Your faith in me wasn't foolish, I promise.

Abe and I have been accused of unspeakable acts. People in this world are so disconnected from the next life, and they see a distinct line between here and there. I assure you that this line is very faint, like the imaginary line that marks one day from the next in ordinary life, and crossing it is peaceful. Please don't worry about me. I am ready. I know the world thinks I am a murderer for what I do, how I help people who are suffering, but you have always seen the best in me. While I viewed my actions as necessary, you have seen them as misguided but compassionate. Still, you stood by my side. I am the luckiest woman in the world. I don't think you know this, so I am telling you now: I love you with all my soul—there has never been a moment since the summer of 2009 when my heart wasn't 100% yours. I never considered being with Abe. It's important to me that you know that, once and for all.

Please do three things for me after I go. One: take care of the children. Help them always remember that I love them and make sure they are okay. Two: cooperate with Cross. Tell him what you know and don't try to protect me or Abe. It will make things easier for all of you. I am aware that this goes against all I have begged of you in the past, but I ask you to trust me one final time. Abe has agreed this is best and he is ready to face the music. Third, and most important: go on living and loving. Your spirit and liveliness are what I fell in love with, and the best way to honor our love is to go on living, from this life and into the next.

I'll be there waiting for you. And I'll wear pink.

I love you,
Kate

Simon sat quietly for a few minutes after reading the letter. This couldn't be happening. He really was losing her. He really had to say goodbye.

"So, here's the thing, Kate—I can't let you go, not yet." He cleared his throat, and continued. "I want to honor our love, as you do. I have no problem with your first request, my darling. The kids are loved, and they are provided for. They always will be. I know you want me to try to understand Maggie and her desire for...him. I don't know if I can, but for you, I'll try. Number two on your list—well, that will be my pleasure. You are the only one who stopped me from turning him over to Cross a long time ago. But I can't let him tarnish your name or make your life not matter.

"As for number three, of course I'll go on loving. Forever I will love you, Kate Lasca-Gray. God put love for you in my heart before I ever came kicking and screaming into this world, and only He can take it out—and He'd have a hell of a fight on his hands at that.

"But...how about I get back to you on that going on living part?

CHAPTER TWENTY-EIGHT

It was nearly lunchtime on Monday after a long weekend with Jack. Kate was by Greta's side, reading from her journal.

> July 4, 1969
>
> Dad is dead, and I don't even know how I feel yet. Elise has been quiet, but trying to comfort me. She puts her arms around me and tells me it's going to be okay. She's an awesome sister, but no one can help me right now. Momma threw herself across Dad and cried and screamed for a long time. Elise and I went into the living room and sat alone talking about how life might be now. Momma loves us, but she can't take care of us. Not like other moms. She doesn't understand. She just keeps telling us to pray.
>
> I saw God again. He was in my room yesterday morning when Dad died. He was just a shape like before, but brighter. No one else saw him but me and Dad. I saw him put his hands on Dad right before he stopped breathing. I think Dad saw him, because he looked up, right into his face, and he smiled with his last breath. I am glad he was happy when he went. What will I do without him?
>
> I haven't found my tears yet.

Regan interrupted with unexpected news.

"Your boss is here, Kate. He wants to see you in the waiting room," she said.

"Jasper is here? Really?" She closed the book. "Okay, I'll be right there." Kate adjusted Greta's pillows. "I'll be right back," she told Greta.

He didn't greet her with his usual mega voice calling out, "Katie-Girl, how goes it?" She was startled by the sadness on his face.

"Mr. Jasper, when did you get here?"

"Kate, I got a phone call this morning."

"Is it bad news?" she asked.

"No, it's not bad—or good." His voice was somber. "It was Greta's attorney. He has been out of the country and just returned. He read about the wreck in the paper and found us, me actually. It's complicated."

"I don't understand," she said.

"You should sit," he told her. She had never seen him like this. "Here's the thing," he said. "It turns out that Greta, about a week after starting at the agency, contacted her lawyer and arranged for an anonymous power of attorney in an event such as this. He has asked that I advise him and also communicate his decisions."

"That's good news, isn't it? You can help decide things now." She felt a weight lift from her shoulders.

"A decision has been made." He didn't smile.

"Well, what is it? Surgery—medications? I mean, are we going to move her to Dallas? I think that's a great idea."

"We are taking her off life support, Kate. We're going to let her go."

"NO WE ARE NOT!" she screamed. "We are not going to kill Greta. No way. I have been sitting by her side, and I will continue to sit here until she wakes up. You can't do this, Mr. Jasper. You can't—"

"Kate, honey." He was starting to breathe heavy. "She's not going to wake up. I just spoke with Dr. D'Angelo. There is definite damage to her brain stem. She can't wake up, ever. We've got to let her go. It's the kind thing. We've got to."

"No, no, please no." She was crying, too. "Please, tell me you won't do this. I'll fight you, I swear—"

"You'll lose. And what's worse, she will too. Kate, you are a smart woman. And a compassionate woman. I adore your spirit, but you know I'm right."

She hung her head and tried to contain her sobs. She shook violently but wouldn't let any sound escape. He sat next to her and gathered her small frame into his huge embrace, rocking back and forth. She cried for a very long time, about a woman for whom, she feared, tears might never before been shed.

Kate sat at their table at Beau's Burgers, sipped her iced tea with extra lemon, and stared into space. She didn't know how to let go of Greta. She didn't know how to do anything. She was numb, body, mind, and spirit. Her heart was breaking. Greta had lost her father so young, and it seemed so tragic. She was trying to take it all in. All the death. All the sadness.

"May I join you, pretty lady?"

She looked up and saw Simon's smiling face. He was holding a tray full of food and looking very handsome.

"You don't really want to," she said. But she really wanted him to.

"Why don't you let me decide?" he asked.

She motioned for him to sit, then looked away, hoping not to cry in front of him.

ALINDA QUINN

"Kate, what's wrong?" His voice was clean and sincere; it grabbed her heart and held onto it.

She broke into tears, and he took her hand gently. She took several minutes to catch her breath and speak.

"Oh, Simon," she said. "I've made such a mess of things."

"I can't imagine that. What's going on? Surely it's not that bad."

"It's worse than anything you can imagine. I have done a terrible thing. Many terrible things."

She told him the story of Greta, as she knew it, from beginning to end.

He listened quietly, never letting go of her hand, occasionally offering her a napkin to blow her nose into.

"Kate, it was a car accident, an *accident*. It's awful seeing you like this. Let me drive you home."

"No, absolutely not. I can't trouble you."

"It's never trouble to help a friend. It's my privilege. And besides, you shouldn't drive."

Kate thought it sounded remarkably like he was trying to take care of her, which made her prickle.

They rode in silence, except for Kate's occasional sniffles, and when they arrived, he clicked the key off and turned to face her.

"I'm so sorry," he said. "I don't know what else to say." He took her hand again.

"There's something else," she whispered.

"What.... Kate, what is it?"

"My father," she said.

She had never told another soul.

"Yes, I'm listening," he said. She knew he was.

"I—I don't know how to say it. I've never thought of it in words. I've never *given* it words. It's unspeakable."

"Take your time. I'm here."

"He asked me to help him—to help him—" She still couldn't say it.

"Kate?"

"He had AIDS and he was suffering terribly. He asked me to help him die."

"Oh my God," Simon said, softly and without judgment.

"And I said I would. I was supposed to give him an overdose of pills. We had it planned. One morning, I crushed his usual pills into his juice, and I was supposed to add the whole bottle. I added a lot, but not enough."

"It's not your fault," Simon told her. "You couldn't have predicted—"

"You don't understand. I knew it wasn't enough. I chickened out. But I couldn't tell him that. He thought I just miscalculated. I left the bottle on the bed next to him, knowing he'd finish it. Knowing I was too weak, but unable to tell him the truth. Unable to do this thing for him—to make his last moments easier."

132

"Kate, you can't blame yourself."

"Yes, I can. I do. And I will. Every day. For the rest of my life. I am a coward." She was crying hard now.

"I let him down," she said. "And I lied to him. It was supposed to be—my eternity in hell, not his. He wasn't supposed to kill himself. Oh, God, I can't—"

"Kate, Mr. Jasper is taking care of this with Greta. And I'll take care of you," he said.

"My mind, and my heart, they are so mixed up right now. I can't untangle it all."

"I know. I understand."

He got out of the truck and came around to the passenger's side, opened her door, and scooped her up. She wrapped her arms around his neck and let him carry her across the path, up the steps, into the cabin, and place her gently into her bed. He pulled a chair up close and tucked her in with her blanket.

"I told you—I'm here," he said again. "I'm not going anywhere. Just sleep now."

She fell asleep, and he sat in the chair next to her bed until the sun came up the next morning.

****

Kate, Jack, Simon, Jasper, Hannah, and Marissa gathered at Greta's bedside. They decided to take turns privately telling her goodbye. Marissa went first, and the others filed into the waiting room. Simon offered to go get coffee for everyone and then headed for the cafeteria, and Kate used the opportunity to confront Jack.

"What the hell is she doing here?" she asked.

"Marissa? She came to support you, and to say goodbye."

"It's true, Shug," Hannah said.

"Stay out of it," Kate told her. Hannah took a few steps back and remained quiet.

"How much time have you spent with her while I've been in Houston, Jack? How much?"

"Kate, honey. I can't talk to you when you're like this. You are hurting, and I won't contribute to it by arguing with you."

"Don't protect me, you bastard. I know what you're up to." Her voice was quiet, but clearly enraged.

"Look, she is here for *you*, not me. I did not invite her."

"Did I cause a problem?" It was Marissa's voice. "I didn't mean to. Should I leave?"

"No," Jack said.

Kate shot him a nasty look.

Marissa spoke in her small voice: "Kate, I just admire you so much. I know I've gossiped about her and I know you don't approve of that, and I hoped I could—I

133

don't know—somehow make it up to you and to Greta." Marissa sighed and put a hand on Kate's arm. Kate pulled away and stormed out into the hall. Jack followed.

He spoke first. "Honey, you are hurting, and you are saying things you don't mean. I understand, but you need to stop before you go too far."

"How do you know what I mean to say?" she hissed.

"Kate, damn it. Listen to me," he begged. "If I didn't care about you, would I leave Houston and fly back two days later to be here for you?" She could tell he was fighting his anger.

"Listen to you? To you? Are you kidding? That has worked so well for me. Yeah, I'm going to listen to you. I don't think so!"

"So, you will listen to what's his name—Simon? Is that his name? Or Abe? Or Jasper? How many are there, Kate—I'm losing count."

She reached back planning to smack him with the force of a mule kick, but Simon caught her hand from behind.

"Hey, folks. I know I'm new here, but this doesn't seem like the time or place for this, don't you agree?" His next comment was directed plainly toward Jack. "Pardon me for butting in, but a lady's getting ready to pass away. Can this wait?"

Everyone was quiet. Kate didn't dare make eye contact with Simon. She was embarrassed by her behavior—both here and the evening before. She hadn't even introduced him to her friends from Houston.

Abe turned a corner and almost ran into the trio. He had just arrived.

"Hi, guys. How are we all doing?" he asked.

Kate looked at Jack apologetically now. She truly was ashamed of herself.

"Kate," Abe said, putting his arm around her shoulder, "I thought you might need me. I'd like to minister to all of you if you are okay with that."

She fully expected Jack to ask him to leave. Talk about bad timing.

Jack reached his hand out toward the minister, and Abe took it and held it, smiling.

"Thank you for coming," Jack said. "Kate could use a lot of support right now. We all could. I'm glad you're here."

They all silently filed into Greta's room. Kate looked at all the faces here—Jasper, Simon, Jack, Abe, Marissa, Hannah—and she saw great sadness. It was a comfort to know that Greta wouldn't die alone.

Abe took Greta's hand and started to pray…

> *The Lord is my Shepherd; I shall not want.*
> *He maketh me to lie down in green pastures:*
> *He leadeth me beside still waters.*

Reagan came in with Dr. D'Angelo. He seemed agitated, but didn't speak.

He restoreth my soul:
He leadeth me in the paths of righteousness for His name's sake.

The doctor nodded at Reagan, and she turned off the respirator. Then, as they all stood very still, watching Greta's chest rise and fall for the last few times, Kate felt like she was in another world. Both of Abe's hands were wound tightly around Greta's, just like they had held Kate's the first night they met.

Yea, though I walk through the valley of the shadow of death,
I will fear no evil;
For thou art with me;

Her breathing slowed a little more. Kate wanted to turn away, but didn't. She had to see Greta through to the end. Reagan gently removed the tubes from Greta's mouth and nose. The doctor's words mixed with Abe's prayer, and Kate felt confused by it all—like she was standing in a human abstract painting. She realized she hadn't privately told her goodbye. She was busy yelling at Jack, and somehow…it was nearly unbearable to think about.

"You've made the right decision," Dr. D'Angelo said. "I applaud your strength."

Thy rod and thy staff, they comfort me.
Thou preparest a table before me in the presence of mine enemies;
Thou annointest my head with oil;

The heart monitor slowed, and slowed again, and they waited for the long beep they had heard on television and in the movies but never in real life. They waited, but it was taking its time. Jack squeezed Kate's hand.

My cup runneth over.
Surely goodness and mercy shall follow me all the days of my life,

Kate watched the clock. She checked it against her watch and saw that her watch had stopped again. Something so ordinary as a broken watch seemed disrespectfully out of place at this moment. She looked back at the clock and followed the tiny red hand, like she had when Greta sat in her office, droning on when Kate had work to do. Two seconds, ten seconds, one minute. Still the slow beat of Greta's heart. Greta's chest rose and fell weakly, slowly. It was time.

And I will dwell in the House of the Lord forever.... Amen.

Abe removed his hands from Greta's and laid them across her chest, feeling her heart.

They all listened as the monitor slowed even more.

Abe closed his eyes and seemed to be saying a frantic, but silent prayer, keeping his hands across Greta's chest. Kate held her breath.

Dr. D'Angelo looked really impatient now. Did he have somewhere better to be? Kate hated arrogant doctors. What could be more important than this moment?

He hastily put one end of his stethoscope to his ears and the other to Greta's chest, pushing Abe's hands out of the way. He squinted as he listened, making eye contact with Abe the whole time.

Another agonizing minute went by before he nodded at the minister, and Abe spoke again.

"Praise God," he said. "She's alive. Thy will be done."

CHAPTER TWENTY-NINE

Jasper had Greta transferred to a long-term care facility just outside Houston two days after they took her off the respirator. She was being fed intravenously, but miraculously her heart was beating and her lungs were pushing air on their own. Jasper and the others were already back in Dallas, and Kate was packing to join them there when she heard a knock at her cabin door.

"I thought I'd see you off, and tell you how much I've enjoyed getting to know you." Simon smiled, but she thought his eyes looked a little sad. Maybe she just wanted them to be sad.

"Well, Dallas calls, and Kate answers, I guess. I'll miss the cabin, but I'm not really needed here anymore."

"That's not true," he said.

Her heart leapt. She looked at him. How could she feel joy and sadness at the same time?

"I think Greta does need you," he said. I think the reading, the company, the human contact, might be keeping her alive."

"Oh," she said. "Maybe."

"No, definitely," Simon said. "We need to be connected to others, to touch them, even when we're in her condition, heck, even more so when we're sick or hurting....or lonely."

"You could be right, but I am so far behind on my work, you know?"

"I understand." He reached out to shake her hand. "Good bye, Ms. Lasca," he said, with the most beautiful smile she had ever seen, "And good luck."

She held his hand and vowed silently to remember the pleasure of his skin against hers for as long as she lived.

"Goodbye, Simon Gray," she said, and watched him climb into his beat-up red pick-up and drive away in a cloud of dust.

Kate looked out the window of the 737 and wondered what it would be like to just fall out of the sky and land somewhere new, where no one knew her, and no one expected anything from her. She could recreate herself. What would she change? Her hair, her weight—well definitely—but what else? Is it possible to recreate oneself? Her brain hurt from thinking so much about her life. Half of her was begging to get back to normal, to sit at her desk at Jasper, to visit hospice evenings and weekends, go to church on Sundays. The other half fantasized about a new Kate Lasca that would shock the hell out of the world.

She drove to Hope Springs first. She had missed the funeral for Chris Stone, but wanted to check on some of her other friends. She was grateful that Abe wasn't there. She couldn't deal with him today.

By two o'clock she was parking in the garage next to Jasper's building and gathering her dusty briefcase and sweater from the backseat of her Accord. Had it only been sixteen days since the accident?

She stopped by Jack's office and stood in the doorway waiting for him to get off the phone. He was turned away from the door, looking out the window, and talking to a client. He hung up and swung around, and smiled at her. He looked so different than she remembered: not bad, not good, just different.

"Jack?"

"Oh, Kate." He stood up and they embraced. "I love you, Kate."

"I've missed you," she said. "I just wanted to say hello, and I'm sorry I was so awful to you in Houston."

"I know," he said. "I'll call you tonight, and maybe we can get together this weekend."

"Yes," she said. "That sounds nice." She felt flat as she spoke these words. Re-entry into Dallas might be harder than she anticipated.

She spent a couple of hours at her desk, making it a point to not watch the children in the park. She kept looking up and expecting to see Greta standing there, bracelets jangling, hair flying, words scratching. Instead, she saw Jasper standing in the doorway watching her work.

"Mr. Jasper. How long have you been waiting? Did you need me?"

"May I come in?" he asked.

"Of course."

He sat in her father's chair.

"Kate," he said. Not *Katie-Girl*, but just *Kate*.

"Yes?"

"You have impressed me beyond words. I can't begin to tell you how grateful I am to you for your level of commitment."

"Thank you for the compliment. And for the opportunity to work the Arlow account. I have learned a lot. And I've grown a lot."

"I know you have," he said. "That's why I want to formally offer you the Creative Director position."

"Really?" She felt a rush of excitement. "You mean—oh of course, I accept." It felt deliciously good to feel happy again.

"Don't you want to think about it?"

"I've thought about it, plenty!"

He laughed and stood to leave. She walked him to the door. Jack and Hannah were in the hallway, eavesdropping.

"Congratulations!" they sang out.

"And Kate," Jasper said. "When I said I'm impressed, I didn't just mean professionally. You're an A+ human being, and I'm proud to know you."

She was sure she blushed.

"I'll leave you to celebrate with your friends." She reached out to take his hand, but he grabbed her into a big bear hug and touched her hair. She held onto these rare minutes in her life when everything made sense again. They were few, and fleeting.

She looked at Hannah, who was standing there with her hands on her hips.

"Oh, Hannah," Kate said. "I'm sorry about my rudeness at the hospital. My life is—I can't describe it. But that's no excuse."

"It's okay, Hon, I know you're going through a lot."

"Kate, we're here for you," Jack said, "and everything is getting ready to turn around for you, Ms. Creative Director."

"Thank you both for understanding, and for the support here at Jasper too. I guess I'm not ready for all this."

"You're ready," Hannah said. You just don't know it."

"And you, Jack," Kate said. "You deserve my trust. It's me I don't trust right now. I have felt so lost."

"Well, now you're found. Welcome home, darling," he said.

"We know you haven't been yourself, and we love you," Hannah said.

"You're right. I haven't." Kate had been feeling like an intruder in her own skin. Her mind went back to the plane ride home, to that fantasy person she would create if she could, the person who knew what she wanted and went for it, not just professionally, but personally. What she wasn't admitting at that exact moment was that the new Kate Lasca was already in the making.

Finally home, Kate attached the book light to a page in the middle of Greta's 1969 journal, where she had been interrupted on that horrible day to talk with Jasper about his decision to turn off the machines. She fluffed the pillows on each side of her. It felt so good to be back in her own bed. She had to keep reading the journal. It had seized her interest, and she devoured every word.

July 5, 1969

The house was quiet last night. Momma and Elise spent the day making funeral arrangements. I stayed here because Momma still thinks I'm a kid. I had to clean house for all the company we'll be having over the next few days. I could see and hear Independence Day celebrations going on out in the street all day: firecrackers popping and sparklers sizzling.

B.J. left to visit his mother this morning. He won't be here for the funeral. He won't be back for six weeks. He came over to bring me some flowers and try to get me to watch the big fireworks show, but I didn't feel like going out. He didn't want to leave me alone, so we sat on my bed together and watched the fireworks out my window. I opened my curtains wide and we just watched quietly. I didn't wait for him to kiss me. I put my mouth on his and I kissed him for a long time, longer than I've ever kissed him before. I don't know what happened. I was so scared with him leaving, and so sad about Dad. I took his hand and put it on my chest and asked him to feel my heartbeat, and asked him to touch me....

Kate inhaled sharply and put her hand to her own chest to feel her suddenly galloping heart. Was Greta going to give herself to B.J.? It was sweet, and sad, and beautiful.

He was so scared and kept asking me if I was sure, if I was okay. Boys! Of course I was nervous, but I wanted to feel him. I wanted to feel all of him. I've never seen a naked boy before. He touched me on my breasts and my stomach and my legs. He was very gentle, and he was shaking. I told him I wanted to do it, to go all the way, and I told him I love him. He said he loved me too. And he cried a little.

It hurt a little bit at first, but mostly it just felt nice to touch him and let him touch me. His body felt so good on top of mine, and I never wanted it to end. With Dad gone, I don't think anyone will ever hold me again, and I didn't want B.J. to ever leave. He is my safe place now and forever. He laid next to me for a long time after, but then I made him leave because I knew Momma would be home soon. I wonder when I'll see him again? Six weeks is a long time.

Kate felt hot wet streaks on her cheeks, and she wondered if she would ever stop crying. She had cried more in the past several weeks than she had cried in five years before it. She opened her bureau drawer and pulled out a bookmark she had made on Father's Day when she was a little girl. She placed it lovingly against the journal's page and closed it. She laid back, held the book close to her chest, and closed her eyes, letting Greta's words soak into her soul and lull her into a deep, dreamless sleep.

CHAPTER THIRTY

2049—Galveston

There were three sharp taps on the front door. Campbell Cross stuck his head into the living room. To Simon, this huge man seemed so small today. This man whose dark suspicions had hung like a fog in their lives wasn't so big and bad right now.

"Can I come in, Simon?" Cross asked.

"Do you have a search warrant?" Simon asked, coolly.

"Hell, Simon—"

"Kidding, Camp. Damn, do you cops ever laugh?" Simon winced at his own question, as a fragment of memory swirled in his brain: this man's laughter escaping from beneath his daughter's bedroom door when he had heard them, had discovered their secret passion, that day so long ago. That day, in other ways, just like any other, but that now was catalogued as one of "those" days in his life, much like this one was destined to become. He had never told Maggie he heard them. She would be devastated by the shame of it.

"Simon, you know why I'm here."

"I told you, I don't know when he's coming back. I'm not going to help you." He wasn't willing to cooperate just yet. Kate still had a few hours left.

"Look," Campbell said. "I think I've been patient. We had a deal."

"Quiet," Simon whispered, rising. "Let's go in the kitchen."

"Fine," Campbell said.

The men talked in hushed tones over lemonade at the kitchen table. Simon could feel Maggie lurking in the living room, and she occasionally glanced their way, through Kate's office, into the kitchen, and right into Simon's heart. He was sure that she couldn't hear them, but also sure she was dying to. Having Zeke, Campbell, and Maggie in the house together produced a feeling in Simon similar to waking up and finding snakes in your bed. One careless move, and it would be over.

"I feel as if, frankly, I've made a deal with the devil," Simon said.

"Shit, Simon, I'm not the bad guy here. You really trust Abe? You are nuts."

"I don't trust you either, asshole."

"Okay, I deserve that. But, you were always blind when it came to Kate. I'll give you one thing—you love unconditionally, don't you?"

"What the hell does that mean? My Katie was faithful, you presumptuous piece of shit! Just because you cheated on Macy—"

"Let's not say something we'll regret," Campbell said.

Simon couldn't believe this guy—his nerve. He was some kind of jerk. Simon never regretted anything he said, especially not to Campbell Cross. Did he not think he owed his family a little more than this?

Campbell and his younger three brothers had played together with Maggie and Zeke on the cabin's lawn, the one now swarming with vultures. Campbell, thirteen years older than Maggie and Zeke, always played baby-sitter, so Simon thought. Simon had taught all the Cross brothers to swim in the pool in the Gray's backyard. He had coached Campbell to victory in college, and he had invited him for dinner every Friday night in an attempt to comfort him, actually to comfort both Simon and Campbell, in the loss of Campbell's father. Simon had become a surrogate for Rudy Cross, who was Simon's dearest friend and the men's basketball coach at University of Houston for many years. After his death, Simon had encouraged Campbell to become a permanent part of their lives. Had he unwittingly nurtured his thirst for his young daughter? He shivered when he thought of it, Camp at age twenty-two, watching a young Maggie dance around the house, unsuspecting, innocent. And later, Camp with his twenty-eight-year-old hands, touching the newly pubescent, soft and smooth skin of his daughter, urging her to kick harder, swim farther. Grooming her for the affair. All right under his nose. Motherfucker.

"You have to trust me," said Campbell.

Simon laughed loudly enough to get Maggie's attention. She stared at them from the living room. Simon lowered his voice. "You are a real piece of work," he said. "Trust you? The man who has devoted his life to proving my wife is a cold-blooded murderer—the monster who spent ten years preparing my baby girl to become his trophy?"

"Come on, Simon, what do you think, I'd rape her? Christ, you know that's not me. She was a willing—"

"Stop!" Simon yelled. Then he lowered his voice again to a low whisper. "I won't have you talk about her that way. Now I need to get back to Kate. Do what you will, but stay away from my girls." A fake smile spread across his face as he looked into the adjoining room at Maggie and continued, through his grin: "I'm warning you. I'll fucking kill you. I swear it."

Maggie nodded and smiled back, blissfully unaware of the blazing hatred in the words he was speaking to the man she loved.

CHAPTER THIRTY-ONE

Daddy, can I marry you when I grow up?
Katie, you deserve better than a guy like me.
There's no guy better than you, Daddy.
And no girl who I love more, Katie.

Kate assumed that Jack would be expecting marathon sex all weekend, after spending so much time apart, but all she wanted was marathon sleep.

He arrived Friday night with a handful of lilies. It seemed uncomfortably late to tell him now that gladiolas were her favorite. She was learning to love lilies, or at least love that he was trying. He asked her where she'd like to eat. He took her out for a nice dinner to congratulate her for the promotion and then he tucked her in to her bed and insisted that she sleep all night. He didn't touch her. In fact, he slept in the guest room. Saturday afternoon, he woke her with hot coffee and yogurt, her usual breakfast. He sat next to her and asked if they could talk.

"Of course, Jack. What do you want to talk about?"

"Kate, I applaud what you've done for Greta. I know I've been a prick about it, but I do think it's great. I can't say I understand, but I'm trying."

"Is that what you want to talk about?" she asked between sips of stout black coffee.

"No. I want to set a date. I want to marry you in August."

"Okay."

"What?"

"I said okay. August is good. But can we keep it simple?" she asked.

"Simple is good," he said, nodding.

"Jack, are you okay? This is what you want, right?"

"Absolutely. But—"

"Is there a 'but'? Let's get married." She pulled out her Blackberry and looked up dates. "August 8th works for me. How about you?"

"Yes, but—"

"Another but?" she said.

"Aren't you worried about the Arlow baby food account starting in July, and having to plan a wedding in the midst of that?"

"Jack, are you trying to talk me into or out of marrying you?"

"You know I want to get married. You are—I'm just shocked. Hell, why the sudden agreement, Kate? You've been fighting this, and, well, I can admit it—I was terrified to even bring it up, and now you open up your date book and pull August 8th out and lay it on the table?"

"Life is short. I'm thirty-five years old. It's time to grow up. Don't you agree?"

He touched her face gently and whispered, "I love you Anna Katherine. I know you don't buy it. I'm no fool. But I love you, and some day you will believe me. I swear to God you will."

He kissed her forehead, and then her nose, and her mouth, and touched her with a tenderness he had never used before. They made love quietly and then lay in each other's arms talking about Jasper, and Greta, and their future.

Winter melts rapidly into spring in Texas, and Kate was grateful for the warmth of the season. April and May danced furiously. She had new business cards printed, moved into her huge corner office, began wedding plans with Hannah, her matron of honor, and made dozens of calls to new clients introducing herself and setting up meetings. She and Hannah shopped for dresses and flowers and tried to diet.

She and Jack planned to have one attendant each, and the guest list was less than fifty. They would marry at Grace Methodist and Abe would perform the ceremony. She and Jack had decided to say in her condo and begin looking for a small house in the fall. They were each selling furniture and giving away belongings and trying to condense their two very busy lives into one harmonious one. Simple was good, that was the plan.

She was close to raising enough funds for a down payment on the building for the Lasca Center, and she had enough volunteers lined up to get things going once that happened. The accident had slowed things down, but she wasn't giving up. She had been trying to put the accident behind her. She anticipated opening the center shortly after the wedding. She had hired a crew to clean the yard around the building, trim the hedges, and plant some flowers. Everything was falling into place. Most of the pieces of the puzzle had been put together, and she was eager to be a bride and get started with the second half of her life.

One evening in late spring, Kate and Jack met with Abe. They had agreed to see him once a week for premarital counseling. The first session went pretty smoothly. They discussed their expectations about marriage, what the wedding vows meant to them, and Abe asked several hypothetical questions about situations that often arise in the first year of marriage. Abe requested that in preparation for their second session, they do some journaling about their early memories of their parents' marriages.

"Well, I think we aced our first class," Jack said as they drove away from the church.

"Jack, it's not high-school mid-terms. It's marriage counseling. There's no passing or failing."

"I know, I know. I'm teasing you," he said. He leaned over and kissed her at the first stoplight. "But we have work to do, I guess. What do you remember about your parents' marriage?"

Kate sighed. "That's a loaded question," she said. "I don't look forward to this assignment."

"What do you mean?" he asked. "I thought they were pretty happy—what little you have told me." He hinted at a subject he knew was touchy.

"I think they were, up to a certain time. Then everything just sort of fell apart. I don't know what happened really. My mom was always very hard to please."

"Well, I just want to get through these sessions. I don't like the way Abe looks at you. It's creepy. He is supposed to be counseling us on our marriage, but he looks like he just wants to pounce on you."

"Please, Jack."

"Okay, okay. What do you want to eat?"

Kate thought for a minute. "A burger sounds good," she said. She was sick of salad.

"I thought you were trying—" he stopped. He wasn't a stupid man. "Burgers it is!" he said as he turned onto Valley View and headed for the nearest burger joint.

That evening, with Jack asleep in bed beside her, Kate returned to Greta's journal and picked up where she left off. She needed to be writing for Abe's assignment, but Greta's story had been calling out to her all day. It had been months since she had read any of it. She was doing everything she could to put distance between herself and Greta. She called once a week to check on her, but there was never any change. And she and Jasper never spoke of it. However, Greta's words were like a snake charmer's flute, and she could no longer resist.

July 7, 1969

We buried Dad today. Then I came home and watched everyone eat. I don't feel anything.

Kate traced the words with her fingers. There were no entries again for over two weeks.

Kate had felt that same emptiness after Frank's death. She remembered looking around the cabin and at all the faces, or more specifically, at all the people stuffing their faces, and her only thought was, do they know what I did? Do they know about the months we spent here, in these rooms, fighting for his life, his spiritual and emotional life, she meant, for his physical one was over by then. She was living for him. She carried him, dragged him, rolled him over, lifted him in and out of the bed, the tub, and picked him up off the floor. *This* floor, where people stood, eating, while her father began to rot in his coffin. Do they know I tried to extend his life, even when he didn't want me to? Do they know I let him down? These were thoughts at the time: merely cognitive activities— electrical discharges in the brain, devoid of emotion. Like Greta, she had watched everyone eat, and had felt nothing at all. Her feelings were in the ground, buried six feet deep.

She kept reading. The handwriting had changed. Everything had changed.

> *July 20, 1969*
> *Something terrible happened yesterday, and I am scared to write about it. If Momma finds out, I'll be so humiliated. She is right—God punishes sinners.*
>
> *Yesterday morning there was a note stuck to the outside of my bedroom window. It was from B.J. It said "Meet me in the shed." He's home early! I thought. I was so happy. I threw on my robe and ran over to meet him. Only he wasn't there.*
>
> *B.J.'s dad was sitting there in the shed with a bottle of whiskey in his hand. He had his pants unzipped.*

Kate prepared herself for a horrific story.

> *I tried to run, but my legs were frozen. I think God froze my legs in place so I had to face my punishment. The punishment I deserve for giving in to lust with B.J. My mind was screaming "Run, Greta!" but my legs couldn't hear me. He turned on the radio, and All You Need is Love was playing. He said, "You like this long haired, pot-smoking music, don't you? I hear you play it when you're with my boy out here." Then he turned it up really loud. He walked over behind me and locked the door. I just stood there and watched him. Then he pulled out a knife.*

Kate gasped. She sat up and turned on the lamp. Jack grumbled and pulled the covers over his head, and went back to snoring.

> *He stood close to me. I smelled the whiskey on his breath. He told me to drink. I said no, but he held the knife up in front of my face, and said,*

146

"Drink, girl." His voice was calm, not mean or angry. I took a drink. He sat down and opened his pants further. He asked me to take his privates in my hand. I started to cry.

"What's wrong?" he said. "You liked it with B.J. I saw you. July 4, I saw you. Take it. Play with it."

Kate felt like she would throw up. She was desperate to save this little girl, and helpless at the knowledge that there was nothing she could do.

He made me touch him, and he made me drink more whiskey. Then he threw a blanket down on the ground. He told me to take off my clothes and lie down. The music was so loud. I wanted to tell him to turn it off, that I wouldn't scream, but I couldn't speak. He said, "You kids, you're into all that 'free love' aren't you? Well, I need some free love." His voice was weird. He laid on top of me and pushed himself inside me quickly. It hurt so bad I started to scream. He didn't seem to hear me. He just kept pushing and breathing hard.

I felt his whiskers on my neck. They were burning me and his penis was ripping into me. He was slobbering and groaning and pushing so hard and so fast, he was breaking me apart. Then he dropped the knife. I don't remember, but I must have grabbed it and started swinging it. I can't explain what happened next. I just heard gasping and gurgling and he rolled off me and I ran. I don't remember unlocking the door, but I must have. I just ran, naked, across the street and into the house and straight to my bathroom. I think I killed him. I think he killed me too.

"Jack…Jack honey, wake up." She shook him vigorously.
"What," he groaned. "What's wrong, Kate?"
"I'm going to Houston. I'll call you tomorrow."
Despite his groggy, confused protests, she packed a bag and drove south as fast as she could, no longer crying, but in a rage.

PART THREE

WATER

CHAPTER THIRTY-TWO

"Ms. Lasca, I appreciate that you've been driving all night, but it's 5:00 a.m., and visiting hours don't start until 8:00. I have to ask you to leave." The charge nurse was a stern, bulky woman, but Kate would not be intimidated. She was on a mission.

"I'm not leaving," Kate said. She looked at the woman's nametag. "Listen, Bethany," she said curtly, "I am here to see Greta Perkins, and I'm not going away until I have seen her. I have something very important to tell her."

"You realize she is in a coma, and—"

"I realize that there is something I need to say, and something she needs to hear!"

The nurse looked her up and down, and Kate grimaced a little.

"In your pajamas and robe..." Nurse Bethany peered over the counter and downward. "...and slippers."

"Call the police if you have to, but I'm not going anywhere." Kate wasn't used to breaking the rules, and her heart raced.

"I don't think we need to call the police," the nurse said. "But if you continue to stand here arguing with me and keeping me from my real work—helping people—then I will call security."

"Here," Kate snapped back. She reached into the pocket of her robe. "Use my cell phone if you need it."

She was grabbed from behind, and she dropped her phone. She didn't scream, or kick, or fight. These were rational people who would think about it and see things her way, she was sure. She was escorted calmly to a small room just off the nurse's station. She lay down on a cot and stared at the ceiling. She wasn't sure how long she had been lying there when the door opened. Finally, someone would take her to Greta.

It was Emily.

"Mom." She sat up. Emily sat next to her on the cot and put her arm around her daughter's shoulder. She gave her a good, long, strange, look.

"Kate, have you been drinking?" she asked.

"No, Mom." Kate chuckled. "Of course not."

"Then why did you drive for five hours in the dead of night in your jammies to see Greta?"

"I have to set things right," Kate said. "A lot of things."

"At five a.m.?"

"Immediately."

Emily gave Kate's shoulder a squeeze and straightened the lapel on her pajamas.

Kate continued: "I know you think I'm crazy, but I have to change, Mom. I can't go on like this."

"I don't think you're crazy, Katie." She kissed the top of her daughter's head. "Well, maybe a little crazy, but there's a time for crazy, and I think you're past due."

"I have to tell her something before she dies."

"I know," Emily said.

"I don't want her to die."

"I know that too." Emily looked deep into Kate's eyes. Something happened. A lifetime in a moment. Kate saw Emily's grief for Frank. Kate saw Emily's brokenness. And she was sorry.

"I miss him, Mommy. I miss him." Kate slumped into her mother's arms.

"I do too. I really do."

"Then, why? Why did you kick him out?"

"Oh, my sweet Kate, do you want to do this right now?"

"No more putting off. Yes. I want to talk about it. I want the truth."

"Will you believe the truth?" Emily asked.

Kate thought about it.

"I will try—I promise."

"Kate, there are two things your father loved—me and you. But there are three things he couldn't live without—me, you, and Derek."

Kate didn't breathe.

Emily reached into her pocketbook and pulled out an old photograph. It was Frank. And a man whose smile she remembered.

"This will be hard for you to hear, but I suspect you know it in your heart. He traveled all the time. I knew what he was doing. I knew it for many years. I loved him, so I pretended it didn't matter. But then, the epidemic came, and I couldn't look away anymore. No matter how much I wanted to stay with him. I let him have Derek, until he stopped being safe about it."

Kate shook her head no, but her heart knew.

"Your father found out he was HIV positive in 1989." Emily's words were calm and even.

"But he didn't tell me until—"

"I know."

"And he told me he got it from—"

"I know." Emily seemed to want to spare Kate from speaking Frank's lies out loud. "Your father adored you, and I know you worshipped him. I couldn't take that from you. Loving him gave you so much pleasure. But Kate, something has changed in you since his death. You're not grieving—not in a normal way."

"Mom, everyone grieves in her own way, and her own time."

"Yes, of course. But this isn't grief, Kate. Whatever is going on with you. It's not grief. You are stuck at anger. My Kate is dying, and I'm afraid."

"I'm sorry I've been angry with you, Mom."

"I'm sorry you've been angry with *you*. That's what hurts me, Katie. Forgive yourself, for whatever it is you think you did. Forgive yourself. Please. Honor him—and yourself—by letting go of it."

Kate and Emily sat quietly for several minutes. Then Emily pulled out a brush and began to run it through her daughter's matted hair.

"You need to look nice for Greta," she said.

"They won't let me in."

Emily shrugged. "Yes, they will."

"Mom? How did you manage—"

"I have a way with people, I guess." She smiled and gave Kate a kiss on the cheek. "They said you could see her. So, go on now."

Kate opened the door to leave, and then she stopped and turned around.

"Oh, I almost forgot. I got a promotion, and I'm getting married."

Emily smiled. "Congratulations, sweetheart. Now go."

Kate stood over Greta and stroked her hair.

"I'm here, Greta," she whispered. "I'm here, and I have something to say. I'm ashamed it has taken me so long."

She climbed into bed and wrapped her arms around Greta's frail body. She held her close the way she imagined B.J. had done many years ago.

"I'm sorry. I'm so sorry. I'm sorry I didn't pay attention, and I didn't listen, and I didn't care. And I'm sorry I did this to you—I put you here. But worse—I didn't let you in. All you wanted was to be my friend, and even though I desperately need friends, I turned you away, again, and again, and again. Because you didn't fit into my plans. But my plans were wrong. I'm sorry. I won't do it again, I promise. Please forgive me."

She heard the door gently open and then close a moment later, and then fading footsteps. Emily. She knew it was Emily.

She lay in the bed next to Greta and held her, listening to all the footsteps—some hurried and light, others heavy and deliberate—footsteps of countless people—nurses, orderlies, family and friends of other patients—walking in the corridor, never stepping inside the door—just walking past. Footsteps of people with their own tragedies and their own secrets.

She spent most of the day with Greta, talking to her and catching her up on her life. She told her about the promotion, and about Jack and the wedding. She talked about her own father and told Greta she understood her pain at losing her dad. She talked until her throat hurt. Around 2:00, she stepped out to the nurse's station.

"Bethany, can you tell me when the cafeteria stops serving lunch?"

Bethany was very pleasant toward her, which she saw as a gift, given their earlier exchange. It seemed she was used to a spectrum of emotion working in a place like this.

"Unfortunately, they stopped about six minutes ago, but there's a machine down at the end of the hall if you're hungry. It takes ones and fives," Bethany said.

"And the sandwiches aren't half bad if you load them up with mustard."

The voice gave her goose bumps. She turned around and saw Simon standing there, sandwich in one hand and large coffee in the other, smiling, as he always did.

She stood there, stunned, and then realized she was still in her pajamas and slippers. She pulled her tattered bathrobe around herself and smiled back at him.

"Kate Lasca, are you actually speechless?" he said.

"What are you doing here?" she asked.

"Visiting. I've been here a couple of times, just—to check on her." He paused. "Just, seems like the right thing to do, I guess."

"And thoughtful," she added.

"Yes, and modest," Bethany said. "Mr. Gray comes twice a week, Tuesday and Thursday, at 2:00. Religiously."

"Come on, let me show you to the machines," he said, clearly trying to change the subject.

He led her down the hall, and pointed to a group of three small round tables with chairs scattered amongst them in an alcove near two vending machines.

"Ladies first," he said. "Have a seat while I get your lunch."

"You don't have to—I can't let you—"

"Only a bum wouldn't buy a lady lunch," he said with a wink. "Now, do you like turkey or ham?"

"Ham," she said, "But really—"

"Stop protesting," he said. "Now if I remember correctly, you're a mayonnaise gal."

"Mustard," she said. "I'm dieting."

"Nonsense," he said, waving a hand at her. He grabbed two mayo packets from a shelf in the corner and laid the sandwich and packets in front of her. He dug into his pockets for more change.

"This machine here has bottles of iced tea with lemon, and it's usually cold," he said, depositing six quarters.

She stared at him, bewildered.

"I pay attention, I guess," he said. His hair still covered his eyes, and they still sparkled out from behind the strands.

They sat quietly while they unwrapped their sandwiches and applied condiments.

"So," she said. "You come twice a week?"

"Yes," he said, "but you were never supposed to know that."

"Why not?" she asked, her mouth full of ham sandwich.

"I don't know. Just because."

"That's not an answer, Simon. I know why. It's because you're kind. Maybe the kindest person I've ever known."

"Now that's a compliment," he said, blushing. "I'm not sure I deserve such high praise."

"You deserve it, and much more." She reached forward, considered moving his hair out of his eyes, but instead grabbed the salt.

He tried to change the subject. "So how are your friends in Dallas?"

"Good," she said, "and by the way, I was so rude to not introduce you that day. Please forgive me."

"It was an emotional day for everyone."

"True, but I'm sorry I didn't handle it better."

"Has anyone ever told you that you apologize too much?" he said, laughing.

"I guess I just mess up too much," she said.

"No. Don't say that. You are too hard on yourself, Kate. I think you're—well, not so bad."

"High praise indeed," she said. They both laughed.

"I was wondering though," Simon said, "and stop me if it's not my business, but how does your minister friend know Dr. D'Angelo? It didn't seem polite to ask the doctor."

"Wait, Dr. D'Angelo comes here? I'm confused—Abe comes here—what do you mean?" She put her sandwich down and listened intently.

"Dr. D'Angelo comes here occasionally to check in. I haven't seen Abe a lot—just the one time. That's why I am asking."

"You have lost me. I had no idea Abe came here, and as far as I know, the two men never met before that day—you know, the day with Greta..." her words trailed off. She was curious, though.

"Look, like I said, it's probably none of my business. The doctor comes here regularly to check her progress. I've seen him four, maybe five times, but I only saw Abe once. And he didn't see me. They were in the hall, whispering, but arguing. I couldn't make too much out. But it didn't feel right. They were definitely upset with each other."

"What were they saying?" Kate realized her voice sounded way too interested.

He smiled. "See, it *is* weird," he said. "I knew it was." He lowered his voice a little. "I heard them argue, but when I came upon them in the hall, they changed the subject and walked away."

"Strange," she said.

"Yeah, and all I could make out was Dr. D'Angelo saying something about how Abe wasn't letting him do his job and Abe was telling him to let him handle it his way. They weren't happy with one another."

"I'll have to ask Abe. He's my minister and I also see him for…. counseling."

"That's great, Kate. I'm glad you're talking to someone," he said.

"It's—well, it's—marriage counseling." She started eating her sandwich again.

"You're married? I—"

"Engaged, actually, yeah."

"Well, congratulations, Kate. That's wonderful news."

She hoped he was lying. She searched his eyes for a sign of disappointment but wasn't sure what she saw there. It hurt her to tell him the truth. She wished she could take it back, but she knew it was wrong to keep it from him. He was a stand-up guy who deserved to know she wasn't available.

Simon took her hand and gave it a squeeze.

"Kate, you deserve happiness, and I hope you find it." She knew he meant it.

"Thank you, Simon," she said.

He lifted her hand to his lips and kissed it gently. She pulled away, grabbed her bottle of tea and took a big swig, hoping to hide any clues on her face and also trying to plug up her big mouth before she said anything stupid.

CHAPTER THIRTY-THREE

2049—Galveston

Simon suspected that Abe had arrived when he heard the doorbell, and Maggie's irritated voice confirmed his suspicion. He knew it was too much to ask for peace today, not with all the secrets of their pasts tumbling together and colliding in his living room, and especially with the simultaneous presence of Abe Archer and Campbell Cross.

"What's going on?" Simon asked as he entered the living room.

"What do you think?" said Zeke, who smiled as he spoke. Simon knew that Zeke always looked for the bright side, the humor in a situation. He was like a youthful Simon in that way, too. One would be tempted to laugh, he supposed, should he or she wander upon the scene: a woman on her deathbed, and in the next room, television coverage of blood-thirsty savages on her lawn, and yet another room over, her accused lover/partner in crime, her two children, the detective trying to convict her of murder, and with whom, by the way, her daughter had been having an eleven-year love affair, and of course, the grieving soon-to-be widow. Simon knew that Zeke saw the macabre humor of it all. And of course, Zeke had that luxury, as he was the only one who didn't look like a total idiot in the situation.

"Welcome, Abe. It's good to see you again," Simon said, extending a hand. All sound and movement had been sucked from the room. Simon looked at his daughter, whose expression was one of shock.

Abe receded silently into the corner with his bible in his hand.

"Dude," Zeke exclaimed, "this is weird."

"Shut up, Zeke!" Maggie wasn't amused.

"Look," Simon began, "There is no need for hostility. Your mother was a grand woman, and she was always calm under pressure. She would want us to behave as such. She allowed Detective Cross into our home without restriction over the years, and she loved Abe very much. We've got to find a way—"

"God, Dad, don't be naïve. Abe is here to kill her," Maggie said. "Check his bag for a syringe."

Abe didn't attempt to defend himself.

"Shit, Maggie," said Zeke. "Don't be stupid"

"What? I'm just saying what we all know to be true," Maggie responded. "Someone needs to say it."

"Really, well, Maggie, are you interested in the truth?" His mood changed quickly. "Maybe someone needs to mention the real pink elephant in this room." All eyes turned to Campbell. Simon tried to think of a way to defuse things, but wondered if he should let the kids speak their minds—get it all out.

"Don't start, Zeke," Maggie whined.

"Mags, why do you act like such a baby? You're a brilliant scientist, and a grown woman, and this guy walks in the room and you start whimpering like a little girl. It makes me sick. You deserve better."

"He has a right to be here," Maggie said.

"You don't want Mom's friend here, but you don't mind hosting the man who devoted the last twenty years to trying to put her in jail." The other thing that Zeke and Simon had in common was their hatred for Cross.

"Campbell is just trying to protect Mom. If he wanted, he could have arrested them both years ago, and you know it," Maggie said, red in the face now. Campbell reached for her in an attempt to calm the situation, but the sight of his hands on his sister sent Zeke over the edge.

"Without evidence, you mean? If he had one shred, Mom and Abe would be in jail. How can you be so dense?" Zeke seemed unsure what to do with his anger. It was an unnatural state for him. Simon stepped in to put an arm around his trembling son. He had never seen him so close to snapping.

"Campbell is the only one in this room with Mom's best interest at heart," Maggie continued, apparently wanting to throw gasoline on Zeke's rage.

Zeke stepped away from Simon's embrace, turned to Cross and asked, "So, Detective Cross, are you here on official duties today or just a booty call with my baby sister?"

Maggie grunted and took a step toward Zeke, but it was too late to shut him up. His next insult stunned everyone.

"And Maggie, do tell…" Zeke chided, "Just how good a fuck is he? Good enough to make you betray your dying mother? Good enough for him to betray Macy, that's for sure!"

Maggie lunged for him, screaming profanities and clawing at him. She tackled Zeke to the floor, and it took all three men to pull her off. She came up with a handful of Zeke's hair in her fist. She ran from the room, screaming and crying.

Zeke stayed supine on the rug, staring at the ceiling, obviously surprised by his cruel rage. Simon sat on the sofa with his face in his hands. Abe and Cross stood on opposite sides of the room, arms folded. None of the men could think of a single thing to say.

CHAPTER THIRTY-FOUR

"Jack, I know I said I'd call earlier today, but honestly, this is the first chance I've had. I'm sorry."

"What's going on, Kate? Why did you just run out of here like a crazy person?"

"Greta needs me. I can't explain it to you. I can't even explain it to me. But she needs me. And I need to do the right thing. I have to stay with her."

"Kate" he said. "We are getting married in seven weeks, and you have a major presentation in four. What the hell are you thinking? Come home!"

"You did not just tell me what to do," she snapped back at him. "I'll come home when I'm good and ready."

"Fine, fine. I can't handle this anymore. You call me when you figure things out," he said, and then he hung up. Kate wasn't angry. She was tired of fighting with Jack, and she knew she was doing the right thing.

There was a knock at the cabin door, and she let Simon in. His arms were loaded with bags of groceries.

"You shopped for me? Oh, that is wonderful. I never have food here, you know?"

"Yes, I do know. So how about I clean up that grill out there and make us some chicken?"

"Great, and I'll bake some potatoes and make salad," she said, pulling items out of the bags and putting them in the fridge. "You love to take care of people, don't you?"

"Kind of like someone else I know," he said, smiling.

Within an hour, they had a meal ready and set out on the picnic table on the porch. She was ready for some home cooking and easy conversation.

"So, do you and Jack plan to have kids?" he asked.

She almost choked on her chicken.

"You are always direct, aren't you?" she asked.

"Pretty much. Tell me if it's none of my business."

"Well, it's not that. It's just—well—we haven't discussed it."

"What? You're marrying him, and you haven't asked him?"

"No."

"Well," he said, "what do you want? Kids or none?"

She swallowed hard and didn't know what to say.

"Kate, did I cross the line? I didn't mean to intrude. Me and my big mouth, I always say the wrong thing."

"I had a baby," she said. Then she was quiet a minute. "Why do I always confess my sins to you?"

"Sins? I hardly think a baby is a sin," he said. "Tell me about it."

"I was twenty-two. There was this boy in college, Lucas. My first love. He was pretty amazing. I swam. He was a cross-country runner. We were the perfect couple. He ended up running in Sydney in 2000. A quarter second shy of the bronze medal. He followed his dream. It was complicated. Are you sure you want to hear this?"

"Every word," he said.

"I fell in love instantly. And I fell hard. We dated all through college. My junior year, I started working with a private coach. His name was Olen Victor. He was a scout and had coached in the 1976 through1992 games. He took me on. My parents couldn't afford to pay him much, but my father, he wanted it for me so desperately, and Olen thought I was gifted, so he took me on for very little money. I guess I always felt, I don't know, beholden, obligated. It blinded me."

"To what?" he asked.

"His intentions. Dark intentions. Lucas saw it and tried to pull me away, but I didn't believe it. I just thought he was being jealous because I was becoming successful and because Olen showered me with praise and attention. I was young and stupid. And then when Lucas left, I felt lost, and so lonely. Olen pushed me harder and harder, and right before the trials in 1996, I slept with him. It was about a month after Lucas left for grad school. I stayed behind at SMU for the summer to train. I didn't want to sleep with him. I don't know why I did. And it was horrible. It was like being—"

"It's okay," Simon said. "You were young. He took advantage."

"But I was old enough to know better," she said. "And then I found out I was pregnant. I've never been so terrified in my life. I couldn't tell anyone."

"Not even your dad? You told me your dad was so supportive."

"He was. But he also thought I was perfect, and I couldn't risk hurting him. My God, I was pregnant and didn't even know for sure whose baby it was."

"I suspect he knew you weren't perfect, Kate."

"I realize that now, but not when I was twenty-two. So, I covered it up. I never went home during my pregnancy. I wore huge clothes. I stopped swimming, and then I left for grad school. I didn't have a plan beyond the moment. And then the baby came, two months early, during Christmas break between semesters. She was beautiful, and perfect, but she couldn't breathe. She lived two days."

"Oh, Kate, I'm sorry."

"Me, too. I was such a fool."

"You were a girl. Just a girl."

She reached into her handbag and pulled out a photograph.

"This is her. My baby."

Simon took the photo. "You're right. She's perfect. She looks like you,' he said.

"You think so?"

"Yes. What was her name?"

"I didn't name her. I know that sounds awful. Like, somehow I could forget her if she didn't have a name. I just had her cremated and tried to move on. Does that make me a monster?"

"No. It makes you human, and imperfect. You were all alone. That's not right, Kate."

"Like Greta. Simon, she needs my help. God is calling me to help her. I just know it. It's as if everything in my life led me here, to this moment. I have to find a way to give her some peace before she dies. You don't know what she's been through."

"So tell me. Let me help you."

They talked for hours. Kate told him about B.J.'s father and the rape, and how she felt a strong connection to Greta and her life. It was as if she and Greta were on parallel planes, and based on the laws of physics, their paths never should have crossed. But somehow, for some reason, they did. Kate told him that she had to find out why and how. She was beginning to believe she was destined to do something great, but she was lost, and Greta somehow held the answers to everything. She told him about what she had learned about her father's affair and how he had really gotten sick. She talked, and consumed her words like sweet wine. He listened all night, and then crashed on her couch at 3:00 a.m. She fell asleep fully dressed, feeling like part of her burden had been lifted.

She only slept a few hours, and woke in time to watch the sunset from her porch. Simon woke early too, and joined her. They watched quietly for a while, and then he told her he had to leave.

"Thank you again," she said. "I have never told anyone all these things, and you have listened without judgment."

"What's there to judge?" he asked. "We all have histories, you know?"

"Maybe someday I'll learn some of yours," she said.

"Maybe…. but for now, I've got to get to work. You'll be back this weekend?"

"Every weekend," she said. "Every weekend until—"

"Until she's ready to go," he said.

"Jack won't like it."

"I don't blame him." He put his hand on the small of her back and rested it there, just a second, as he said goodbye. Then he was gone.

She knew she had a lot of explaining to do, with Jack and Jasper, and Hannah, and she worked through the words in her mind as she packed her bag, loaded it into her car, and headed for Dallas one more time.

****

Hannah jumped up from her desk and grabbed Kate's arm as soon as she got off the elevator at Jasper Agency.

'Girl, you look like hell. What is going on?" she asked.

"It's a very long story," Kate said.

Jack saw them from his office and followed them all the way to Kate's. They didn't even wait for her to get her door unlocked to bombard her with questions.

"Calm down," she told them. "Come in and we'll talk."

"What happened?" Hannah asked. "We have been worried sick."

"We?"

"Jack and I. We don't know what 's going on with you, but it's getting…disturbing. You are going to ruin your life for this woman."

"This woman?" Kate said. "You mean the one I almost killed and now am trying to give some dignity before she dies."

"Just let it go, Kate. Why can't you ever let things go?" Hannah asked.

"It—things?"

"You know what I mean," Hannah said.

"She doesn't have much time," Kate said.

"Thank God," Jack whispered.

"What did you just say? How can you be so callous? What is wrong with you people?"

"You people?" Jack said. "We are your friends for God's sake! We are protecting you. Are you aware that there are people in this office who would love to take over Arlow for you, and who also think maybe you don't deserve this promotion? People talk, Kate. I'm tired of making excuses for you."

"So don't," she said. "I don't need you to. I talked to Jasper from the road. He is fine with this."

"Of course he is," Hannah said, under her breath.

Kate inhaled deeply and slowly several times, trying to find her composure.

"Okay, here's the deal," she said. "Jasper is okay with my taking off early on Fridays and spending the weekends in Galveston. The Arlow presentation is good. Hell, I could do it today, in my sleep, blindfolded. So don't worry about Arlow. Jasper is supportive because he knows I have it under control, not because he has been sleeping with Greta. But because he supports me. He is a good man who wants to make sure that she is taken care of."

There was a knock at the door. It was Marissa.

"Hannah, Mr. Dowling is on the phone, says it's urgent. Sorry to interrupt."

Hannah excused herself and shut the door behind her. Jack plopped down in Kate's chair and twirled side to side, watching her like she was some strange phenomenon he couldn't figure out. She came to him and sat in his lap, and then put her hands on his chest.

"I know I've asked a lot of you."

"Hell yes, you have," he said.

"Just please give me a few more weeks. Just 'til the wedding and then this will be over."

"Over?" he asked. "Kate, I don't mean to sound crass, but what if she is still...."

"Alive?"

"Yes. Sorry."

"I don't know Jack. But I have to do this. Please try to understand. If you love me, you have to try."

"I don't have a choice, do I?" he asked.

She took another deep breath, and faced him squarely.

"No. I don't think you do. Not if you want to marry me. I'm sorry."

"I love you Kate. So, do what you have to do. But you need to know something. I will be standing in that church on August 8, with or without you, and then I am moving on with my life, with—"

"Or without me. I get it. Thank you for your blessing."

"I didn't give you my blessing, but I'm not going to fight you anymore."

"Thank you, Jack." She laid her head on his chest, and together, they watched the children playing in the park.

CHAPTER THIRTY-FIVE

2009—Galveston

Kate loved the cabin in the summer. She had nothing but happy memories of this part of her life. She brought a few small furnishings and photos from her condo to make the cabin feel more like home. Coming here on weekends to be with Greta was the right thing to do, for Greta and for her. At the same time, she knew she was being unfair to Jack. Their relationship was definitely on the line, and she was constantly testing the limits of his love for her. She was confused, too, by her feelings for Simon. He was a gentleman, but even with his politeness, she sensed that maybe he felt attracted to her too. It was an innocent crush, she told herself. She and Jack had everything in common. She and Simon were great friends, but she wasn't sure they could ever be more. She doubted he could tolerate her drive and perfectionist's nature, whereas Jack loved those things about her.

A few weekends had passed, and she hadn't seen Simon since she had decided to come back regularly. They had talked once on the phone, and she knew he was still visiting Greta Tuesday and Thursday afternoons. He had called Friday night and asked if he could see her Saturday morning.

Saturday morning arrived, and Kate was on her knees refinishing the old picnic table when she heard thunder reverberate in the distance. She took a break from her work and moved to the porch steps to watch the lightning and count seconds before the thunder. She sat still, listening and counting for half an hour. Then it began to sprinkle. She reached her hand out beyond the porch's protection and let the drops hit her skin. It was delightfully cool and calming. She brought her moist hand up to her lips and tasted the droplets. She loved the rain. She was awed by its power, its gift—or maybe its curse—to both nurture and destroy. Near the end, she and Frank sat here on these steps and watched the storms roll in across Galveston Bay. Later, when he was too sick to leave his bed, she sat alone, watching and listening with the tape recorder in her lap, capturing the sounds she hoped would comfort him later. When he could no longer make the twenty steps to the porch, he had smiled and held her hand as they listened to her recordings. It had provided less solace than he deserved. She hated her powerlessness.

On the tail end of a huge thunderclap, Kate heard Simon's truck pulling into the sandy driveway. He parked and got out, waving at her. He was wearing a red ZZ Top tee shirt, snug Wranglers, and his old brown work boots. She watched him approach; he moved slowly and easily, undisturbed by the drops gathering on his shirt and in his hair.

"I come bearing donuts," he said, holding out a box proudly. "Don't tell me you're dieting. Not today."

She took the donuts and let her hand linger a second longer than necessary on his freckled and calloused hand.

"Come in, and join me," she said. I made coffee for us."

"Thank you, ma'am. I could use a cuppa joe."

"It's the least I could do. You have been here clearing brush this week, haven't you?"

"I don't know what you're talking about," he said, smiling.

She wondered if the girls who swam for him at U of H saw him as handsome. He was so kind, but she imagined that he was a firm coach, pushing hard but always supportive. In her twenties, she probably would have never looked twice at Simon Gray, but she knew now that he would be a great husband for someone, some day. She was trying hard to distance herself, remove herself from temptation. She was a loyal friend and fiancée, and she had no intentions of hurting Jack.

They sat down to their coffee and donuts. She handed him a towel and asked him why he needed to see her.

"Well," he said. "I just wondered if you would be in town next weekend. I mean I know you come every weekend, but with the holiday and all, I just didn't know if maybe you had plans."

"Independence Day? I usually don't even notice July Fourth."

"Seriously?" he asked. "Oh, come on. That's the saddest thing I ever heard."

Kate was embarrassed. "I guess it kind of is."

"You are severely depleted in the fun department. All you do is work and deal with dying people. Join me in town for the parade, and then let me barbecue for you. What do you say?"

"I don't know, Simon. I'm not sure I should."

It was embarrassingly quiet for a moment.

"Right," he finally said. "I am overstepping. My apologies."

His eyes were sincere and so damn blue. He was the least threatening person in the world, but she was terrified of him at times.

"You know what—let's do it," she said. She wasn't sure who was controlling her lips and her voice, and she knew it was a bad idea to spend the day with him.

"Okay, great!" he said. "I'll pick you up at ten?"

"Okay, but before you go, I want to show you something." She pulled out Greta's 1969 journal and showed it to him. She watched his face as he read.

August 10, 1969

I am leaving Dallas. I can't be here anymore. B.J.'s dad showed up yesterday and talked to Mama. He came in and asked for us to speak, the three of us, in the living room. He had bandages on both arms and his neck, and I think they were from knife wounds. I must have hurt him. But he just sat there, in our living room as if nothing had happened. He even asked Mama for some lemonade. Then he told her about how he saw B.J. and me through the window on July 4. He told her he watched us make love, but he didn't say "make love." He told her everything he saw. She was quiet, and I wondered if she would hit me. She never has before, but this is big. I can't believe he did this. There's no way I can tell her he raped me. She'd never believe me now that she knows what a terrible sinner I am for losing my virginity the day my father died.

She gave him more lemonade and thanked him for coming over. When he left, she didn't say a word. She took me to bathroom, undressed me and pointed to the shower. She turned the water on, really hot. Then she pulled out her bleach and scrub brushes from under the sink. She silently scrubbed every inch of me, even down there. My legs and stomach were bleeding, but she didn't stop. Not until Elise came in and grabbed her.

Mama didn't even fight her. She just walked away and still didn't speak. I think she gave up on me, and I deserve it. I wish she had yelled at me and told me to pray or something. The silence is awful. Elise bandaged me and asked me what happened. I told her everything. Including something Mama must not know for a very long time.

I missed my period. Elise is going to take care of me. She is using her college money to send me to a home in Phoenix where I can have the baby. I begged her to come with me, but she wants to stay behind and take care of Mama. I understand. I will be back in Dallas someday. I will make Mama proud of me again. She will say that I am a wonderful mother, and she won't have to be ashamed. I will pay Elise back every cent. She was supposed to go to school next year, and she gave that up for me. She is so smart, but she loves me more than anyone. I won't let her down. I will love this baby forever, and never give him away, or give up on him.

Kate took out the photograph of Greta and the teenage boy. She handed it to Simon. He looked at it, turned it over, and saw the words *Arizona, 1985* on the back.

"It's her son," he said. "Greta has a son."

"Yes," she said. And I am going to find him."

Two hours later, Kate was on a plane to Phoenix. Armed with the photos and a couple of Greta's journals, she was determined to find someone who Greta had once loved and who had loved her equally. That person would be by her side soon.

She had lain awake most of the previous night re-reading the journals, thinking about how much Greta must have loved her child. What they didn't mention was who the father was. Did Greta know whether it was B.J.'s or his dad's? It was an agony Kate knew too well. She couldn't wait to find Greta's son and tell him how amazing she thought his mother was.

It was one of those compelling thoughts that sometimes come to us in the dark of night. She had an address. Why hadn't she thought of it before? Why was she busy making calls and searching the Internet? She would go to #46 Windswept Road in Phoenix, the address on the blue card, the one attached to the name *Isabella Marquez*. Her web search revealed that this address existed, but she couldn't find a resident or business name, and the phone numbers were a dead end. No one knew Isabella Marquez, or if they did, they weren't talking. She was ready to face this head-on and the best way to do that was to go in person and ask questions.

She pulled up in front of #46 and sat in the car for a few minutes, collecting herself. This was the place. She could learn so much here, or she could be sent home with nothing.

It was time. She marched confidently to the door and rang the bell. She was determined to find out who Isabella was. She had lived here once, and someone had to know something.

What she didn't expect was that the mystery woman would answer the door. She looked right into her eyes and knew them instantly from the photograph. The door was only half-open, and the woman stuck only her head out.

"Isabella Marquez?" she asked, biting her lip.

The woman examined her up and down. "Who are you?" she said.

"My name is Kate Lasca, and I'm from Dallas—"

"There's no Isabella here. I'm sorry."

"Then you must be her sister, because you look…" Kate reached into her bag and pulled out the photo of Isabella and Greta and handed it to her. The woman's eyes widened, and she stumbled out onto the porch.

"Where did you get this?" she asked, her eyes filling with tears.

"I'm a friend of Greta's," she said. "I need to find Isabella—for her."

Mi Lucero? Dear sweet Greta. You found her?"

"Found her? I didn't know she was missing. Do you think we could talk for a minute?"

"Jorge, come here," she called out, and let the door fall open slightly. A young boy, about sixteen, came out and took the woman's arm.

"Yes, Mima."

"Help me and Ms. Lasca into the den. We need to talk." As she opened the door wider, Kate saw that the woman used a cane. Her stiff unsteadiness suggested she wore leg braces beneath her lavender slacks. Jorge helped his grandmother scoot slowly onto the sofa, and she motioned for Kate to sit in the chair across from her.

"Would you like something to drink?" she asked. She straightened her white silk blouse, and Kate considered that her hair was nearly as white as her blouse. Her hair had been hidden in the photo, but certainly nothing visible had changed about her. She was stunning even now, in her sixties. She was calm elegance and grace.

"No thank you," Kate said, eager to ask questions. "I had a soda on the way over." She could barely contain her excitement. "I'd like to know how you know Greta," she blurted out.

"First things first," the woman said. "I am Isabella. I don't know how you found me, or why, or what's going on, but if you know where Greta is, I need to find her. I must find her."

Kate decided to tread lightly. She knew nothing about this woman, and she came here to ask questions, not answer them. She couldn't know what Isabella's motives were, and she didn't have reason to trust her.

"I work with Greta," Kate said. We work for Jasper Agency—"

"Jasper?"

"Yes, do you know it?" Kate asked.

"No...I don't."

"Well, we work there together in Dallas. I met her several months ago and we became friends. She asked me to find you. All she gave me is your name." Kate lied because she sensed that this woman wasn't ready to hear that Greta was dying. Or was it that she wasn't ready to tell her?

Isabella's posture changed. She didn't trust Kate either.

"Kate, where is Greta now?"

"In Houston."

"Why?" Isabella asked. "You said you were from Dallas."

Kate avoided answering. She pulled out the 1969 journal and opened to the last page, the entry about leaving Dallas.

"What do you know about this child?" she asked. Did you know him? I believe they were in Phoenix together, which is what connected me to you. But this is her last entry, so I know nothing else."

"No, it's not her last entry." She sent for Jorge again. "Corazoncita, bring me the books."

He left and came back, arms full of notebooks of varying sizes and colors. He placed them on the table between the women.

"Oh my God," Kate whispered. "She was here."

"From August 1969 to December 1992. Then she disappeared. My beautiful Greta vanished seventeen years ago. You must be the angel I've been praying for."

CHAPTER THIRTY-SIX

2049—Galveston

"I'm going after her," Campbell said.

"Leave my sister alone, Cross," Zeke told him. He was still angry, but much calmer now.

"He's right, Camp," said Simon. "Let her be. Come—sit with me a while. They left Abe and Zeke in their still stunned silence and moved to Kate and Simon's bedroom. As Simon walked, he felt every muscle, every bone, every skin fiber of his eighty-one years, pushing, pulling, and pulsing. His life was on fire with sensory input, and he saw colors and smelled odors that he had long since forgotten. His world was changing. He motioned for Cross to sit down next to the bed, and he went to the shelf in the far corner of the room. There were two rows of old journals along the top, and beneath those were photo albums containing the picture history of the Gray family. He pulled a few out and thumbed through until he found the right one. Then he pulled a stool over next to Cross and sat down, holding out the album.

"Look at it," he said.

"What is this?" Campbell asked.

"Just look at it."

Cross began to flip through pages, quickly, almost disrespectfully in Simon's view, but Simon also knew that his demeanor would shift. This broad-shouldered detective was just as afraid of his feelings as the rest of us. He had seen it over and over. Cross's expression was hard now, maybe even blank to most, but simple-as-pie to read for Simon Gray. He continued to flip through quickly. Simon saw a moving picture show of Cross swimming with the Gray children, Cross holding up trophy after trophy in regional, state, and national swim meets, Cross going to his senior prom, Cross in front of a Christmas tree with Macy—the first photo ever taken of them. He stopped there, but his expression didn't change. He stared at the photo.

Then slowly, he turned to the next page, his and Macy's wedding photo. Their smiles were jubilant. On the opposite page was a picture of Macy in her wedding gown, arms wrapped around Kate, her matron of honor, the two of them dancing and laughing at the reception.

"This doesn't change anything," Cross murmured.

"No…nothing has changed."

"And yet, everything has changed." Campbell's face began to soften, as Simon expected it would.

Simon cleared his throat. He could see the searing loss in Campbell's eyes as he looked at the picture of the love of his life. He looked over at Kate for the first time. There was no way he would cry. Losing Macy almost killed him, but he thought he had to pretend. He thought chasing Kate and Abe would change how he felt, ease how pissed off he was that Macy was gone and never coming back.

"Kate loved you and Macy with all her heart," Simon said. "She has suffered more loss than anyone I know, and her heart broke when Macy died. But she carried on, doing her work, without anger."

"Her work, that's why I'm here."

"You know Kate. You know she would never hurt anyone. Why can't you let this go?"

"Because euthanasia is against the law. Your wife is a killer, in the eyes of the law."

"What about your eyes?" Simon asked.

"My eyes are the eyes of the law."

"Bullshit. What about *your* eyes?"

Campbell slammed the photo album shut and thrust it back at Simon. "I don't like your tactics, Mr. Gray."

"I know that. I know everything about you, Campbell. I watched you grow up, I watched you fall in love, get married, watched you and Macy go through years of agonizing fertility treatments, and I watched you watch Macy die a slow torturous death. I watched you hurt as much as she did. And Kate watched it all too. And Macy was her friend. I'm not a begging man, but today—I'm begging you to stop this."

"I'm going to wait on the porch," Campbell said. "You probably need some crowd control." He stood in a huff and turned to leave."

"I know your secret," Simon said, just loud enough for his words to tap Cross on the back of his head.

Cross stopped mid-step and shot an angry look over his shoulder at Simon. "I don't have any secrets," he growled.

"Not anymore, you don't." The gloves were off.

"Look. I have a job to do, and you have a lot to do too. So let's stop playing games."

"I agree. I hate games. Today is the day we all come clean."

"I'm clean," Cross said, anger building.

"So, it's legal, then, murder for hire?"

"What the fuck, Simon—spit it out!"

"You know that Kate is innocent. You know it in your heart."

"Okay, I'll bite. How do I know any such thing?"

"Because you tried to hire Kate to kill your wife. Mercy killing. And she turned you down. It's all right here, my friend." He opened the box and pulled out a letter and held it up. "Now why don't you sit down here and let's talk?"

CHAPTER THIRTY-SEVEN

"Make a left up here onto Promenade. Then go straight for a while."

"Where are we going?" Kate asked.

"In time, you'll know," Isabella said. "For now, you need to understand Greta's life as she lived it here in Phoenix."

"I'd like nothing better. I came a long way to learn the truth."

"The truth, young lady, is a slippery thing. But let me start at the beginning, and somewhere along the way, maybe you will find some truth...

"Greta arrived in Phoenix thin, pale, and terrified. She had $3,000 in her pocket, a huge sum for 1969. She was two months pregnant. She came to me because her family doctor told her about me. In 1969, #46 Windswept Road was a home for pregnant teens. It's still not publicly known, so we don't trust others easily. We spent so many years hiding that it just became part of our nature. Back then angry parents would show up and drag their girls away if they hadn't sent them with their blessing—situations such as Greta's. Sometimes boyfriends would show up demanding their rights to the child; we even had stalkers from time to time find our girls. We had runaways here, we had young women whose parents kicked them out or shipped them to me, we had rich girls, poor girls, girls of all ages and stations." Isabella's narration was sweet and slow, like pouring warm honey from a jar.

"But Greta...now that was a special young lady," she continued. "I remember that day she arrived, standing on my porch, shaking and scared, dark circles under her eyes, one small travel bag in her hand, and a box of notebooks at her feet. Everyone here fell instantly in love with her. She had a way of being herself—a quality so hard to find. She worked tirelessly to earn her way while she was here. She had other rare qualities—she felt a sense of communion with people, she believed in interdependence. She nurtured that amongst the girls here. She paid her share of utilities, and worked in the garden and cooked for us. She took on duties for girls who were sick or having a bad day, expecting nothing in return—just wanting to be part of a normal family. Funny, yes, that she thought we were normal."

"So, what happened?" Kate asked.

"In the spring of 1970 she gave birth to the most beautiful seven-pound boy, and her life changed completely. She finally had someone to hold onto. Someone who loved her the way she loved him. She was the most joyful mother I've ever seen. Praise God, she decided to stay on here and help me with the girls. In return, I gave her room and board, childcare, and a small wage. She was happy here, very happy. And she made me tremendously happy as well.

Kate was having trouble watching the road and listening to the story.

"She went about the business of raising little Steven, and when he was three, she started college. She majored in Art. She also paid her sister back all the money she borrowed, a few dollars at a time. It was a good life, but no life for a young woman like Greta. She was too big for this place, but I couldn't make her see that. People like Greta, people brimming with love for life, can't be contained—they have to keep moving or they break places open, like a giant in a doll's house."

Kate soaked it all in. How blessed she had been to have this woman in her life. God had given her a gift, and she had turned her nose up at it, like it wasn't good enough for her.

"Over time, the need for homes like ours diminished, and so I retired in 1985. She planned to stay with me until Steven graduated high school, and then the plan was to stay until he finished college, and then he joined the Navy during Desert Storm, and by then, we were...I don't know.... settled into our lives. She got her paintings into a few shows and sold a few, and she taught art workshops to children from the community. I loved her like my own daughter.

"And then, one day, a few days before Christmas in 1990, we saw them. We were watching *It's a Wonderful Life* on television. It was a Jimmy Stewart movie marathon. He was always her favorite. We looked out the window and saw the Naval officers, walking up the drive. Steven's plane went down in Kuwait and there were no survivors—just ashes—nothing left of the plane."

"Oh, no," Kate said, wiping her eyes.

"Pull in here, Ms. Lasca." Isabella motioned to a narrow driveway on the right side of the road.

Kate held Isabella's arm to steady her as they weaved their way through tombstones. Kate looked across the vast expanse of land. In a way it was beautiful as intended, well-kept, lush green grass and warm purple and white trees. But the verve of the backdrop couldn't quell the sadness of rows and rows of gray stones—wide, thin, tall, short, with no real expression of the life that was buried here. Kate hated cemeteries.

"Here we are," Isabella finally said. She pointed her cane toward a small bench shaded by a recently trimmed crepe myrtle. The afternoon sun flickered through its white flowers and sprinkled dots of light across a nearby headstone. As Kate eased Isabella down onto the bench, she noticed on the back an inscription: "In memory of Steven. Sit a while and remember his life."

Isabella was pale with exhaustion, and Kate pulled a package of tissues and a bottle of water from her oversized bag. "Are you okay?" she asked, handing her the items.

"Better than I've been in many years, child." She pointed at the headstone. Kate turned her whole body, and then fell to her knees when she read the words:

Steven Jasper Perkins: Beloved Son, Friend, and Hero
March 28, 1970-December 20, 1990

"Jasper." Kate whispered. "Oh my God, Jasper." Suddenly the sun was beating down on her, melting her, vaporizing her breath. "Their son is buried here. *Their* son. Right here at this spot."

"No," Isabella said. "In this casket are bits of debris, a teddy bear, a lock of his baby hair, mementos. But this grave doesn't contain Steven."

"I didn't mean any disrespect. Of course, his—"

"Kate, you misunderstand. He's not in there. Steven is alive. Please, I beg you— take us to Greta."

****

Greta's room was dark. It was early morning, and no one had opened the blinds yet. There was a small glimmering candle on the table near Greta's bed. The air smelled of sandalwood and disinfectant. Kate stood in the doorway for several minutes watching Jasper sit next to Greta, holding her hand, talking to her, laughing.

She had been so blind. She knew nothing about life, about true love. She was a child learning to walk, falling again and again until she got it right. She was a slow learner with skinned knees, and bruised head to toe, still tripping and tumbling downward a lot. But she knew she would keep getting back up. Right here, right now—she understood what love was. She would never forget this feeling. Someday she would make it her own.

"B.J." she said.

Jasper turned to her. "Katie-Girl, you're here. She's having a good day. I thought I'd make a quick trip to check on my favorite gals."

"Bob Jasper. B.J. It's you." It was exultation more than a comment. "It's you!" She was crying now.

Jasper didn't speak. Kate approached the couple. She wrapped her hands around their entwined hands and held tight. "You still love her, don't you?" she managed to say between tears.

"Always," he said. "Since I was sixteen years old. She disappeared that summer— so many years ago. And then, she just called me one day. After forty years of nighttime, the sun rose again for me. I picked up the phone, and my beautiful Greta was on the line." He was barely holding it in.

"Mr. Jasper, I have brought someone who wants to meet you." She motioned for Steven and Isabella to come in.

Steven was six-feet, five inches tall, and prematurely balding at age 39. He had Greta's cat's eyes, and Jasper's broad shoulders. His face was tan and smooth, except for one large, circular white area, where his right eyebrow had once been, a very old burn scar. He walked with a slight limp, and his left arm hung loosely at his side.

Steven had managed to jump from his aircraft when it went down in 1990, but not before suffering burns over part of his face and torso. The landing was rough, and he had broken his left tibia into two pieces and crushed his left arm. He had been found by Iraqi soldiers and taken prisoner. He wouldn't speak of the torture he experienced, or the guilt he felt at being the only survivor from the plane. He spoke instead of the miracle of being released alive two years later and the devastation of coming home to discover that his mother was missing.

Kate faded into the corner with Isabella, and they watched the two men first shake hands, and then, as Steven talked, no doubt telling Jasper who he was, she saw Jasper grab him, hold him tight, and sob into his son's shoulder.

"So," Kate said to Isabella. "Jasper never knew?"

"No. It was what she wanted."

"How does Greta know that Steven was B.J.'s? Could it have been his dad's?"

"Remember, Kate, I told you the truth is a slippery thing. Sometimes what we don't know, we have to substitute what we believe. Greta believed in her soul that Steven was B.J.'s child. So, that is her truth."

Kate thought about her childhood book. That message had been with her all along. She had tucked it away somewhere deep down. She thought of the lines she had recited to Simon that day at Beau's Burgers. She repeated those words aloud now to Isabella, to Steven and Jasper, and Greta, but most of all, to herself:

"It is only with the heart that one can see rightly; what is essential is invisible to the eye."

CHAPTER THIRTY-EIGHT

2049—Galveston

Dearest Campbell,

You know I adore you. Simon doesn't understand that, but he is blinded by his love for me. That's just how he is. And how lucky am I to have been loved like that? The same way you loved Macy.

I remember when I first met you. You were sixteen, skinny, and one hell of a swimmer, maybe the best swimmer I've ever seen. Simon was still coaching the women's team at U of H, and your dad was the new coach for the men. They became best friends, Simon and Rudy. When we lost Rudy, Simon hurt more than I've ever seen him hurt. He almost didn't take the job as head coach of the men's team. He loved your father, and he felt a calling to take care of you and your mom and brothers. He has a sense of duty, my Simon. That's why I love him.

The reason I love you? I think it's because we are a lot alike, you and I. You are committed to doing what you believe is right, just like I am. You are doing a job you believe you are called to do, and so am I. God manages to sort these things out in the end, and He will this time too. In the meantime, you need to understand some things. I never broke any laws, God's nor man's. Neither has Abe. The reason you haven't found any real evidence is that there isn't any. I never administered drugs to a single person. You want to believe me, but you don't—you can't. I realized that when you came to me and asked me to help Macy die eleven years ago. It broke my heart to tell you no—because I understood. I've been where you were, and I almost lost myself in my grief. However, you misunderstand my purpose in this life. I couldn't help her until it was her time. That's how it works. I know you are torn between your job and your love for the Gray family. I admire you for fighting the fight all these years. I know about the clue you have been holding back from the press. I know about the clocks in all the homes of the "victims." I know that they all stop at the time of their death. You have been holding onto that like it would solve the mystery. Camp, there's no mystery. Watch the clock at 11:38 tonight and maybe you'll have your answers. I hope they are the answers you want. Be open to them.

Maggie has told me everything. How the night after you came to me for help, you went to her and made love to her. You were hurting—crazy with grief. I don't blame you. Three days later, Macy was gone. Campbell, do the right thing and walk away from my Maggie. You don't love her, and you must tell her that. She isn't a substitute for Macy. She deserves more; she wants more. This on-again, off-again affair is killing her spirit. Free her to find real love…like I did, and like you did. I'll be gone soon, and Abe is probably in the cabin right now. I imagine it's been a crazy day. Abe won't run from you anymore. We have only one more request. Wait until tonight after I'm gone to arrest him. He will go with you if you still think he's guilty.

Well, I guess I actually have one more favor to ask. Take care of Simon. He is a good man. He was a father to you. He will forgive you in time. He has a big heart. Make sure he takes care of himself and keeps going. You owe him that much. I do love you Campbell. I want you by my side when the time comes. I want you to know everything. No more secrets.

All My Love,
Kate

"Jesus, Coach. You read this?" Campbell asked.

"Yes. Don't make me have to hold this over your head, Camp. Can we just do this tonight with some dignity?"

Defeated, Campbell muttered, "Of course, Simon. Of course."

CHAPTER THIRTY-NINE

2009—Houston

Kate put Steven and Isabella in a cab and sent them back to their hotels with promises to meet again after the holiday weekend. She sat waiting for Jasper in the snack area where she had talked with Simon a few weeks earlier. As she watched him approach, she thought that he looked tired, but pleased. He had changed too. He wasn't weaker, but he was somehow more human, more real to her. All the one-dimensional figures from her world seemed to be springing to life. She saw everyone with new eyes.

He walked slowly and shuffled his feet ever so slightly. For the first time since she met him, he looked his age, not in years, but in knowledge. His dress shirt was untucked, and he carried his suit jacket draped over an arm. He was looking down, and was taking his sweet time getting down the hall. When he did look up, she saw in his eyes a certain peace that she never realized had been lacking in him.

"I'm losing you, aren't I?" he asked.

"No…of course not," she said. "But Jasper Agency is. I—I quit, Mr. Jasper."

"So, you can call me Bob now." His eyes were clear and calm.

"I can't," she said. "You are Mr. Jasper. You are a role model to me. Do you understand?"

"I understand that it's time for you to move on. Jasper Agency isn't big enough to hold the Kate Lascas of this world."

"I'm flattered. Thank you. For everything. You have always believed in me."

"So, what are your plans?"

"I thought I'd move into the cabin full-time and maybe start up the AIDS center in Galveston. There's a need here, and it's where I belong. I can swing a down payment soon. I've got over fifty-thousand dollars now, with many thanks to you."

"Me? What do you mean?"

"Come on, Mr. Jasper. A mystery man comes forward with an anonymous donation of over thirty-eight thousand dollars last Christmas. Pretty flimsy secret."

"Kate, that's wonderful news, but the few hundred dollars here and there I donated you knew about. No private donations from me."

"Whatever you say," Kate said. "I will start looking for a place to house the Frank Lasca Center right after the Fourth. And of course, I'll finalize things with Arlow before I move on."

"I wish you well, Katie-Girl. You are one hell of a woman."

"Thank you, Mr. Jasper. Enjoy your son."

"You can bet your backside I will." He winked at her and wrapped his huge arms around her. "Thank you, Kate. For your courage, and for falling in love with Greta."

CHAPTER FORTY

July 4, 2009—Galveston

Bursts of color and light zipped through the black sky above them. There was a gentle, merciful breeze that kept Kate from sweating as she sat on her porch with Simon, enjoying the radio's music and a basket of ribs he had barbecued for them. She looked over at him, and, starting with his reddish hair, she let her eyes float down, past his shoulders, still broad and powerful, she knew—she had watched him many evenings from this porch, swimming back and forth under a descending sun. Her gaze lingered a moment at that place where a man's chest blends into his waist, that place just where her torso would make contact with his, should it ever have occasion to....and then her eyes drifted to his hands. They were large and strong, like Jack's, but completely different. These were hands that did important work, like cooking ribs, clearing brush, planting flowers, washing windows. She felt unable to stop her fingers from inching slowly toward his. They stopped just short of touching him. It was crazy, she knew. She looked at his face and discovered that he had been watching her.

"Kate, are you blushing?"

She looked down.

"Hey," he said, "have another rib." He held the basket out to her. She took one, and nibbled on its corner. They finished their ribs in silence.

"You're good...I mean, a good cook," she said, after polishing off two ribs. She looked up at him shyly.

"Anna Katherine, are you flirting with me?"

She stammered something incoherent, and he bailed her out with an invitation— a welcome distraction.

"Let's go swimming," he said, nodding toward the water.

"In the middle of the fireworks show?" The idea secretly excited her. She followed his gaze out onto the water and smiled.

"Heck, yeah. Why not? We've got our suits on, it's a warm night. And, well, come on—let's just do it!"

She stared at him a minute. "You're right," she said. "Let's just do it."

He grabbed her hand and pulled hard, too hard, accidentally yanking her up and into him forcefully. They both stumbled. Their vigorous impact stirred desires she had been fighting for months. Her heart sank a bit when he seemed unaffected by their collision.

"Come on," he said, before she could sort all her feelings. He ran down the steps, and onto the sand, dragging her behind him.

She caught up with him, exhilarated. It occurred to her that to him, perhaps her touch was merely incidental. *Cool your jets, Kate*, she thought. *Breathe in. Breathe out.*

They swam way out, toes and elbows occasionally bumping one another in their aquatic endeavors. There was no competition. Instead, their goal was to swim together, side by side. In the water she could celebrate the complete fusion of her body to her spirit. Only in the water was she complete. Alive. She delighted in the flow of the cool liquid along the sleek lines of her extended arms and legs. In the months of traveling back and forth between Dallas and Houston, searching for answers, working on Arlow—she had barely remembered to eat. Almost every free moment had been spent in the water. So, although her mind was tired, her body was leaner and stronger than it had been in ten years.

With each stroke, she met the water with her fingertips, inviting a smooth rush down her arms and into her shoulders, caressing her breasts and abdomen, and slithering down her thighs and calves, and finally, pushing itself off her toes. She allowed herself to feel every drop of water and every inch of herself. A few hundred feet out, they let themselves go limp, floating on their backs, watching the dazzling display overhead. The electric booms reverberated in her chest like thunder. As they floated silently, dreamily, she attempted a few times to drift discreetly toward him. Then she would lose her nerve and lean away from him. For several minutes, she continued this back-and-forth dance, while they bobbed along, still not speaking.

When the show ended, they took their time swimming toward the shore, playfully showing off for one another, like a game of horse, but with water and their bodies instead of a basketball, and without a net. The moonlight shone on the dark water in cascades, alternately surrounding them in light and shadows. She enjoyed his stunts and giggled like a schoolgirl. When they were closer to the land, they stopped and stood in shoulder deep water, facing one another.

"Wow," she said, breathless, unthinking. "That was better than sex."

There was a pause. Nervously, she added, "I can't believe I just said that."

He chuckled, putting her at ease. "Sounds like you've been having sex with the wrong person," he said.

"Why, Simon Gray, are you flirting with me?"

"Yeah.... how am I doing?" he asked. She liked his frankness, and the fact that he always seemed slightly embarrassed by it, but didn't let that stop him.

She was thoughtful a moment. "You're doing pretty good, actually," she said, nodding.

"I'm sure you've heard a lot of crummy pick-up lines, a pretty lady like yourself," he said.

"A few….and thank you. I suppose you're kinda cute in a…Howdy Doody sort of way." They both laughed. She loved that she could be honest with him too.

They looked up at a passing plane, its light flashing in a now empty sky, like the cigarette after the passion. She wondered what the show had looked like from up there—actually both shows—the fireworks and the encounter unfolding between them. She imagined that the passengers probably felt her attraction to Simon from thirty thousand feet above. But Simon didn't seem to sense it from three feet away.

"So, what's your favorite?" he said.

"My favorite what?"

"Pick up line."

"Oh, please," she said. "Let's not dredge up my bar-hopping days."

"Really, I want to know," Simon said.

"Okay…" she bit the side of her lip and smiled at the same time. "Umm…here goes." She took a few seconds to mentally establish her best big-dumb-oaf voice. Then she said, "Hey, baby, I bet I'll have a hangover in the morning, because tonight, your beauty is intoxicating." Then she made herself belch, a big hairy lumberjack belch. They both laughed out loud.

"That's pretty weak," he said, "But the belch was impressive." He looked up and watched the plane until its lights faded from sight. Then he looked at Kate. His face became serious, and he nervously scratched the side of his nose. "It's true, you know?"

His meaning didn't register. She was still smirking, wondering if he liked girls who could burp on command.

"It's true, Kate. Your beauty, I mean, it is intoxicating."

"Stop," she said, and waved him off.

"No. It's not a line." He grabbed her hand. Boom! There was no doubt that his touch was deliberate this time. Defibrillator paddles couldn't have zapped her heart with greater force.

"Listen to me, Kate. I go to bed every night thinking of you, drunk with desire for you, as goofy and *Howdy Doody* as that must sound. I spend every sleeping moment dreaming of you, your hair, your skin, your smell, the way you bite your lip, dear God, you make me crazy." He put his hands on her shoulders and leaned in closer, their faces only inches apart. His words came out with such a surprising force that Kate wondered if he was going to get sick. She felt his hot breath on her cheeks. Then when he touched her face with one of those wonderful important hands, it was almost too much to experience all at one time.

"But Simon—"

"Don't stop me or I'll lose my nerve. Kate Lasca, you are an amazing woman. Now I know you're used to more sophisticated people than me, or *I*, or whatever the hell…I'm simple. I'm not rich. I'm only borderline handsome, really. But I swear on everything I own, I'm telling the truth. I dream of you, and it's so real, that I wake up missing you, feeling you, tasting you. Never in my life, I mean, I open my eyes, and your scent is on my sheets, on my skin, in the air. Now I know I may be overstepping here, but—"

"Simon, wait—" She put a finger to his lips. He grabbed it and put her hand against his heart, which was flailing in his chest. She was scared by her feelings for him, but excited to feel his heart racing as quickly as hers.

"I said don't stop me. I hate waking up missing you. And please excuse me for the bedroom talk and all, because I don't expect you to, or even want, well I want to, but—oh hell!" He took a deep breath and started again, with a quieter passion this time. "It occurred to me recently that there's only one way to wake up and not miss you. Does that make sense, I mean, do you understand what I'm saying? I know I'm not as eloquent as your crowd, but, well…. there it is."

He was wrong. He *was* eloquent. In fact, they were the most beautiful words she had ever heard—broken, out of control, but spoken with clarity unmatched by every previous conversation in her life. Simon's face inched closer, and she thought maybe it was she who would be sick now. His kiss couldn't come quickly enough. *Stop teasing me* —she wanted to scream, but realized that only a millisecond had actually passed. Her lips took on a life of their own, moving toward his, silently urging his lips to reciprocate. For once in her uptight, stressed out, goody-two-shoes life, she was not going to let anything stop her from enjoying this kiss.

"Kate!" A voice sliced the warm air above them. "Kate, is that you?"

At first, she thought she was imagining it, or maybe it was her conscience she heard saying her name. Or maybe God was telling her to stop. She was suspended on a tightrope, and she didn't dare move. Simon pointed up the slope toward the voice, and she turned her head in the same direction. "It's Jack," she said, sighing. "It's my fiancé."

The harsh July sun pierced the windows of the cabin, and Kate's head was on fire. She looked at the nightstand and saw the culprit, a half-empty bottle of tequila. Everything came back to her in crude pieces, like shards of glass on the floor after dropping a mirror. The reflections she saw were disturbing.

She had introduced Simon and Jack more formally, as it seemed she hadn't really done so properly. There had been no arguing at the cabin. Jack seemed oblivious to what he almost interrupted, which made no sense considering his jealous nature. She had been terribly embarrassed as she watched Simon crawl into his truck and drive home in his swim trunks and flip-flops. He refused to come in to get his clothes. Of course, Jack wanted to make love, and that's when she had started drinking. Did he realize that she *had* to drink to get through it? She lay in bed, in the aftermath of their sex, disgusted with herself that Jack's scent was all over her. She ached for Simon. She reached up and touched her breasts, felt them come alive under her hands, as she imagined Simon's hands on her. Then his breath, and his mouth…

"Kate, honey?" Jack leaned into her, throwing an arm around her torso. "What do you want for breakfast?"

"I can't do this anymore, Jack."

"Breakfast?"

"No. I think you know what I mean."

He sat up and looked at her. He was half-asleep, but waking up quickly. "What the hell are you talking about?"

"Surely you've seen this coming."

"Kate?" There was a hint of panic in his voice, but he kept smiling. "I love you, Kate." He reached for her, still smiling his Ken doll smile, and she realized that she was tired of playing Barbie. And the Dreamhouse was not what she had dreamed, at all.

"You see, that's the problem. You don't really. Not the way I want you to."

"What can I do any differently? Come on, you have had me on a short leash—"

"I know, and you have done everything right. Everything in your power. That's why it's over, Jack. You are a great guy, you are. But you are not *the* guy. The guy wouldn't have to do anything. He would just—be. Does that make sense?"

"Hell, no. You are some kind of crazy, you know that?"

"Yeah, I do. I am crazy. And it feels fan-fucking-tastic!"

"Listen, Kate. We'll postpone the wedding. It'll give you time to get used to your new job. We'll wait until Greta is gone…"

"See, Jack. You just listed all the reasons we don't work. You are too willing to wait. How much can you really love me? And I can't stomach waiting for Greta to die. She means something to me Jack. Don't you get that?"

"I'm sorry. I didn't mean to sound cruel. Of course, she does. But just come back to work with me Monday and we'll give it some time."

"I quit."

He jumped out of bed and grabbed his robe and put it on.

"You what?" He shouted, and he pushed his hands through his hair like a dump truck pushing dirt. "Oh my God. You are nuts, Kate. I was kidding before, but I swear to God. You are certifiable. Everything you worked for your whole life, everything you ever wanted—"

"Is right here, in Galveston. This is what I want. I am going to start the center here and stay here."

"But you are a kick-ass advertising executive. Why would you give that up?"

"Because I'd rather be a kick-ass human being. That's why. Now, I'm going into town. Please be gone when I get back."

"I'll call you—"

"Please don't," she said. She went to her closet for jeans and a tee shirt while Jack went into the bathroom. In the bottom of her closet were Simon's shirt, jeans, and boots. She held the shirt close to her face and inhaled. She rubbed it against her breasts, and leaned against the door for support. She couldn't wait to find him—to feel him again. She dressed hastily and drove into town to Beau's to pick up hotcakes and sausage for two. She would call Simon as soon as she knew Jack was gone.

She pulled up into the parking lot and saw Simon's truck. Her heart raced with anticipation. She jumped out of her car and ran to the front door of the restaurant and threw it open. In their spot sat Simon, looking beautiful, and attached to his neck was a bosomy blonde, looking equally gorgeous.

CHAPTER FORTY-ONE

Kate sat on her sofa, wrapped in a blanket, and stared at the TV, waiting for the sun to go down so she could sleep away the hideous knowledge that she was an idiot. She had rented *It's a Wonderful Life*. She sipped her hot chocolate slowly. It was ninety-one degrees at nine in the evening, but hot chocolate with marshmallows was the best way she knew to soothe a broken heart.

She had dug herself into this hole, and she would be truly alone now. Greta was dying, she was leaving Hannah, her only friend, back in Dallas, and she had dumped Jack. And she had no job. Now Simon was out of reach. She couldn't go crawling to him. She had led him on all those weeks, and hadn't really meant to, but at the same time, she knew she had been unfair. She had a safety net in Jack. She was ashamed to admit that she had thought of him that way. He didn't deserve that, but a small self-serving part of her had indeed entertained that notion. It was easy for her to flirt and to reach for Simon in times of need. She hadn't imagined, though, that he might have a safety net too. She doubted he thought of anyone that way. He wasn't as selfish as she was. He had confessed his deep feelings for her, and, well—she had smashed them to bits. What had she thought, that she could go bursting into Beau's exclaiming, "I choose you Simon!" and he would respond, "Oh, thank you, Kate. I thought you'd never fall in love with me." Yeah, right.

She heard a car door shut in front of the cabin. She jumped up to run to the door and then thought she should slow down a little. Wait for him to knock at least. It had to be him.

She opened the door tentatively, unsure what he would say when he saw her. She also wasn't sure what she should say.

"Kate," he said.

"Simon."

"Umm, I need to get my clothes. Then I'll be out of your way." He held up a small duffle bag.

"Come in," she said.

"Thanks." He smelled delicious.

"Coffee?" she asked.

"No, thanks. Just my clothes and I'll be out of your hair."

She pointed him in the direction of her bedroom and followed him there.

"You're not in my way, or in my hair. You are...my friend." Damn it. She still couldn't say it.

"Kate, I'm sorry. I've been encroaching on your life these past months, and I pushed you too far last night."

"I'm the one who's sorry. I continue to screw everything up."

"Stop it," he said. "Just stop." His voice was harsh.

"Excuse me?"

"Well, I've already stuck my foot in it, so I might as well speak my mind. From my vantage point, you are teetering between life and death. You want Greta to survive, you want to bring your father back to life, and somewhere along the way, you've forgotten how to live. It's admirable what you've done for others, it is. But Jeez-Louise, wake up and get a life. You deserve one."

"I can't believe you are saying this to me."

"Yeah, well, believe it. I'm saying it. You've got to forgive yourself for your dad's death. He asked you to kill him, for God's sake. I think that was real shitty of him. I mean no disrespect. He must be some kind of man to have raised you, and your mom is a wonderful person. I'm sure Frank was too. But he made a mistake, not you."

"What do you know?" Her voice was raised.

"I know I love you. And I'd never ask you to do such a thing for me. I don't judge him. Hell, he was dying and out of his mind in pain. But after years of fooling around and being careless, and putting you and your mom at odds and putting your mom at risk, how can you take the blame for everything? Christ, Kate, yank him down from that pedestal."

"Are you one of those? Are you saying he deserved AIDS? Because his love knew no gender?" Her temper was flaring.

"You know better. Listen, I should go before I say things that will ruin any friendship we have left."

"No. You are not walking out on this. Say what you need to say."

"Okay. Fine. Kate, do you know why you still have the nightmares? It's because you can't bear the thought of never hearing his voice again. You hold onto these dreams, Kate, just like you hold onto him. You wake up frightened and depressed, but you refuse to let them go."

"That's unfair," she said.

"Shut up Kate, and listen. Your whole life is about your grief for Frank. You don't have room for anything else, anyone else, because you don't *make* room. You may have been a victim of circumstance five years ago, and my heart goes out to you, but you're not the victim anymore. He's dead. Let him die."

Kate swung her arm wildly, intending to slap him, but he grabbed her arm. "How dare you?" she cried. "You miserable bastard. You don't understand my pain. You don't know what I feel."

"That's because you don't let me know. You let me in a little and then you push me away. I'd be willing to bet you do the same thing to Jack. The only person you talk to is a ghost, and ghosts can't talk back. They can't touch you or hold you, and they can't make love to you." He grabbed her and held her firmly against his chest. He lowered his face until it was an inch from hers. "So, no one else gets to either." He released her. "I'm tired from loving you, Kate. It's too hard. I've known you six months, and I've loved you every minute of those six months. And every minute you have made me work for it. You've trained me well."

"I can't let go. I can't. I failed him. I let him down. There's no excuse for that." She refused to cry. She was angry, but she wanted his arms around her again.

"There is an excuse. A good one. The best. You didn't help him commit suicide because you loved him." His tone softened, but she could sense he would cut her no slack. "When you love someone, you don't want him to die. So, you told him no. Do you think you're going to make it right by trying to kill every other man who loves you? Or by killing yourself? Because that's what you're doing, Kate."

She looked up, her face tight—fighting tears.

"I'm leaving, Kate. Do you even understand why?"

"Because everyone leaves," she said, quietly.

"That's bullshit, Kate. No one wants to attend that pity party with you anymore. If everyone leaves, it's because you kick their ass out the door. I'm going because, just like you, I will not help the person I love commit suicide. I won't help you die, and I won't watch, either."

She was quiet. He walked to the closet, opened it, and began to gather his clothes.

"There's a storm coming," she said. "Wait till it passes."

"I don't mind getting wet," he said, and he began to fold his clothes.

Kate watched him unzip the bag. Everything about him excited her—from his habit of scratching the side of his nose to his love for hamburgers and strawberry ice cream. Her excitement for him emanated from a now familiar place that had been foreign and distant for too long. He just wanted to love her. And he knew her; somehow, he knew her. Incredibly, he thought her thoughts with her and spoke her words with her—and in times of weakness she suspected he would do it not just with her, but for her. She saw herself have his babies, grow old with him, die in his arms.

Simon sat on her bed and put the clothes into his duffle bag. She wanted to reach for him. After a handful of wordless minutes, he turned to her and spoke, not stiffly, for God knows that would make this too easy. No, he spoke as if each syllable were a gentle finger tracing the memory of every moment of the previous months. She couldn't help but relive them, too, and wonder why in the hell she was letting him walk away.

"I'll miss you, Kate."

It was getting dark. She considered switching the lamp on, but she knew the sight of him in full light now would be unbearable.

"I'm sorry," she whispered. She couldn't bring herself to say she loved him too.

"So, I guess that's it," he said. When she didn't respond, he stood and picked up his duffle bag. Just like that—just casually picked it up, leaving no clue to the bystander that this might be the last time they ever saw each other. He walked slowly toward the door like it was any other day. Except today was the day that Kate's heart would break. Exactly what she wanted to avoid in the first place. She followed him into the living room and toward the front door. He didn't turn to look at her. The door joists groaned under the age and weight of the wood. As he flung it open, the pre-storm air hit her cruelly in the face.

And he was gone.

CHAPTER FORTY-TWO

"Good morning, Bethany," Kate said as she walked past the nurse's station at the care center.

"Hey, Kate." She looked up from her paperwork. "Whoa, you look like awful."

"Yeah, I know."

"Out late watching fireworks this weekend?"

"Yes, you could put it that way. How is she today?"

"Not so good. She has a visitor. It's Abe Archer. Minister from Dallas, says he's a friend of yours."

"Hmm, really?"

"Yeah, he and Dr. D are in there. Kate, I think you should go in. I think it's almost time."

Kate had prepared herself for this moment, but she knew she wasn't truly ready.

"Have you called anyone?" she asked the nurse.

"Not yet. I can."

"Let me, okay, Bethany?"

"Sure," she said, and added, "I'm here if you need me, Kate."

Kate called the hotel where Isabella and Steven were staying, and she called Jasper. He was staying in town, too. She asked them to come as soon as possible. Then she walked down the hall, bracing herself for what she might find. When she reached the door, she heard muffled arguing between Dr. D'Angelo and Abe. She pushed the door open, but just barely.

"I told you this would happen. I warned you, Abe. But you had to do things your way. No one's happy about this. You didn't follow protocol."

"Listen,   Rick.   This   is   my   assignment."

"You stole it from me. To be close to her. You know that's against policy. You are bordering on big trouble, Abe. You'd have been terminated if I hadn't covered for you."

"It was worth it. I love her."

"You know the rules on this kind of thing. Now today you must do it. You were supposed
to do it months ago!"

"Do what?" Kate asked, swinging the door open.

"Kate!" Abe said. "You remember Dr. D'Angelo. We were just talking about who would take care of funeral arrangements and such. Don't worry yourself."

"I'm out of here, Abe. I want no part of this," Dr. D'Angelo said. "Take care of it now," he added, as he stormed out.

"What's going on?" Kate asked.

"How have you been, Kate? I'm looking forward to this week's counseling."

"Stop changing the subject. And there won't be a session. I just broke the engagement."

She thought she saw Abe smiling. In fact, his smile broadened, and he wasn't even trying to hide it.

"Are you happy about this, Abe?" She was offended.

"Kate, you don't love him. I know that."

"It   still   hurts."

"I'm sure it does. I want to be here for you." He came over and put his arm around her.

It didn't feel right to her at all. She had always been comfortable with him, but today her skin prickled at his touch.

"There is something I have to know," he said.

"What, Abe?"

"How do you feel about me?"

"I respect you. I'm incredibly grateful to you."

"That's all?"

"I think so."

"Kiss me."

"What? No." She tried to pull away, but he grabbed her hard and pushed his lips into hers. She fought him for a moment, and then her strength was suddenly gone. She felt weak and dizzy, as if she were entering a dream-world.

What happened next would alter the course of her life forever. As he held his lips to hers, she was pulled from herself and taken somewhere else, somewhere dark and quiet. Stained glass windows lined a long narrow hallway, with a door at the end of the hall. She began to walk, and in the colored glass she saw many faces, some she knew and some she didn't. Her Grandmother, Maddie, made her stop in her tracks. She touched the glass likeness with her fingers and a memory jolted through her. Gingerbread in the oven, cider on the stove. Paper dolls on the table strewn about. Modeling clay and beads on the floor. She pulled her hand away and the memory gradually faded and swirled away. She was left with feelings of love. She had adored her Mama Maddie, who died when Kate was seven.

She kept walking, looking at the glass. Many of the faces were familiar, but she couldn't place them exactly. Then one she knew. Jackie Grubner from junior high. They had been friends, and then Jackie fell in with a bad crowd. She had overdosed on heroine when they were sixteen. She touched the glass and was once again pulled into a memory. Jackie's bedroom. Rapture-me Raspberry body spray in the air, Duran Duran blasting from the cassette player in the boom box. Her toes felt cool and wet, and she looked down and saw fresh red-hot-love#6 polish on her toes. "Jackie," she called and reached for her friend, but Jackie was dancing in front of the window, oblivious of her presence. She wore a purple, off-the-shoulder sweater with silver sparkles that glinted in the fading sunlight as she gyrated and grooved to the music. A tight white mini-skirt outlined her tiny waist and drew the eyes down her thin legs and into white ankle boots adorned with purple Conchos. Kate's heart ached for her friend. She pulled her hand away, and the memory vaporized.

Kate felt very tired, but kept walking. Then she stopped, paralyzed, at one of the images. It was her, the nameless child she had lost. She forced her legs to move forward and tried to go past the window, but Abe's voice whispered to her. "Touch her," he said.

"I can't," Kate called out. "What is happening to me? Is this a dream?" She was scared now.

"Touch her," he repeated. His gentle tone wasn't enough to comfort her.

Her hand was shaking as she reached up and let her finger barely graze the glass.

She was lying in a hospital bed. Everything was white, blinding white, except for the pink blanket wrapped around her baby girl. Kate felt her heart exploding with love as she looked down into the face of her daughter, and then seize tight with fear as the nurse removed her from Kate's arms and explained that she was taking her to Intensive Care and that she was very sick.

"No!" Kate was screaming, but no one answered. 'No!" she screamed again and again, until she fell on the floor of the hallway in a heap, crying. The memory snapped itself free and flew back into her past. She tried to hold it for a moment, but it was too powerful for her to contain. She sat on the floor, rocking back and forth, screaming at Abe.

"Get me out of here! I can't take it."

"You can," he said. "You have to keep walking, Kate. Get up and walk."

It took every bit of strength she had to walk again. Her single purpose was to reach the door and get out of here. She forced her gaze straight ahead to protect herself from the images. It was all too painful.

She reached the door and grabbed the handle. She didn't care what was on the other side; she had to get out of this hallway.

She swung the door open wide and saw a huge room that was so bright with colored lights, she couldn't make anything out, except one emerging shape in the middle. Slowly, it came to her: facing away from her was a large chair, made of brown leather with coppery studs along the top and sides of the back. She knew this chair. She knew there was a small tear in the left arm, where her cat Zippy had scratched it when Kate was five. She saw the blue cotton magazine holder draped across the arm, and knew the latest Reader's Digest and his reading glasses were inside. She thought she smelled Old Spice and mud-black coffee.

A small tuft of sandy gray hair was poking up from the other side. As she approached the chair, she began to recognize other elements of the room around her. A red brick fireplace took shape, and on its mantle were photos of her as a child. Hanging above it was a family portrait of her, Frank, and Emily, painted by a friend and given to Emily by Frank as a twentieth wedding anniversary gift. Kate had argued with Frank about wearing the yellow dress that day. She hated it, but he had convinced her to wear it. "It's her favorite," he told her. "Do it for your mother."

On the other side of the room was a huge window overlooking the oak tree she and Frank had planted together. She tried to retreat, but her feet were frozen. She panicked and started to scream. "Abe!" she shrieked. "Stop—I can't do this!"

The chair slowly turned, and she found herself face to face with her father. No way could she walk away now. His eyes were so clear and so real. His white tee shirt was wrinkled, and his jeans were faded. He had been working in the yard, she knew. He was healthy and strong, and he reached his firm tan arms out to her as he spoke.

"Katie-Girl," he said. "Come to me." His words were released into the air and caressed her from head to toe, and all the fear inside her broke apart and disintegrated. She felt complete love for the first time in a decade. She ran to him, arms extended.

"I'm here Daddy. I love you Daddy. I love you," she cried as she fell into his arms and held onto him as tightly as she could.

"I love you too, Katie. I don't have much time—seems there's never enough time," Frank said, stroking his daughter's hair. "But there is something I have to say to you."

"What Daddy?"

"It wasn't your fault. We go when it's our time to go. I lived a blessed life. I loved you and your mother more than anything."

"I know you love us," she said, curling up in his lap. She was finally home, finally safe.

"And it wasn't your mother's fault either."

"I should have been here for you."

"Katie, now listen to me." He took her face into his huge calloused hands. "This is the last time we'll see each other until it's your time. So, you have to hear me. You did everything you could. I am the luckiest man in the world, and the happiest. There's no more pain, no more fear. And the pain I felt on earth—it was my own. I made choices, and I live the results of those, just as we all must ultimately do. The only way you can hurt me now is by holding onto this guilt. Do you understand?"

"I do. Please don't go."

"The only way I can find true peace is to know you and Emily are moving on with your lives. If you feel you owe me anything, give me that. That's all I want."

"I'll try." Her mind couldn't comprehend what was happening to her. It was like her dreams, but it wasn't a dream. She knew it wasn't. But here she was, in her father's lap, smelling him, feeling his arms around her, tasting his skin beneath her kisses.

One thing was clear—he was happy. The smile of their early years was back.

"Kate, this is a gift to you. Abe is risking everything to give you these minutes, but I'm afraid they're almost over."

"Abe? I'm confused."

"Bye, Katie. I love you." He kissed her cheek.

She had a vague sense of Abe holding her. "Not yet!" she yelled, and she found herself fighting him again, this time to stay in this place rather than avoid it. All went quiet. She opened her eyes, and she was standing next to Greta's bed again, Abe's lips against hers, his arms wound tightly around her. She pulled away, took a step back, and stumbled into a chair. She grabbed its arms and lowered herself uneasily.

"Who—who the fuck are you?" she stammered.

"I'm Abe Archer. I'm your friend."

"What are you?" She felt sick. "Where's my father? Where have you taken him?"

"I think you know that."

"In heaven? Is that where I was?"

"Sort of. It's—I'm not allowed to discuss certain things with humans."

She laughed. "This is insane. What the hell is happening?"

"Again, I think you know. You see it with your heart. You always have."

He came over, sat on Greta's bed, took Kate's hand, and stared into her eyes. They sat there like that, until it came to her. The déjà vu.

She whispered, "You were there. I was up that whole night, tormented by my father's request, trying to decide what to do. I felt you, your hands on mine, counting pills, enough for him to rest, but not enough to die. I felt you pushing me forward, helping me talk myself through it. Then crushing and mixing. I felt you. But I didn't see you."

"Only the heart sees certain things, right Kate?"

"But, Greta, she saw you, with her eyes and with her heart. You were with her father when he died. She said it in her journal. Was it you or another—one of you?"

"An angel, you mean? You can say it, Kate."

"No. I won't say it."

"Why not, Kate?"

"I think I'm going crazy."

"Or maybe you're finally not crazy? I was there, and yes—Greta saw me."

"Because she believes?" Kate began to understand.

"Yes, because she believes."

"Then how come I have been able to see you since we met last year?"

"I was hoping you wouldn't ask me that."

She just stared at him.

"It's complicated. Hard to understand."

"Try me."

"We—angels—I mean, we can take physical form if we see the need, to right a wrong or fix an urgent situation."

"What situation?"

"You."

She was quiet.

"I came here to—"

"Fix me?"

"No, to be with you. And that is strictly forbidden. I was supposed to be here in February to take Greta from this life. But I saw the job opening at your church in December, and well, who knows the bible better than an angel, except God I suppose, so I—"

"Orchestrated everything to be with me? Why?" She felt the gradual emotion of this like feathers dusting her skin.

"Because I love you, Kate. I fell in love with you that night, in the cabin, when your father was dying."

"But, Abe, you know—"

"I know. You love Simon. I thought maybe you loved me, a little, but that was just me dreaming. You need to be with Simon. I see that. I hope you do too."

A thought flashed through her mind. "Wait, the argument with Dr. D'Angelo—is he—"

"Yep. He will be disappearing this afternoon, though."

"I'm so confused."

"He won't be needed—because—it's time to complete our assignment, the one we argued over."

"Greta? No. Please Abe. Please." She fell, and he caught her, held her close.

"Today," he whispered. "Now."

The door opened, and Isabella, Steven, and Jasper entered.

"It's time." Abe looked at them and nodded. "I am so sorry."

They gathered around Greta's bed, each with a hand on her, and Abe, pulling a weeping Kate into his chest, began to pray,

The Lord is my shepherd, I shall not want...

CHAPTER FORTY-THREE

2049—11:20 p.m.—Galveston

Once again, Abe and Simon faced each other from opposite sides of the bed of the woman they loved. The box sat open at her side, empty except for one envelope.

"Do you ever wonder," Abe said, "what might have been? What turns your life might have taken, given—"

"Different opportunities?" "No, not exactly," Abe said. "I'm talking about making different—choices. Do you ever think about it, Simon?"

"No, I live for today."

"But you never wonder?"

"Doubts about the past are very expensive, comrade."

Abe smiled. "Indeed."

"I think I have to open this now," Simon said. He reached into the box, pulled out the envelope, and opened it slowly. He looked up at Abe. "Are these the last words I'll ever hear from Kate?" he asked.

"In this life," Abe said. "But you'll see her again, I promise."

"How can you be sure?" Simon straightened the creases in the paper, taking his time, postponing the inevitable.

"I just am," Abe said. This morning, I promised you the truth, and so here it is."

Simon pursed his lips, slowly inhaled, and exhaled a gust of breath. He tentatively began to read:

> *Simon Darling:*
>
> *It's time for me to go now. Call everyone in and surround yourself with all their love. My love is all around you already. I am happy. You gave me everything I needed. And now I am giving you what you have always needed, what you lived without for forty years.   You know I have seen much suffering*

and grief, in my life and the lives of others. The center has been successful, and Abe and I have helped thousands of people find peace. I couldn't be happier with how my life turned out. I spent that last four decades with the love of my life. Simon, you made all my dreams come true and never asked for a thing in return. You have a special place reserved for you in Heaven I'm sure. And I'll see you there soon. You were right to believe in me. Abe and I never broke the law. We were doing God's work, just like I told you. I told you as much of the truth as I could without hurting Abe.

Abe is not who you think he is. I know this will be very hard to swallow, but you have to trust me one last time. Remember the summer after we met? Remember July 4? And the argument in the cabin the next day—when I thought I'd lost you forever? That was the day before Greta died. I was there with Abe, and something extraordinary happened....

CHAPTER FORTY-FOUR

2009—Galveston

The waves beckoned her, this keeper of secrets, hoping to coax its first confession of the morning. She made her way down the steps and onto the path she and Frank had cleared six years ago when they had been here together. He had grown weaker each day as they worked. They had gathered stones together all summer, just like they had done when she was a girl. As she walked the path today, she carried with her all of her memories, and some of Greta's too. She had fallen in love with both their pasts, and she knew it was time to start moving beyond those events; but this morning, she wanted to grab hold of them one more time.

Her childhood summers swirled in her brain with fondness and a little sadness. Mom and Dad had been more in love than anyone in the world. She envisioned them walking hand in hand and laughing. How she had loved their laughter. She would awaken in the mornings and hear her parents talking and laughing in the front room, and she had felt safe.

The weekend mornings on the beach had always been even better. She remembered smelling coffee and pancakes, or bacon sometimes, and she remembered how they would let her sleep late. Then they would all three go down to the shore, she and her mother on their treasure hunt, while Dad fished or lay in the sun. He joined them occasionally, but mostly it was Kate and her mother on their excursions. She loved searching and digging for anything interesting in the sand. She had known even then that her mom didn't really care about those items they found. She cared about being together, and she, too, had cared about their laughter. She wished she had appreciated those times with Emily more. Those warm days were marked by collecting not only stones, but seashells, little sticks, and myriad other useless items. But her favorite had always been the feathers.

The summer after first grade, she had become obsessed with feathers. They had covered a unit in Science called "Traces of Living Things," and she had marveled at the endless supply of such treasures on the beach that year. All that evidence of life.

She had wondered if she might collect enough feathers to make herself a bird suit and fly to the sun. She also had learned in science class that no one can fly into the sun, but in her child's mind, she thought maybe the teachers were wrong. She knew extraordinary things were possible. She had collected feathers and stones, just as Greta had collected words and pictures. Their collections had saved her.

She cupped her hands into a visor across her brow and looked into the rising sun. She felt its warmth across her exposed neck and shoulders, and she remembered something her father often had said: "With morning comes hope." She walked steadily along the path, stopping every few steps to clear pieces of tree branches and trash from the sandy trail. This was a different world. It used to be her safe place, until a very different summer nearly six years ago. She felt a flash of anger at herself for allowing her only source of pure happiness to be marred by a stabbing grief. She didn't want to be angry any more.

Kate's life had been hit by a tornado, and Greta had helped her sift through the debris and recreate herself, helped her find the Kate she was meant to be. Kate remembered standing in this spot the day after her father's funeral. She had packed up the cabin, covered the furniture, gotten her bags ready, and then put on this dress and walked this path. She had intended, on that day, to walk into the ocean and never look back. The pain had broken her, and she hadn't believed she could face life without him. But something had stopped her that day.

She continued on her little stone path toward the water. She and her father had passionately built this path together, so she would be able to enjoy it for many years to come, and so she could remember the happy times. But she had stayed away for too long. That life was someone else's now, someone she didn't recognize. She heard that other self, the Kate who still had a father, giggle and say to him, "You know, we could go to Barney's and buy a bag of rocks for five dollars. Big rocks that would do the job." But he had wanted them to collect their own stones, one pebble at a time, as if each little rock could buy him another day with her. She had believed that too, in a way. She had always believed him, even when he had lied to her. She had forgiven his lies. She knew she had much to forgive. And now, he was begging her to move on. Frank had spoken to her from the other side with his true final wish: for her to live. She bent down and touched the rocks. They felt cold on her fingers, and she was surprised to see that time had not changed them. They were just as she remembered, just as she had left them.

She looked at the little rocks for a long time, wondering how she had never noticed there were so many shades of brown. She mused, what a miracle brown is! She shoved her hands down into the pockets of her faded orange sundress and felt their cool emptiness. She had loved those deep pockets. She had looked for two weeks for a sundress with deep enough pockets to carry her rocks from the shore each day. She had hated the color, though, and her father laughed out loud at the sight of her in it at first. Over the short months, they had collected enough stones to line this path. *The path to paradise*, he had dubbed it as they drank a toast to their accomplishment. That was a Sunday morning. On Friday afternoon, she was burying him.

She scraped the mud from around the embedded stones and began to fill her pockets. She hoped the small stones weighed enough to sink to the ocean floor. It had been quite a struggle to get her father and her rocks back up along the path, especially in the final days, so she felt strangely reassured that they would be heavy enough. She added more to her pockets, slowly at first, then faster, as her father's words whispered to her over the waves: *One pebble at a time.* She worked feverishly now, trudging up sand and muck to dig out as many rocks as her pockets would hold. When the seams were pulled tight and bulging, she stood up and followed the trail down to the shore. She stood there a long time, holding the memories in her head. She took a step forward. Then another.

She had swum here with her mother for the first time thirty years earlier. She thought she caught a glimpse of her now: her then risqué pink bikini rising and falling along distant waves. She wanted to swim out to her and to her father, the way they were then, to look into their young, satisfied faces. She wanted to hear her father's reassuring voice cheer them on as she and her mother danced to the Beatles on the old gray and white radio. She wanted life to make sense again.

She stopped, chin deep in her little piece of the ocean, and looked into the sun. For a moment, she let it melt her.

She began to untie the straps of her sundress. Then she let it fall into the ocean, the weight of it freeing her, because yes—she was finally free—from the pain, the regret, the anger. The old Kate floated down, and down, and down. She reached with her arms and pushed with her toes into the waves and rejoiced in their coolness. She tasted the salt water and remembered a silly song her father made up and sang to her when she was barely more than an infant, when he taught her to swim. She felt his hands holding her, pushing her, reassuring her, and she heard the love in his voice and knew that he was proud of her. She heard him sing:

> *How many tears to fill the ocean?*
> *How many tears to fill the sea?*
> *My sweet baby, when you get the notion*
> *Don't forget to come back to me.*

She finally understood. He hadn't meant, "Come back to me," as in "Don't let me go." No. He had been asking her to go back to that place where she was most happy and to reclaim it.

She swam hard and fast, faster than ever before. She opened her eyes wide and dove deep into the breast of the morning tide. She peered into the silent black water, eager to reach that place of delicious void, to celebrate her new life, pure as a newborn baby.

That's when she felt hands grab her by the waist and a strong body embrace hers and pull her upward. She tried to squirm free, but together they went higher and higher until they reached the surface. She gasped for air and turned to see that it was Simon who was holding her tight.

"What are you doing?" she asked. She couldn't believe he was actually there.

"I love you Kate." He was breathless and very serious. "I love you, you crazy, impossible—"

She grabbed his face with both her hands and kissed him hard.

"Shut up," she said.

He kissed her back. They were both gasping now.

"Oh my God," she said, "I have wanted to kiss you, to just grab you for so long."

"So, do it," he said, kissing her again.

She reached for his boxers, and hesitated, afraid her heart might explode. He put his hand on hers and slid them down and kicked them off. He pulled her close.

"I thought you would never get rid of that God-awful orange dress," he said. She saw the smile in his eyes rather than on his lips.

She tossed her head back, laughing and crying, and he put his lips to her neck and shoulders. She inched his wet tee shirt slowly up and over his head. She wanted her hands all over him at once and wanted to be touched all over by him at the same time. She had waited so long, she wanted to experience every inch of him as quickly and as slowly as possible. They held each other and kissed each other for a long time, and she really believed she might break into pieces if he didn't make love to her.

"Are you sure, Kate?" he asked. "I can't just be one more guy. And I can't take advantage of you. This is it for me. For life. Forever. I have to know you feel the same."

"I love you, Simon Gray," she said, and she moved his hair out of his eyes. "Please make love to me."

She leaned back slightly and let herself float a moment, savoring the cold water touching her shoulders and buoying her breasts, and his hands clutching her waist. The waves pushed them together, and he gently moved into her. It was as if God had made her body just for this moment, just to receive his. She felt him everywhere, inside and out, and she loved him more than she had ever loved anyone. She pushed her body quietly against his, knowing she could make love to him forever. She didn't want to die, not today in the ocean, not today, in the soft sunlight, with Simon Gray inside her. Not today, when she was finally fully alive.

CHAPTER FORTY-FIVE

2049—11:36 p.m.—Galveston

Simon folded the single page neatly back into thirds and slid it into its envelope. Abe waited patiently while he tried to absorb the letter's contents.

"So, how will this work?" he asked the minister.

"Is that your only question?" Abe said.

"Should I call the others? It's time, isn't it?" Simon didn't want to discuss the letter.

"Yes," Abe said. I'll get everyone.

Kate's most cherished loved ones filed into her room and gathered around her. Maggie's eyes were red and swollen, and she was shaking. Zeke took her hand and kissed the top of her head. "I love you, Mags," he whispered. "And she loves you too."

They stood around her bed, Simon, Zeke, Maggie, Abe, and Campbell.

Abe took one of Kate's hands and looked at the clock. 11:38. He started to say a silent prayer.

Zeke opened Kate's favorite book, *The Little Prince*, and began to read the passage that Kate had marked for this occasion:

> "All men have the stars... but they are not the same things for different people. For some, who are travelers, the stars are guides. For others, they are no more than little lights in the sky. For others, who are scholars, they are problems.... But all these stars are silent. You—you alone—will have the stars as no one else has them—

> "In one of the stars I shall be living. In one of them I shall be laughing. And so it will be as if all the stars were laughing, when you look at the sky at night... you—only you—will have stars that can laugh!

".... And when your sorrow is comforted (time soothes all sorrows) you will be content that you have known me. You will always be my friend. You will want to laugh with me. And you will sometimes open your window, so, for that pleasure... and your friends will be properly astonished to see you laughing as you look up at the sky! Then you will say to them, 'yes, the stars always make me laugh.' "

CHAPTER FORTY-SIX

August 8, 2009—Dallas

Kate quietly entered the church and walked down the aisle. The sun broke through the stained glass and dappled the floor with colored light. It felt like a lifetime had passed since she was last here at Grace Methodist.

She took a seat on the very front row, right next to him. His hands were folded, and his head was bowed.

"Jack?"

"How did you know I'd be here?" he asked. When he looked up, she was hurt to see the sadness in his eyes.

"You said, no matter what, you'd be here on the 8th. I knew you'd keep your word."

"Hmm," he said, half-smiling. "What are you doing here?"

She reached into her purse and pulled out the box containing her engagement ring. She put it in his hand and closed his fingers on it.

"You keep it," he said, extending his hand to her.

"No, that would be wrong. I took enough from you. Sell it. Buy another ring for the future Mrs. Jack Finnegan."

"There's no one else for me Kate. I'll never love anyone the way I loved you."

"You did love me. And I'm sorry I never really believed you. That was wrong of me. Jack, I was a mess. And you put up with me. Thank you."

"I still love you Kate Lasca."

"I know." She reached into her handbag again and pulled out an envelope. "That's why I can't keep this either." She held out the envelope.

"What is it?" He didn't reach for it.

"A check for $38,000. Your Christmas donation to the Frank Lasca Center."

"How did you know?" His eyes brightened a little.

"An angel whispered it in my ear," she said. "It's incredibly generous, but considering everything, it—it's just not right."

"Kate, you have to keep it. You deserve it!"

"No, I don't."

"Take it—for him—for Frank, and for me?" He smiled and winked.

She looked into his eyes, and saw that Jack Finnegan was a beautiful man. Misguided, but good, truly good. She put the envelope back into her bag. She promised herself she would do important work with the money.

"Goodbye, Jack," she whispered, and kissed him lightly on the cheek. "And good luck."

****

It was August in Galveston, and Kate wore pink. Her chestnut hair was swept into a loose bun, and wild wisps of hair hung loosely about her freckled shoulders, reflecting hints of red in the late summer sun. She stood on the porch of the cabin waiting for Simon. They had planned a small ceremony with just the two of them, and Emily, and Simon's mother. Abe would marry them on the spot where they had met eight months earlier.

Emily came out of the cabin, looking beautiful in her sea-foam green dress and baby's breath in her hair. She carried a small box.

"Something old," she said, as she handed the box to Kate.

"Mom, how sweet. I hadn't even thought of—well, what's in here?"

"One way to find out," Emily said, tapping the lid.

Kate had no idea what it could be. She removed the lid and looked inside. "Oh, Mom. Oh—my—gosh. You—"

"Put it on," Emily said.

"You knew about this?" Kate said, tears filling her eyes.

"Mothers know everything," she said, and put her arm around her daughter.

Kate slid the clunky bubble gum machine ring onto her right ring pinky finger and held it up in the sunlight. "It's beautiful. Thank you."

"No, you're beautiful!" Simon shouted and grabbed her from behind. He picked her up and twirled her around and around until they were both dizzy. Kate thought back to the moments in her bathroom, towel on her head, ring on her finger. Her imperfect fairy tale husband had arrived. It was the happiest moment of her life.

He put her down gently and got down on one knee.

"Kate. Will you marry me—right now? And love me forever?"

"I will," she said. She reached down and moved his hair out of his eyes. "I will love you forever, Simon Gray."

CHAPTER FORTY-SEVEN

"Okay, Detective Cross, I'll go with you, but I need to talk to Simon first. Please, give me one more minute."

"Alright, Archer. But hurry."

"Simon, I'm sorry about Kate's death. I would give anything—anything, to bring her back."

"Don't you have that power?"

"No, I'm afraid not."

"Kate was ready. It was her time."

"Yes, and I have to tell you something. Remember what I asked you before, about past choices and consequences?"

"Yes."

"You don't wonder how things might have been different?"

"You mean like if I hadn't taken the job at U of H when I did? Or bigger, like if I hadn't ever fallen into that pond and nearly drowned, never fought my way back and found a passion for swimming?"

"No, not bigger events—smaller ones. Like one day you're at the hospital visiting a sick friend, for example." He paused.

"Yeah?"

"And you go for a cup of coffee from the vending machine. Only you drop your quarter under the machine, and while you are bent over retrieving it, the future love of your life, the one visiting her sick father, walks by, and you miss her."

"No, I can't say I've ever had such thoughts."

"Well, these things happen you know?"

"I guess they probably do. They seem so small, in fact very small and specific, why would I think about that, Abe?"

"Because small events mater. And we never think about them."

"What are you trying to say?"

"Just that things happen, you know, trivial things, and people don't notice. Things like dropping a quarter under a machine."

Simon thought for a moment. Then it struck him with such wattage that he had to sit down.

"You're right," he said. "People don't notice, and that works to your advantage, doesn't it?"

"Sometimes."

"My memory fails me, but perhaps I went to see a sick friend in....2003?"

"Yes."

"Ah. And I suspect Frank Lasca might have been hospitalized during that time."

"Yes." His voice was softer, ashamed.

"And I have a hunch I might have dropped a quarter that day."

"You might have."

"You're making a confession? You want forgiveness?" Simon smiled broadly.

"You're not angry?" Abe asked.

"Nope."

"I thought you'd be angry. I messed things up for you."

"Look around, Abe. Does this look messed up? I have had an amazing life. In fact, I have the life you wanted. Isn't that what this is really about? You thought you could wave your magic wand and—"

"We don't use wands."

"Whatever, wiggle your nose or lay your hands on a vending machine. You think you can do your thing, and change the trajectory of everyone's lives?"

"I think I did." He sounded smug.

"But you still didn't get what you wanted. I did."

"True. Because some things—"

"Are supposed to happen? Like me and Kate?"

"I did everything I could to control the universe. All kinds of things—big things and small ones—and I got to be with Kate. But I couldn't make her love me."

"Thank God for that."

"I'll pass it on, when I see him next."

They laughed.

"You're one crazy bastard, you know that?" Simon said.

"Yes, I do, and you're one tough son-of-a-bitch."

CHAPTER FORTY-EIGHT

2009—Galveston

Warm and satisfied after making love to her husband, Kate decided to take a shower, and her husband decided not to let her out of his sight.

"It's all so fleeting," she said. They held each other and let the water cascade off their skin, both still elated that they were actually husband and wife.

"You're still young, Kate," he reminded her.

"Yes, but it all goes so quickly. What's the difference between 35 and 75?"

"A lifetime. But don't worry, it will be a lifetime *together.*"

"It feels like every day just slips out of my reach before I've used it. I don't want to do that anymore."

"I think you use your days pretty well." He smiled and pulled her closer, grabbing her backside and squeezing.

"It's like this water, you know? It's here now and it feels good. But it hits us, bounces off, runs down us, and swirls into the drain, gone forever."

"Hmm." He seemed unsure what to say.

"And it happens so fast. I mean, how many times have I showered in my life? And how many of those moments have I truly savored? It's the same thing."

He pulled back slightly so he could look directly at her.

"You're right," he said.

She was surprised to hear him say this, and her expression must have told him so. He laughed lightly and kissed her.

"Life is like this water. It hits us, sometimes gently, barely noticeable, like in the early September rain. And it feels refreshing, that's true. And other times, well, it practically beats us to death, you and I know that."

She put her head on his chest. She loved listening to his body vibrate beneath his words.

"But it's not gone forever, Kate. Yes, it hits us, and evaporates or runs down us into the drain. But it becomes part of us and we become part of it. The ecosystem, you know? Just like your kindness, and Greta's words. They're not gone. They merge into something bigger than us."

"I like that," she said, and kissed his shoulder. "But what if I want to hold onto it?"

"I don't think we're meant to. I think life is sometimes about holding on, but mostly about letting go."

Kate knew she would remember this day. As frightened as she was that it wouldn't last, that Simon, too, would go away, today she was experiencing true, soul-piercing joy. Greta had changed her, by loving so deeply and sharing that love with Kate through her words. She couldn't imagine wanting to be anywhere else than here with Simon at this moment, and for as many moments as she might have left. If the next forty years could be as happy as the past twenty-four hours had been, then she had plenty to look forward to. No more looking back.

She turned the shower off. They touched each other and held each other, feeling all the droplets of water until they finally ran cool against their warm skin. They didn't bother to dry off before moving to the bed. The beads of water cushioned their bodies against one another as they made love for the second time, slowly and quietly. They didn't have to vocalize their words any more. They felt them in every touch— in one another's fingertips, and arms, knees, and bellies. Kate loved him, and she knew he loved her. She had fought it so hard for so many months that accepting it felt like falling asleep after a very hard day. Better than that, even. It was like having an orgasm for the first time—new and strange, but fantastic and comforting—and knowing that there was a lifetime of them ahead of you. Knowing that he would move you inside and out and show you parts of yourself you didn't know—parts of yourself that he loved and that maybe, yes—maybe, you could love, too.

CHAPTER FORTY-NINE

2049—Galveston

"Dad, can we come in?" Maggie and Zeke stood at the door to Kate and Simon's bedroom.

"Yes, of course."

"The coroner will be here soon for Mom. Are you sure you don't want to sit with us in the living room?"

He shook his head.

"Yeah, that's what we thought." They sat on the love seat opposite him.

"We also thought you'd want to know some other news. Abe's gone," Zeke said.

"In jail, you mean?"

"No—disappeared. This whole thing has been on the news all day, and then his arrest even interrupted the season premiere of *Survivor*.

Simon chuckled.

"But he is gone. They lost him. He was in his cell, and then—he just wasn't. That's all they're saying."

"There's nothing else to say," said Simon. "But somehow, I don't think I've seen the last of Abe Archer."

"And—well—" Maggie said, "I broke up with Campbell."

"Oh, honey, I'm sorry," Simon said. He truly was. He knew how much she was hurting.

"I'm sorry too. That he didn't love me, that is." She managed to stay calm as she spoke.

"You've still got me, Mags," Zeke said, spreading his arms dramatically, wrapping them around her, and then giving her a good noogie.

"Stop!" she yelled, and then gave in, wrapping her arms around him. They held each other and began to cry.

"We'll miss her," Zeke said. "But we have a lot of good memories, and she made sure we had a happy life."

"Just make sure you keep it that way," Simon said. He waved them out. "Go on, now, you don't need to sit here with us."

They left, and Maggie shut the door gently behind them.

He turned to his wife, who was still and peaceful beside him.

"Well, Mrs. Gray, since today has been all about confessions, I suppose I should make mine while you're still here. I swore I wouldn't let it go to the grave with me, so I better spill it."

He walked to the window, opened it, and stood quietly a moment.

"Do you remember the day we met?" He paused, as if waiting for "Yes, darling."

"Of course you do. You threatened to shoot me," he said cheerily. He opened the curtains further and then began to push their bed up against the window.

"Well," he continued, out of breath from the hard work. "The night before that, I came to see you, to meet you, and see if you needed help cleaning the place up." The bed was flush with the wall now, and he crawled in and wrapped his arms around his wife, holding her for the very last time.

"You stood at this window, just as it got dark, just as the first stars became visible, and I saw you. I watched you. I had no idea at first—" He leaned close and kissed her hair.

"Remember that strip tease you did? I don't know why you did it. You have always been full of surprises. My only thought at the time was 'I am one lucky son-of-a-bitch,' and God forgive me, but I watched you. I couldn't help myself. I knew it was wrong, but you were so God-damn gorgeous." He looked at Kate and thought about all the times he had watched her undress in four decades together. She still made him shiver.

"I knew I should look away, but I couldn't. And there you were, taking it all off and fluttering your eyelids, here, in this moonlight, in this room. I knew my life was about to change. So yes, you can tell Abe that I do believe that our choices shape our future. I chose to stop by that night, and my life was never the same." He re-tied the pink ribbon on the front of her nightgown.

"I just thought you should know," he whispered. "I hope you forgive me for the transgression. And I'll see you soon, my love."

Simon lifted Kate's hand to his lips and kissed it softly, already looking forward to kisses in their next lifetime together. He looked out the window, and thought he saw her in the stars, shining brightly down on them.

And he began to laugh.

References

Dickinson, E. (1960). *The Complete Poems of Emily Dickinson.* (T. H. Johnson, Ed.) Boston: Little, Brown and Compnay.

Saint-Exupery, A. d. (1943). *The Little Prince.* New York: Harcourt, Brace and World.

ABOUT THE AUTHOR

Alinda Quinn has been a freelance writer for over fifteen years. During her graduate work in English, she became interested in how narrative is crafted and comes to have meaning. Then as a teacher of writing, she became passionate about exploring the ways in which meaning-making promotes healing. That's why she recently founded a non-profit whose mission is to aid recovery from sexual trauma through creative expression. She has three beautiful children and a lovely daughter-in-law who bring her much joy. She calls Dallas her home.

Made in the USA
San Bernardino, CA
01 May 2018